By B.G. THOMAS

Published by DREAMSPINNER PRESS
http://www.dreamspinnerpress.com

THE BOY WHO
CAME IN FROM
THE COLD

B.G. THOMAS

Dreamspinner Press

Published by
Dreamspinner Press
5032 Capital Circle SW
Ste 2, PMB# 279
Tallahassee, FL 32305-7886
USA
http://www.dreamspinnerpress.com/

The Boy Who Came In From the Cold
Copyright © 2013 by B.G. Thomas

Cover Art by Aaron Anderson
aaronbydesign55@gmail.com

ISBN: 978-1-62380-713-9
Digital ISBN: 978-1-62380-714-6

Printed in the United States of America
First Edition
May 2013

This is for Jonah Markowitz,
and Brad Rowe and Trevor Wright, of course.
Thank you for giving us *Shelter*.
May this be some small way to express my gratitude.

Special thanks to my wondrous editors—Rowan Speedwell, Kat Weller, Sal Davis, P.D. Singer (who opened my eyes a time or two) and C.L. Miles—Thanks ladies, you make me look good!

And of course Andi Byassee! Thank you, thank you, thank you. It is a wonderful thing to find an editor who really "gets" you.

We blink over 22,000 times a day,
and I bet you thought you only woke up once.

~ Michael Lee

Becoming hurts.

~ Kat Howard

CHAPTER ONE

IT WAS cold outside. It was really cold. *Freezing* cold.

Todd Burton, freezing himself, watched as a man with a big industrial broom swept what was an obviously already shoveled sidewalk. The snow was falling harder than ever and was piled everywhere.

Jeez, it's snowing like a son of a bitch out there. Todd glanced nervously over his shoulder into the lobby of the apartment building. No one seemed to be watching him.

What the hell am I going to do?

If this had happened to him a week ago, it wouldn't have been so bad. Not good. But not nearly as bad.

Luckily, one of the building's residents had let him in out of the cold in the first place. A big guy–good-looking, tall and wide—wearing a long woolen (and obviously warm) coat.

Todd would have done almost anything for that coat. His pale-tan lightweight fall jacket barely kept out the chill of late autumn. It didn't stand a chance against the snowstorm outside the warm lobby.

"You'll wear it and *like* it," his mother had screamed. "We ain't made of money!"

If he hadn't chosen to wear a sweater to the New Year's Eve party last night, he didn't know what he would have done. It was the only thing keeping him from being chilled to the bone. His gloves were a joke—the simple one-size-fits-all type bought at Family Dollar, with a hat purchased at the same place—and all but useless. He might as well have been naked.

So it had been a stroke of luck when the big man had asked Todd why he was standing under the awning of the Oscar Wilde apartment building.

"Waiting for a ride," Todd replied, even though it was a lie. He was no more waiting for a ride than he was waiting for the results of a pregnancy test. But it got him out of the frigging cold. Todd flexed his wet toes in the confines of sneakers worn to death. His feet were still frozen and aching after nearly an hour. Lord yes, his toes hurt.

This sucks, he thought. *This sucks zombie dick.*

"What am I going to do?" he muttered as the snow, abundant as the feathers from a high-school-girls' pillow fight, fell thickly to the ground. Icicles, looking like the teeth of some primeval creature, hung just outside the large plate-glass windows. *I'd hate to be the poor guy that one of those fell on.*

"Still waiting?" came a voice from behind Todd, and, startled, he jumped and let out a cry. He spun around and found himself gazing up into the face of the man who'd let him into the building. No longer in his winter wear (where was that coat?), the man had changed into jogging shorts and a T-shirt that stretched over a massive chest and proclaimed that he was 2CUTE2BSTR8.

It took Todd a moment to figure it out, but when he did, his mouth dropped open. Too cute to be straight. The guy was queer. It was a little more than Todd's small-town naïveté could take in. This guy? A fag? It just didn't seem possible. The guy was a powerhouse. A total class-A stud. This was no swishy, limp-wristed, pink-wearing gay boy.

The man eyed him suspiciously, and Todd realized he needed to say something. "Uh-uh, yeah, I don't know what's taking... uh, George... so long." *Piss. Did I actually say "uh George"?*

The man nodded, went to retrieve his mail, and on his way back, stopped again and looked Todd up and down. But this time his gaze lingered just a bit. Todd felt his stomach give a weird sort of flip-flop.

"Look," said the man. "Watch yourself, okay? The building manager has been known to have a shit fit when hustlers come in the building for, well, *whatever* they come in here for. Just don't get caught."

Todd stiffened. Hustlers? Did this guy think he was looking to sell himself? Before he could think of how to respond, the man crossed the lobby and disappeared into the elevator.

He thinks I'm for sale! Todd shook his head. Cursed under his breath. *Do I look like a hustler?* he wondered and thought about the boys who sold themselves in the park. *Maybe I do*, he realized, horrified. He touched the scruff on his face—he hadn't shaved today and his facial hair grew like wildfire—and looked down at his dirty jeans and worn-out sneakers. Would someone want to buy something so... dirty? He tried in vain to catch his reflection in the big lobby windows. *Not enough light in here,* he thought.

He glanced around the lobby, seeing what at one time must have been elegance, but was now just a few levels above run-down. Brass elevator doors, once shiny and beautiful, now tarnished with age; hardwood and marble floors now scuffed; banks of fluorescent lights hanging from the ceiling; what looked like the faded remains of a huge mural—all probably gorgeous when the building was made. All just sad echoes of a different age.

Todd thought of the man who had let him into the building. From the look of his business attire Todd was surprised he didn't live in a much fancier place. That coat hadn't come from Walmart. Couldn't the guy afford an apartment in a better building?

There was the pinging from the elevator as the doors opened, and speak of the devil, it was the same man. He was carrying what looked like a plate and a mug and was heading in Todd's direction. When he got closer, the wondrous aroma of coffee hit Todd and he saw the man had a sandwich as well. To Todd's surprise, the man handed them both over. His mouth fell open. The day had been one of the shittiest ever in a year of total shit. And here, out of the blue, a complete stranger was showing some small-town kindness?

Todd only hesitated for a second, all but snatched the food and coffee from the man, sat down on the windowsill, and practically gulped everything down. Both were a relief beyond words. Todd almost swooned. He hadn't had so much as a bite all day, and with barely twenty bucks in his pocket and no idea when he'd get more, he'd been afraid to buy so much as a dollar grease burger from Mickey D's. He ate the food so fast he barely tasted it. Oh! And the coffee filled him with a warmth that finally let him shake off the cold that had plagued him all day. He actually gave a shiver as it lifted.

"I'm Gabe," said the man.

With only a few bites left, Todd nodded but didn't offer his own name.

"What are you doing out in this weather, anyway?" Gabe asked.

Todd stopped chewing. Boy, was that a question and a half. He swallowed hard. How did he explain it? It was awful. He was ashamed. How did he tell a complete stranger that he felt like a total failure?

Todd gave the guy a quick look, then a longer one. The guy was huge. A good head taller, at least, than Todd's five foot nine and downright massive: really built. He obviously worked out. A lot. Like the guys in the muscle mags that Todd collected.

(*"Jesus, Todd, how many of these things do you fucking have?"*)

Not like the men who were all gnarly and knotted like mutants or something, but the nicely built, Hollywood TV-star kind.

(*"It don't make no sense a boy your age having so many of these. You a faggot or something?"*

"I just use them for exercise tips.")

Gabe's pecs looked as big as dinner plates, and Todd could see the man's abs even through his shirt. His waist seemed almost as small, his hips as narrow, as Todd's, impossible as that should be.

And good-looking. *Really* good-looking. The man had short light-brown hair (dark-blond? It was hard to tell) and light blue eyes (the color of a country summer sky) and a face like a movie star. This guy could have any woman he wanted. Why had he chosen to go gay?

"Okay, so if you don't want me to know—"

Know? Know what? Did I miss something?

"—can I at least get that name?"

"Uh, Todd."

"Todd what?"

What the hell? "Why do you need to know?"

Gabe shook his head. "Okay, Mr. Uh Todd Whydoyouneedtoknow, I'll leave you alone."

The man started to turn away, and suddenly, Todd didn't want Gabe to leave. "I was kicked out of my apartment," he cried out in a rush.

Gabe stopped, turned back.

"Surprised the shit out of me too. Got home this morning from a New Year's party, and the lock had been changed."

Gabe's eyes widened just a bit. "Damn."

"What kind of asshole kicks someone out on the streets in this kind of weather?" Todd asked. He began to wring his hands. "I thought there were laws that protected you from that."

"I believe there are, but that's not going to do you any good right now," Gabe said.

"No shit." Todd sighed. He looked at the man again. God what he'd do to look like that. He'd worked out all through high school and bought weights for home, but no, he just couldn't do it. There was a level of baby fat that didn't want to go away for anything.

(*"Ha! Look at you, working out! You trying to get a body like the guys in your magazines? Give it up. Ain't gonna happen. You Burtons have the bodies you have. Skinny as shit."*)

At least he didn't look like his stepfather, with his big beer gut and his flat ass. Todd was in decent enough shape, but he'd come to realize he'd never have a body like Gabe's. "You really queer?" he asked without thinking. His lack of a filter from thought to spoken word had bounced him against the walls of authority all his life.

"You don't think before you speak," his freshman teacher—Mr. Grombeck—would say over and over.

"The word is 'gay'," Gabe said, "and yes I am."

(*"I remember when gay was a good word. Homos have ruined that word!"*)

"It still is," Gabe returned.

Shit, I said that out loud? He heard me. He must have six million dollar ears.

"Gay is a joyful and happy word."

Gay and proud of it, Todd thought with wonder. "Sorry," he said and meant it. After all, the guy had helped him when no one else would. So what if he chose to fuck a dude instead of a girl? It was his choice.

"Any idea what you're going to do in the meantime?" Gabe crossed his arms over that expanse of chest. "You got a place to stay? A friend?"

Todd felt the last of his strength leave him and his shoulders slumped in defeat. "No." The people he'd met since moving to Kansas City had been total jerks. Or drug addicts. Thieves. Users. Girls as well as dudes just trying to get him into bed. All he'd wanted to do was get out of his small town and into a big city. Fat lot of good that had done him.

"What about the friends you partied with last night?"

Todd jerked. A few people he'd met at Gilham Park a month or so before—a far different park than the one that catered to male prostitution—had asked him if he wanted to party, and, desperate to get away from his tiny studio apartment, he'd agreed. He'd no sooner gotten to the party than a couple of boys younger than him tried to give him some crack. No way was he going there. He might be small town, but he knew that stuff was no joke. A couple of beers later and he was buzzed and sitting alone in a corner watching the freakiest things. Two, then three, guys making out on a couch. Another guy with his head under the skirt of a girl who couldn't have been legal. Lots of drugs, but mostly marijuana. He'd even taken a few hits of something that made the pot he'd occasionally smoked with his friend Austin seem like grass clippings.

Then, right after midnight, two girls who had been watching him, giggling (when they weren't kissing each other), had pulled him into a dark bedroom, yanked off their tops, and tried to get him to have sex. One girl with no bra and huge breasts had grabbed his hand, pressed it against one tit, and squeezed his fingers over it. He couldn't yank away fast enough, and he didn't know why. "No," he said, then got the hell out.

"No," he said again to Gabe. "No way." The people at that party hadn't been his friends.

There was a pause, and Gabe looked him up and down once more. Not rudely, but it made Todd feel weird anyway. He couldn't quite describe the feeling. The guy wasn't drooling or any fucking thing like that, but still....

(*"Perverts. They like little boys. They kidnap them and they cut them...."*)

Gabe was a guy. And despite parades and gay marriage, the end of Don't Ask, Don't Tell, and gay and lesbian support groups in high schools, men with men wasn't—

(*"... normal! They ain't normal!"*)

—anything he was used to. The guy seemed nice. Had given him food. Gabe had shown him more kindness than anyone else in this fucking city, so—

"Look," said the big man, "I've never paid for it, but you're awfully cute, and it would give you a place to stay for the night, and...."

Todd started. "What?"

"I mean it's not going to be like *Pretty Woman*, where I have to pay extra to get you to stay the night, right? I mean, I'm getting you out of the snow and—"

"I'm not a whore," Todd snarled. "And I'm not a fucking *queer*."

Gabe's face froze, his warmth vanishing as if it had never been there. He reached out and took Todd's now empty mug. "Good luck," he said, voice icy. "And like I said, don't let the building manager catch you, or you'll be back out on the street, blizzard or not." Gabe turned and strode back to the elevator without looking back.

Great. Shit. Why did I do that? "I gotta stop losing it," he said aloud. *I could have just told him I'm not gay, not a hustler. The guy—Gabe—was nice. He would have taken no for an answer.* Todd turned back to look out the lobby windows. Gasped. The snow, which had been coming down hard, was now a writhing wall of white.

"Look at that," said someone to his right. Todd turned and saw a couple of people had wandered into the lobby from who knew where? Upstairs? An office?

"My mom just called and told me the governor declared a state of emergency," said another onlooker. "I sure would hate to be out in that."

No shit, Todd thought. He looked back to the elevator. But Gabe was gone, of course. *Why did I act like an asshole? Maybe all he wanted to do was suck my dick. Not like I haven't ever had my dick sucked. Just because Joan didn't like giving them.... And of course there was the one that....*

"Just look at that!"

Todd jumped at the voice and looked outside again. What had been bad had become downright scary. It was like some kind of special effect from a horror movie.

Wouldn't it have been worth a blowjob to get out of that?

"It's easy money," a hustler from the park across from his apartment building—his *ex*-apartment building—had told him a couple of weeks ago. A day that had been pleasant, a few orange and red leaves still hanging bravely from the trees; a day when his lousy coat had kept him warm enough. "*Easy* money. I make fifty a blowjob. *Getting* a blowjob! I can shoot two, three times a day for sure. The third time not as much, but if he's an ugly old troll, he's lucky to get what he gets."

The guy—a redhead named Doug—and a friend had been smoking a joint and regaling Todd with the gainful job opportunities in the world of male prostitution. "I just lay back," he continued, "close my eyes, and pretend it's Katy Perry givin' me head. Who doesn't like to get his dick sucked? And get *paid* for it."

Somehow, Todd doubted Doug's sincerity. If it was all that great, why wasn't everybody champing at the bit to be a prostitute?

"Don't let him fool you, girlfriend," said Chaz, the second young man, a kid of mixed ethnicity, maybe twenty years old. "Doug here ain't thinkin' 'bout Katy. Channing Tatum is his thing. And I tells you this…. We all suck cock at least now and again." He shifted his hip, rested a hand upon it, and then snapped his fingers with the other. "*Especially* in these hard economic times."

Todd had shaken his head doubtfully. "I don't think…."

"You could suck dick? After that first time or two it isn't a big deal," Doug said, thereby admitting he did indeed give at least the occasional blowjob. "And if you can swallow, you make more money."

"Why you guys telling me this?" Todd had asked, as if he didn't already know.

Chaz took a hit of his joint, apparently not worried in the least about who might see, and passed it to Doug. "Cuz you ain't got no job, and you're trying like a motherfucker to get one. Am I right?"

Todd was startled but didn't answer.

"No need to deny it," Doug replied casually and hit the joint. "You leave your place all different times, and you're always wearing a tie." He reached out and flicked the thrift-store paisley one Todd had loosened but not removed. He held out his joint.

Todd shook his head.

"And because you don't want the grass. You're studying for a test."

"A test?"

"A piss test," Chaz explained.

How does the guy know so much?

"We know all kinds of stuff about you," Doug said and raised an orange brow.

"Like you is from a small town, ain't ya?" Chaz asked.

Jesus. Todd gaped at the young man in disbelief. "How do you know all this?"

The boy-men laughed.

"Because we're *all* small-town," Doug cried.

"We knows our own," Chaz continued and snapped his fingers again. "We all comes to the city to get away from a big bad daddy who can't keeps his hands to his self—"

"Or to make big money or get famous," Doug added.

"Or what-the-fuck-ever, and instead we winds up sellin' ourselves. Story as old as fuckin' time, baby."

Todd hadn't taken them up on their offer. Hadn't even considered it. *I'll never get that low*, he'd told himself.

But now? He watched the swirling maelstrom.

Gabe would have been better than some old toothless "troll" picking him up off the street. At least Gabe was hot. Maybe he could have laid back and let the man give him some head. It couldn't be any worse than those his so-called girlfriend had given him back home.

He shuddered at the thought.

Or any more disastrous than....

And Gabe would have given him a place to stay for the night.

What if Gabe wanted the blowjob? Could you do it?

He shrugged.

Memories of a basement…

Hell. Maybe. Didn't every dude wonder what it would be like once or twice? He remembered a time in the locker room at school. He was sitting down untying his shoes when he realized the penis of one of his classmates was less than a foot from his face. He could actually smell it, it was so close, the heat from the showers bringing out the boy's natural male musk. Todd had toed off one shoe and as he slowly worked on the other, he was able to look up through his bangs without his buddy knowing he was checking out his cock. Todd found he wasn't repulsed by it at all, as Joan seemed to be by his own. Why, it was rather handsome. Longer than his, it draped over two largish testicles, one hanging slightly lower than the other in a fleshy, silky-looking sack. The scrotum was hairless, and he wondered if his buddy shaved his balls (*and where that thought had come from?*).

"Hey Burton! Whatcha lookin' at?"

Luckily his big mouth served him well that day. "I don't know what the hell it is," he'd replied rather loudly. "But whatever it is, it's about the ugliest damn thing I've ever seen in my life."

The roar of laughter was probably the only thing that had kept him from being called a faggot for the rest of the school year.

But a few days later, while Joan was making another sloppy and unexciting attempt at giving him a blowjob, gagging like he was twelve inches long or something, he'd wondered what it was like to suck a cock. What if he had been alone with that boy in the locker room and he had just leaned forward and taken it into his mouth? Or his friend Austin. The cute boy's face filled his mind. The image of him from when they'd gone skinny-dipping over the summer. Evenings at his friend's house. What would Austin's cock feel like in his mouth? Taste like? Strange, those were the thoughts that allowed him to finally cum, to his girlfriend's noisy complaints—"Toddy! You said you'd warn me."—in a voice like rubbing two balloons together.

So if Gabe had taken him to his apartment, gotten him out of the snow, maybe he could try it? As clean-cut as the man was, Todd was sure he would be clean down there.

Strange also that Todd felt his own cock shift about then. Just in time for a bellow like an elephant that startled him so badly he gave a shout.

"Hey you! Who the hell are you?"

Todd turned to see a huge man descending on him like doom. "Goddamn drifters and hustlers always coming in my building. Get the hell out of here!"

What was he supposed to do now?

CHAPTER TWO

THE elevator doors had barely closed behind him when Gabriel Richards was hit with guilt. *Shitfire. Why did I snap at that kid? What must it be like to be on the streets in weather like this?* He—Todd—had to be cold and frightened.

But dammit, the kid had used the words queer and faggot, and Gabe hated those words. They were ugly. He knew activists said using them took away their power, but he didn't agree at all. People used those words to hurt. Hadn't the kid meant it that way?

Gabe let himself into his apartment on the top floor of the Oscar Wilde and threw his mail on the small black lacquered table just inside the door. He paid extra for the larger apartment so he had a bedroom, a study, and a workout room. Having all three was important to him. A bedroom for only what bedrooms were for—sleeping and making love (which he hadn't done in what felt like a thousand years, surely the reason he'd offered to pay the kid—*Todd!*—for sex.). The study/office, where he could take work home without cluttering up the whole apartment. And his workout room, which was meant purely for improving his body. Each had its place.

Working out had been his plan too—what he was going to do right after grabbing the mail. That's when he'd seen Todd was still standing there, a good hour after he'd let the young man in. The look on his face, pure desperation, told him Todd must be in trouble. But what could he do?

Well, get the kid something to eat, surely.

Very nice-looking kid as a matter of fact. Creamy pale skin, dark hair with two masculine slashes for brows. He was scruffy, but when had he had a chance to shave last? Besides, it suited him. He looked a little stocky, but it was hard to tell. He had a nice mouth too. Wide. Full. *Kissable.* And then there were those eyes. Deep dark brown. And sad, like deer eyes.

So Gabe took Todd the corned beef sandwich he'd brought home from work and hadn't had time to eat, and a big mug of coffee. Only to have the kid get rude.

And why wouldn't he? Scared. Desperate. Cold. And accused of being a whore? Did he have one shred of proof that Todd was a hustler? No. He'd assumed it. And one thing Gabe never did was assume.

It makes an ass out of me, and forget the you.

Assumed it all because—no. Don't go there.

Suddenly, Gabe didn't feel like working out. It was a big part of his day, but now? How could he run on his three-thousand-dollar NordicTrack treadmill, or work out with his equally expensive Bowflex Revolution Home Gym, knowing there was a young man downstairs who obviously didn't have enough money to even afford something to eat?

Shower.

That was the ticket. A hot shower, clean off the day's grime, chase off the chill of the inclement weather, and he'd not only feel better, but he'd be thinking—excuse the expression—straight. Then he could make up his mind what to do about Todd—if anything.

And oh God, he could just hear Tracy, his friend and co-worker, now: "Oh no! No you don't. Not another stray. And especially not one so young. You know what happened last time."

Halfway through his shower, he heard someone at the door. Pounding on it, in fact. *Now what the hell?*

He stepped out of the shower, wiped his feet on the bathmat (something he hated to do), wrapped a towel around his waist, grabbed a second for his hair, and went to answer the door before someone knocked it down.

When he opened it, Gabe wasn't at all prepared for what he saw. Standing outside his apartment was Mr. Martinez—a man almost as wide in the middle as he was tall—and Todd, who looked desperate, his pretty, dark eyes wide and pleading. *He wants me to go along with his lie.*

The building manager was holding the young man by the arm, and it looked like he was being quite rough about it. "Sorry to bother you, Mr. Richards, but I found this kid downstairs, and he claims to be your boyfriend."

Martinez's words startled and amused Gabe. "Oh?" he asked, raising both brows.

Abruptly, Todd shrugged off the fat man's grip and to Gabe's complete astonishment, threw his arms around him and pressed his scruffy cheek against Gabe's bare chest. "I'm so sorry, Gabe," he said. "Please don't make me go."

It was hard not to laugh. Having to hug a big wet gay man couldn't be easy for Todd. But the devil was in Gabe, and he couldn't resist teasing him. "I don't know, Todd." He pretended to pull away. "You said some pretty shitty things."

The pleading look on Todd's pale face made Gabe bite the insides of his cheeks. It really wasn't humorous. He knew the kid was in trouble. He didn't want to make Todd feel worse.

"I said I was sorry," Todd all but whined.

Gabe made up his mind in that second to help the boy, but he was going to get in one last shot, mean or not. He really did hate when people used words like faggot. "Well…," he said, then paused again. "Oh, all right." With that he pulled Todd close and kissed him. Really kissed him. Hard. Todd started to struggle but then must have realized how that would look. Todd submitted, even allowing Gabe to ease a bit of tongue into his mouth. And damn! Gabe hadn't realized how much he must have missed kissing. Heart beginning to race, it was all he could do to stop. He could feel his cock shifting under the towel. Would Todd be able to miss it?

"All right, all right! Break it up. Break it up," said Mr. Martinez. "Son of a bitch, you're gonna be fuckin' in the hall in a minute. Get inside." The large man laughed and started down the hall. "Lover's spats! *Chrrrrrrist.*"

When the building manager was gone, Gabe let Todd go. The young man fell back, breathless. "Jeez, man! You sure know how to take advantage of a guy, don't you?"

Gabe blushed. It had been a shitty thing to do. "Sorry." Then, to his surprise, he noticed his cock wasn't the only one to respond. The front of Todd's jeans was telling a very different story from the one Todd had told Gabe. *Well, well, well. Interesting.* "Sorry," he said again. "I shouldn't have done that. But you were an ass."

He opened the door wider, and when Todd didn't move: "Are you coming in, or are you just going to stand there?" Gabe asked quietly.

Todd gulped visibly, looked up and down the hall, and finally nodded. Gabe stood aside and the youth passed him, then let out a quiet gasp. "Wow," he said. "Nice place."

"Thank you," said Gabe. "Why don't you sit down and stay awhile? I'll go put something on. You caught me in the shower." Without waiting to see what Todd would do, he padded out of the room and down the hall to get dressed. He could feel the kid's eyes on him, which was doing nothing to make his erection go down. *Does Todd even know he's watching me?*

Gabe dried quickly, pulled on some sweats and his 2CUTE2BSTR8 shirt and, not bothering with socks, returned to the living room. Todd was still standing there, looking around the room as if he had never seen anything like it.

Maybe he hadn't? Gabe hadn't bought any cheap shit. He shopped for top-of-the-line furniture, modern without being wild. Pieces that would look good for years and not tacky because they'd gone out of style. Three walls were painted a light blue-gray and the fourth a much darker shade, providing a dramatic backdrop for the furnishings: A black leather couch and two deep and comfortable chairs in a color that matched the darker wall. Coffee table and end tables of black lacquer, like the small table by the door, and a matching buffet against one wall. A large industrial piece of art, metal gears and cogs with a clock, dominated one wall. The lamps were metallic and industrial looking as well. A fireplace in the original white and black marble was the centerpiece of another wall, above it a painting done in an impressionist style. He'd liked it the minute he saw it. It reminded him of Claude Monet's "Boulevard des Capucines," a painting he'd fallen in love with when he wasn't much more than a kid. He couldn't resist the piece, especially when he discovered it was done by a local gay artist. What could be better than that?

Then there was his sixty-three-inch flat screen TV. Why go small? If he was going to watch television, why not make it as enjoyable as possible? The area rug, drapes, blinds, and lampshades offered a splash of red and cream, keeping the room from being too cold. It was a man's apartment, no doubt about that. He had even had the hardwood floors redone, though they weren't his and he had no intention of living his whole life in the apartment.

"Sit down," he said, and Todd jumped, spun around. Lord, the kid was jittery. "You okay?" Gabe asked him.

Todd stared, not saying anything, then finally shook his head, dark-brown eyes big and sad. "Not really," he said. He ran fingers through thick dark-brown hair and sighed deeply.

"Let me have your coat," Gabe said. "And sit down. Relax."

Todd pulled off his coat, handed it over, and almost flinched when Gabe took it. *God. He needs to calm down.* "Would you like something to drink? Coke? Ice tea? Beer? Glass of wine?"

"I'm only twenty," Todd said and sat down on the end of the couch farthest from Gabe.

"I won't tell if you don't," Gabe said and offered him a smile. *Be careful. You could say that kind of thing was what got you into trouble last time.*

Gabe's expression must have helped because Todd gave a half smile in return. "Whatever you're having," he said.

"Well, I've been planning on opening a bottle of wine I've been saving for a special occasion. Why not tonight?"

Todd's mouth turned into a straight line and he nodded.

Gabe hung up Todd's coat and paused, realizing how lightweight it was. Not a goose feather or bit of quilting between the layers. *Shit, the kid* must *have been cold.* He went into the kitchen, which he'd also had redone, even stripping the cabinets and replacing the counter. Tracy thought he was crazy for doing it.

"You already pay rent. Why fix up the place?"

"Because I live there, Tracy. I want to enjoy living there."

"I don't know why you just don't buy a house," she said. Tracy was a statuesque brunette with a tendency to wear red. She called it one of her two power colors. She certainly got the attention of the men around her, clients as well as co-workers, gay as well as straight. "Get something really nice in Hyde Park or even Brookside. Make improvements that'll benefit you and not the owners of that building."

"They've let me skip rent on quite a few occasions with what I've done to the place," he'd told her.

"Not equal to what you're spending I bet."

"You're missing the point," Gabe said. "I like it there. I like having mostly gay neighbors. And it tickles me thinking of the prize somebody's going to get when they get my apartment after I leave."

"They're going to defecate a brick is what they're going to do," she replied. *"Hopefully, it won't be wasted on some lesbian who can't appreciate it."*

"Now Tracy...." Defecate. Not shit.

"I can just see some gay boy's face. Mother skeeter! When he walks in, he's gonna think he struck the jackpot." She grinned. *"It'll be Christmas, no matter what month they move in."*

Gabe smiled at the thought. He wasn't sure what Todd's sexuality was; he suspected the young man didn't know himself, despite his denials. Todd sure seemed to be dazzled by the apartment, though. Would a straight kid even have noticed? Todd was acting like Alice in Wonderland. It was sweet. Speaking of which, would Todd want the Schwartzbeeren he'd been planning on opening, or would *it* be too sweet? Should he just play it safe and go with a merlot? Or would that be too dry? He started to ask and then remembered a teenhood of Boone's Farm cheap wine. Sweet was the order of the day, he suspected.

Gabe opened the bottle, poured two glasses, and returned to the living room and handed Todd one of them. Todd reached for it, and Gabe saw the young man's hand was trembling. Not a lot, but shaking all the same. Nervous? Something far worse? He hoped the kid wasn't some kind of addict, although his instincts told Gabe it was nerves. He had to help the kid relax. "Music?" he asked.

Todd gulped again. "Whatever you want," he said, his voice actually cracking.

Gabe stifled a sigh and went to his sound system, turned it on. It was already set to a soft jazz station, and he thought that should soothe the savage beast. He joined Todd on the couch, and once again the boy cringed. *What the hell?*

Then it hit him. Todd thought he was going to have to have sex with Gabe. *Well, shitfire.*

"Todd," he said softly. "Drink your wine. Relax. If you're tired, I'll make up the couch now if you want."

Todd's brown eyes widened. "Couch?" he asked.

Gabe nodded. "I don't have a guest bedroom, so the couch will have to do. I'll put a couple of blankets on it. It's really quite comfortable."

"I-I don't understand. I'm sleeping in here?"

For just a moment, Gabe thought Todd was going to cry. "Sure, Todd. You can sleep in my room if you want. It's a king-size bed, plenty of room, but with you being straight, I figured you wouldn't want to share with a 'queer'."

Confusion filled Todd's face. "I-I don't... I'm sorry about calling you that."

"I'll forgive you this time. In the meantime, I want you to unwind. I'm not paying for you. You told me you're not for sale." He gave Todd another reassuring smile.

The confused look came back. "But I figured... since you let me in...."

Ah, sweet boy. "I don't take advantage of people. Especially not people in trouble. I'm sorry about the offer downstairs. I just thought—"

"I was a whore," Todd muttered.

Gabe's heart sank. "Todd, I'm sorry about that. I fucked up. So tonight I'm giving you a place to stay. Get your head together. That's it."

With those words, Gabe watched the tension run out of Todd, saw his shoulders lower, his posture relax. A smile flickered at the corners of his mouth, but Gabe saw that tears still threatened. What had this kid been through?

Todd sipped cautiously at his wine, and then smiled for real. He took a bigger taste. "Gosh," he said.

"You like?" Gabe asked, taking a drink himself.

"Yeah. I do."

Gabe held his glass toward Todd. "Then let's drink to getting out of the cold."

Todd nodded and clinked glasses with him, though misunderstanding still shimmered across his face.

Talk to him. "Where're you from, Todd?"

"Buckman."

Buckman?

"It's a little town a couple of hours from here. Lived there my whole life."

"And now you're in Kansas City?"

"I had enough of small-town life. I wanted to find myself. Saved up and got out of there."

"What's wrong with where you're from?" Gabe asked.

"Well," Todd said with a snort. "If there's a bright center to the universe, Buckman is the town farthest from." Todd looked away, stared out the double glass doors that let out onto the balcony. The snow was still falling furiously. He looked back. Gabe could see a battle going on there on Todd's face as he tried to decide what to say. Gabe nodded encouragingly at the kid.

"I left because my parents are crazy," Todd said finally. "My Mom.... She... I... I left because I have an alcoholic stepfather who... who...." Todd stopped talking a moment, then continued. "I figured it would only be a matter of time till I got a job here, but it's not that easy. Not one that pays for shit or will give you enough hours to even pay for the electricity. I wanted to go to culinary school. Cooking, you know?"

Gabe nodded. "Cooking, huh." Now that was a surprise.

"That's not working out so much. And when the little savings I had was gone—boom!—I was out in the cold." Suddenly, there were tears springing to his eyes. He wiped at them angrily with the heel of his hand.

"My old man beat me," Gabe said and placed a hand comfortingly (or at least he hoped so) on Todd's knee. At least the kid didn't flinch. "Until I got big enough to hit back. He never laid a hand on me again."

"Well, I can't beat up my mom. And my stepdad could break me over his knee."

Gabe watched, saw the muscles in Todd's jaw clench, a quick tremble, as Todd struggled desperately to fight back the tears.

"You know, man, it's okay to cry." He squeezed Todd's knee.

"I'm not crying," Todd shouted, and then suddenly the tears came. They were pouring out of the kid. Gabe moved closer to Todd and put an arm around his shoulders, but that seemed to only make him cry harder.

Gabe stroked the boy's back. "It's okay," he whispered. "Let it out. Let it all out."

The intensity of the emotions almost frightened Gabe. *What do I do?* He scooted a little nearer to the boy—taking a chance, not wanting to scare him—and pulled him a bit closer. There was a moment of hesitation, and then Todd seemed to just surrender. It was as if Todd flowed into him, like water filling a vessel. Todd wrapped his arms around Gabe and began sobbing, near convulsing with tears. Gabe did the only thing he could. He held the boy—rocking him, hugging him—and just let him cry.

CHAPTER THREE

TO HIS horror, Todd found himself sobbing like a baby. All the pain and suffering and heartache. It just started to pour out of him. His frustrations, the lost hopes....

He cried for parents—a hard mother and a cruel stepfather—people who might as well have been as dead as the father he couldn't remember. He cried for Joan, and all that she wasn't, and for betrayal and the final shock of realizing he really didn't care what she'd done. Or with whom she'd done it. Did it really matter in the end? He cried for the pain of taking chances, believing in his dreams—looking for the best only to find the worst. For a fantasy that wasn't coming true. For having never fit in a world where he wanted nothing more than to find a place that was his. He cried until he could cry no more.

Through it all, Gabe was there. A queer. The kind of man he'd been warned about—the worst kind of man—was there for him when no one else was, not even flesh and blood.

What's more, he couldn't believe how it felt in Gabe's arms. He felt so safe. Gabe's embrace was strangely soothing, peaceful even. The huge pecs were a wonderfully strong pillow for his head, and the big, muscular body made him feel so protected.

Was this how it felt when a father held you? He had no idea. No frame of reference. He couldn't even remember being held by his dad. There was a picture of it—him still in diapers, sitting in his father's lap in a porch swing—but that was it. That man had been smiling. But he was dead and the man Todd's mother married six months later (the bitch!) had never smiled at him. Not that Todd could remember anyway. Unless it was when Todd was in pain.

Yet here was a total stranger, one who'd smiled at him, and more.

Todd knew his mother held him once. There were pictures of that too. And he thought he remembered one time when he was very little— he'd been crying then also; he'd scraped a knee or maybe an elbow— and she'd even kissed him. But that was it. All Todd could remember.

Sometimes Todd wondered what his life would be like now if his real father had lived. What if that smiling man on the porch swing had raised him? How might life be different? Would the man be willing, or even have the desire, to just give him a hug every now and then? Wouldn't that be amazing?

When Joan wanted to be held, he thought he might like it. He'd been looking forward to getting intimate with a girl for forever. All his friends said it would be great, and that he would love her tits. But he never had. Not really. Being so physical with her felt alien and somehow wrong, although that didn't make a lick of sense.

And now? This man holding him? *It felt good.*

It was the first time Todd had felt good in as long he could remember, and he didn't even know the guy's last name. Did he? Had the fat man said Gabe's name? He couldn't remember. All he knew was that it was a wonderful feeling, lying in Gabe's big arms, resting his head on a hard yet pliant chest. The tears began to abate, slow down. It was like some heavy blanket had been lifted off of his body. Not even knowing he was doing it, Todd snuggled in even closer, melted against the man, was amazed at how their bodies fit together, like two puzzle pieces, even though he was so much smaller than Gabe.

That was when Todd realized his body was responding. He was getting hard—*No!*—and he didn't know what to do. *No, no. Why am I...?* Why was this happening to him?

No. No. No!

He couldn't be getting this aroused while in the arms of a man.

Not the first time.

He'd gotten hard when Gabe had kissed him.

No. Can't be.

And it wasn't the first time something like this had happened.

No. He couldn't be getting a hard-on over a guy.

(*"You a faggot or something?"*)

Todd pulled back and as he did his arm brushed a hard knot in Gabe's lap. Fuck! The guy had a hard-on. "No," he cried and pulled away as if he'd been burned.

Gabe was turned on too!

"Todd, I'm sorry."

Not a fag! I'm not!

Todd trembled. Saw his glass of wine on the coffee table—when had he put it there?—snatched it up and swallowed it all in two big gulps. He looked at the empty glass, turned to Gabe, looked away.

"I'll get more," Gabe said and seemed to almost run to the kitchen.

Memory: Cooking breakfast for his mom when he was ten. It was Mother's Day. Pancakes with white chocolate chips. Dribbling dark chocolate in flower petal patterns on the plate before placing the pancakes in the center. A few real flowers added made it all even prettier. He wanted a smile from her. A "That's lovely, Son."

"Todd!" His stepfather. "What the hell?"

His stepfather standing over Todd, looking down at his creation.

"What the hell is that?"

"Pancakes?" Quiet, tiny voice.

"What man makes pancakes like that?"

"They're for Mom."

"I don't care. What are you, a fucking fag?"

He didn't take the breakfast to his mother. Threw it out. Made new, boring pancakes and used Mrs. Butterworth instead of the syrup with just a hint of cocoa that he'd invented out of his head.

Todd looked up and somehow Gabe was standing over him with a bottle of wine. He hadn't heard the man return. "More?" Gabe asked, and Todd saw he was tugging his shirt down in a ridiculous attempt to hide an all-too-prominent erection that traveled down one leg of the man's sweats. They weren't exactly made from a fabric that could hide anything.

Jeez. Look at it. It must be huge.

Dammit. Look away. Stop staring. Not a fag! I can't be a fag. Not that too. Not fair!

Trying not to even look in the man's direction, Todd held out his glass for a refill, left it held out when Gabe only half filled it. Gabe took the hint and poured more of the deep-red, almost purple, wine.

Todd gulped half of it as fast as the last time, then caught himself. He was probably sucking down wine more expensive than he could possibly guess.

"I'm sorry," he muttered.

"No," Gabe said quietly. "I'm the one who should be sorry."

Todd looked at the handsome (sexy) man and saw the anguish in his (beautiful) eyes. What did Gabe have to be sorry for?

"Your wine," Todd said.

"Wine?"

"I'm sorry for gulping down your wine."

"Todd, it's just wine. I can buy more."

"Aren't you having any?" Todd asked, and for some reason thought he might cry again. But there were just no tears left.

Gabe sat down on one of the two chairs instead of the couch, placed the bottle on the coffee table, and picked up his own glass, barely touched. Took a small swallow, closed his eyes, leaned back in his chair.

Todd looked at his own glass. He sipped the wine this time. Closed his eyes. It was sweet. Was there something more he was supposed to be getting out of it? He peeked out at Gabe and then closed his eyes again. Another sip. Then, to his surprise, he did note something. He hadn't noticed at first because the flavor was so intense. Blackberries. This was made from blackberries. And just taking a sip… why, your tongue just soaked it up. God. What would happen if you warmed this up and poured it over ice cream? Would that be crazy?

"You want something stronger? Scotch? Whisky?"

Todd opened his eyes again, shook his head. "Don't like them," he said even though he'd only tried the latter. "I was just wondering what this would be like over ice cream."

Gabe beamed. "I love having it that way."

"Really?" Todd asked, pleased.

And she threw me out of her restaurant!

"I'd get you some, but I don't think I've got any," Gabe said. "We could always put it over snow."

Todd shuddered. "No snow for me, thanks."

"I was just kidding," Gabe said with a smile.

They sat, quietly enjoying their wine, neither saying a word for a while.

Then Gabe: "Do you want to watch TV? A movie?"

Todd looked at the big screen and wondered what watching something like that would be like. He glanced back through the balcony doors. The aforementioned snow was gathering outside the doors despite the fact that the balcony had its own roof. Tomorrow he'd be back out in that. Why experience something that would only make the truth of homelessness feel all the worse? "I don't think so," he said.

There was another long silence. With each passing second, Todd was all the more uncomfortable. Should he say something? What, for God's sakes? And what might Gabe say if he didn't say something first?

"Todd, I know this looks like the end of the world, but the years I have on you mean I can tell you this. It gets better. Things will get better."

"Oh yeah," Todd said, trying to swallow the sarcasm.

"A good night's sleep and everything will be better in the morning."

That was it. Todd snapped. "Better in the morning? Better? How's it going to be better? Tell me!" He stared at the man.

Gabe didn't say anything right away. Of course not. What could he say? Was he going to give him some new age bullshit about how the sun always rises in the morning? "Do you know the son of a bitch that locked me out of my apartment has *all* my stuff? Did I tell you that? He won't even let me have my clothes."

"Jesus," Gabe whispered.

"He's got my laptop. Everything is on my laptop. Stuff I can't replace. Screw the other shit—" well, most of it "—but my laptop! My pictures. My music. But most of all, my recipes."

"I'd assume going home isn't an option?"

"No way. I can't. I can *not*. It's not pride either, if that's what you're thinking. My parents—Mom, my frigging stepdad—told me if I left I can't come back. Can you believe that? I'm twenty. You move out by the time you're twenty. It's normal. Most kids move out when they're eighteen. Most of my classmates have kids already." Todd looked away. "My stepdad says only faggots want to be chefs. He said that if I went to Kansas City, I'd be nothing but a dirty cocksucker in no time, and he didn't want a cocksucker in his house. *His* house? It's my mom's house." Todd took a shaking breath. "I left anyway. I couldn't live with *him* anymore and I didn't want to live with Joan."

Especially after what she did.

"Joan?"

"My girlfriend." He laughed. "Yeah, right." *Except....*

Except somewhere along the line it all went wrong, didn't it? When we decided it was time to be doing what everyone else was doing? And when she....

"So you came to Kansas City to learn to cook?"

Todd raised an eyebrow. "Oh, I *know* how to cook," he said, nodding emphatically. "I may have only worked at a Pizza Hut and a McDonalds, but I know how to cook. What I need are the certificates.

A school. I wanted to learn from Izar Goya. Boy did I want to. But she wouldn't take me."

"The chef of Izar's Jatetxea?"

"You've heard of her?" Todd asked, surprised.

"Of course. I didn't know she teaches, though."

"She doesn't. Not really. She has a show, and I watch it and do what she's doing, and sometimes it turns out great—"

(*"What the fuck is this? Can't you just make a goddamn burger or a friggin' meatloaf? What is this supposed to be?"*)

"—and sometimes it doesn't. How can you learn by watching on TV? You can't smell or taste or feel what they're doing. I need someone to watch over me. I was hoping I could talk her into it. But she threw me out of her restaurant."

Gabe sighed and shook his head.

"So I went with my backup plan. I checked out the culinary schools and realized I hadn't saved up near enough money. I *did* find a school that's all but free if you can show that you need financial help. I filled out all these forms and shit, proved how poor I am? It's part of those programs where they want to help people start a career. Cooking basics and stuff like that. But the waiting list is like a year long…"

"Damn…."

"… and before I knew it I didn't have any money left."

"Surely you could get a job as a cook somewhere. You said Mickey D's?"

Todd sneered.

"Chubby's. *Some*place. Aren't small restaurants always looking for cooks?" Gabe asked.

"I worked for McDonalds until they fired me for being late. *Once.* My van broke down. It was a piece of shit, but it was mine." He paused, looked into Gabe's amazing blue eyes, felt his heart speed up, and found himself blushing for about the hundredth time in the last hour or so. *Change the subject.* "What kind of car do you have?"

Gabe opened his mouth, but nothing came out. He shrugged.

"You don't know what kind of a car you have?" Todd asked.

Gabe sighed. "A Saturn Sky."

"A Saturn Sky? I'm not sure what that is," he replied.

"It's no big deal. Just a little sports car."

"Something sexy?" Todd asked before thinking. He blushed. Now why had he said that? Thoughts to words again. Why didn't he ever think before the words tumbled out?

"I guess so." Gabe looked away. "Where is your van now?"

Todd's face and mood fell that fast. "Gone," he replied. "It was already on its last legs and didn't like the almost three-hour drive to Kansas City. It acted wonky ever since we got here. Then one day it just died. I had a local guy look at it, and he said it would be cheaper to get a new piece of shit than to fix *my* piece of shit."

"Fix it anyway," Gabe said.

"Can't. Damn landlord had it hauled away as an abandoned vehicle. They kept it in a lot, adding twenty dollars a day to get it back—which I couldn't afford on the first day, let alone all the added ones—and then it vanished. I guess they took it to a junk yard." Todd sighed. He gave a humorless laugh. "Ironic, isn't it? The junk yard? That's where I'm headed."

"Todd, you aren't headed to the junkyard."

"Then where am I headed?" Todd asked.

"Well, from what you're saying, just about any place is better than where you were."

Todd surprised himself when he laughed. "No shit. The Dove sure isn't paradise."

"Not sure I know it," Gabe said.

"It's on Main by the Red Garter. I lived right next to a strip club."

"Okay. Sure." Gabe gave a little chuckle. "I know where it is. It's an eyesore. And I guess I knew there were apartments there—"

"Roach-infested firetraps is more like it. But it was home."

There was another long pause. "Todd, I don't know what to say to you that won't sound like total bullshit. I want you to believe me, but I can't make you. I'm sorry that you took a chance on your dreams and got kicked in the teeth. But that doesn't mean chances aren't worth taking. You just have to try again."

Todd shook his head.

"I mean it. What have you got to lose?"

Todd turned to make another biting comment, then just stopped.

He thought about it. Shit. He had no job, almost no money, no home—not even a roach-infested firetrap. What *did* he have to lose? There was nothing left *to* lose. All he had was that twenty bucks and the clothes on his back. And one night out of the cold.

"The only way is up, right?" Gabe asked him.

Todd sighed. "I suppose so."

Gabe reached out and patted Todd's knee.

"What am I supposed to do?" the kid asked.

"Well, tonight you're supposed to relax. Tomorrow will take care of tomorrow. You never know what's just around the bend in the road."

"A sign that says 'Bridge Out'?" Todd asked in reply.

"Maybe."

Todd looked up from his lap and into Gabe's eyes. God, those eyes. Like glass marbles or polished stones. They sparkled. They were gorgeous. So blue and so.... Shit. There he went again. He looked away. Away from those eyes. *Why do I feel like this? What's he doing to me?*

"You know I was driving home from my mom's in Arkansas once—"

"Arkansas?" Gabe was from Arkansas?

"Yes." Gabe raised a brow.

Todd smirked. "You're from *Ar*kansas?"

"No. I'm not from Arkansas. But my mom moved there with her sister after she divorced my dad. I was visiting her. Can I finish?"

Todd nodded.

"So I was driving these really winding country roads and came around this sharp curve and I swear I saw a UFO."

Todd gave a bark of laughter. "What?" Was he kidding? He looked into those eyes again, trying to judge if the man was pulling his leg. That meant, though, he was indeed looking in those eyes again, and he quickly turned away. Dangerous. Those eyes were frigging dangerous.

"I know it sounds crazy. But I will believe it forever. It was all black and big and had all these weird angles, and it looked like something that shouldn't be able to fly. I saw it for half a second and then it was gone just like that"—Gabe snapped his fingers—"right into the trees."

Todd dared a glance back at Gabe. He had to talk to the guy after all. "Were you smoking some wacky-tobacky?"

"Daniel, my boyfriend at the time, swears to this day that I was. But I wasn't. I don't smoke pot."

Of course he doesn't, Todd thought. "You're crazy, then."

"Maybe. I don't deny it. But once—not as long ago as you might think, but longer than I would like to say—life was pretty bad for me too."

Todd looked around the room. It was hard to imagine.

"Then something happened and something else happened and finally I was here."

"You've got it all," Todd replied.

Gabe shook his head, a sad tone in his voice. "No. I don't have it all. But one day. One day I will."

The confidence, Todd thought. He looked around the room again. But why shouldn't Gabe be self-assured? He had a great apartment, even if it could be in a fancier building. He obviously had a good job or he wouldn't be able to afford all this. He had a great body, and he was handsome (*gorgeous*). What did he need? "A pet," he said aloud without even being aware he'd done it.

"A pet?" Gabe asked.

"A dog or a cat. That's what's left."

Gabe looked doubtful. "I don't know. I'm not home a lot. That wouldn't be fair to a pet."

"What? Why aren't you home? Where do you go?" Todd asked. "Hitting the town? The terror of men, gay *and* straight, everywhere?"

Gabe laughed. "Just really cute *straight* ones," he replied and it took Todd a moment to realize Gabe was referring to him. He blushed. He was doing a lot of that. "I spend most of my time at work. My friend Tracy says I work too much, but what else is there? There's no reason to rush home."

"A cat, then," Todd said. "They're more independent. You don't have to walk them and you can get home late. Just make sure they have food and water and they're happy."

"I would want something that wants me," said Gabe, and they locked eyes. Gabe's seemed to go dark, and how could that be with eyes as light-blue as his?

(The color of a country summer sky…)

"I love cats," Todd said. "It was the only thing that my stepdad would let me have. I left Leia behind, though. I didn't know if I could take care of her. Now I worry."

"You don't think your stepfather would hurt her do you?"

Hope not. He might. "I think he would ignore her, maybe kick her out, and she could get hit by a car," he said. He looked away. "They didn't even call on Christmas. My family. I don't have a phone, but they had the manager's number in case of an emergency. I waited all day—thought Mom would at least leave a message." He gave a laugh. "No. I didn't think she would. I just pretended. Fantasized, you know? Of course, with the asshole apartment manager, she could have called and he wouldn't have told me."

"Todd. Shit. I am so sorry. What—what did you do for Christmas?"

"Swanson's," Todd answered, quietly.

"Excuse me?"

"Swanson's frozen turkey slices. It was good. And watched my DVD of *How the Grinch Stole Christmas*."

"Oh, Todd."

Todd shrugged. Could have teared up again, but the pesky things were all gone.

Good. Only a fruit cries.

There was another of those infinite pauses. "Are you sleepy?" Gabe asked. "Would you rather me shut up and make the couch?"

No. Yes. He wanted the man to go away, and he wanted him to stay. All he could say was, "I *am* tired."

"Of course you are. You've had a really bad day. I'll be right back."

Gabe went to get the bedclothes and was back in a flash. He turned the leather couch into a comfortable-looking place to sleep just as quickly. "I'll leave you to it," Gabe said. "You can turn the music off as you like, same with the lights."

Todd nodded. "Thank you, Gabe. Thank you for—" and felt himself leaning toward the man as if Gabe were a magnet. *God. What is happening to me?*

You want him to kiss you again.

"It's okay," Gabe said. "It was nothing."

Todd felt his throat hitch. Then straightened himself. "It was everything."

The two men stood facing each other for another long moment.

Finally, Gabe: "Night, Todd."

"Pleasant dreams," Todd replied.

"Pleasant dreams."

And as Gabe left the room Todd realized that it would be enough if he could just get through until morning without a nightmare.

CHAPTER **FOUR**

IT WASN'T until Gabe got to his room and had slipped out of his sweats and T-shirt that he saw the alarm clock and realized how early it was. Not even eight thirty. Todd might be tired, probably was and should be, but Gabe didn't usually hit the sack until after ten at least. Tired he wasn't.

Can't even watch some TV. Hadn't *he* decided there was no place in the bedroom for a television?

"If you won't let me watch CNN," Daniel, his ex, would whine, "then what about porn?"

"We don't need to watch porn," Gabe had said.

"What about your Logan McCree videos," Daniel had replied with a lascivious tone.

"We don't need to watch them in our bed," Gabe had said, blushing.

"Is that the reason you got a leather couch?" Daniel asked. "Easier cleanup?"

Whatever the reason, Gabe was in his bedroom, without porn or his flat screen. A bedroom was for sleeping or making love. Gabe had been firm then, but now? Was hindsight 20/20?

But hell. A little porn might be just the ticket right now. Not only did he feel restless, he was horny. He couldn't believe how he was reacting to Todd. Like he was some kind of randy teenager instead of a grown man.

Just admit it. He reminds you of Brett.

Brett. God. Don't think about Brett.

Shitfire. Jerking off might be what he needed. But without the porn, he knew that all he would think about was Brett or Todd, and for some reason, he didn't want to think about either of them that way. If he pictured Brett, he would just feel lousy five seconds after he came. And somehow it felt wrong to allow himself to fantasize about Todd. Like he would be intruding or being a voyeur. It was silly, but it felt that way. Wrong. Objectifying Todd. Turning him into a mental pornographic movie, when in fact, Todd was human and alive and had feelings.

Of course, so were porn stars. But they'd volunteered to be sexual objects. Todd hadn't. As a matter of fact, he'd already blundered by coming on to Todd, who hadn't appreciated it one bit.

And what about that kiss? What was that about? Why did you kiss him? Talk about objectifying.

Todd liked it.

Gabe knew he did. Was the kid gay or not? Every instinct told him Todd was, but it was hard to tell. Todd was confused. But hell. So was Gabe. Mixed-up feelings to be sure. But feelings. Very real feelings.

Shitfire! You don't need to bring someone out.

Wasn't that the truth. Hadn't he learned anything? What had bringing someone out accomplished in the past?

Shitfire, I am never going to get to sleep.

Read. That usually helps.

Gabe pulled on a nightshirt, left his bedroom, went quietly to his office, and took a look at his bookcase. There had to be something. The middle shelf, the one with family pictures, was where he kept the few books he was reading.

What *was* he reading? He couldn't remember.

Was it the new Patricia Cornwell? No, wait. *The Third Gate*. And it was good. Why had he put it down?

Because you're a workaholic, that's why.

Not a workaholic. I just don't really have anything to come home to.

You've got friends. Tommy and Jude, Harry and Cody. They're all right there, right downstairs.

Not friends. Acquaintances. If I knocked on their door, they'd answer and look at me strangely and ask if there was something wrong. I'm just not all that social. I like living alone.

Liar.

"Gabe?" came a call from the living room.

Gabe looked down at himself. No bottoms, but he decided the nightshirt he'd pulled on covered everything and went down the hall. "You okay, Todd?"

"I don't know how to turn off the stereo."

"Oh. Sure." He entered the darkened living room and saw Todd standing next to the sound system. "It's the red light there on the left," he said, approaching the young man. Todd was shirtless, and even in the dim light, as Todd turned to him, he could see what a nice chest he had. Quite nice in fact. Not as developed his own—

It's not like he has a home gym.

—but defined and with a fine dusting of dark hair across his pecs.

Gabe started to reach for the off button, but Todd was standing right in front of it. "Excuse me," he said and reached past the young man, barely keeping from grazing him. Todd's nipples were standing hard and erect, and Gabe wondered what they would feel like, taste like, in his mouth.

Damn. Get a hold of yourself.

He shook himself, turned off the sound system, took a step back.

Todd looked up at him and their eyes locked for what seemed forever. "Thanks," he said quietly.

"No, problem. I was just getting up for a book. It's a little early for me—"

"I'm sorry," Todd replied. "I can stay up if you want."

"No, no. That's fine. You need your rest. Look. Did you want to shower before you went to sleep?"

A smile crept across Todd's face. "God, yes. I wanted to ask, but—"

"Then you should have. Come on. I'll get you some fresh towels."

With Todd following behind, Gabe went to the end of the hall, entered the bathroom, and reached up into the cabinets he'd installed over the tub. With the tall ceilings in such an old building, there had been plenty of room, and the space had only been wasted. It was only as he was grabbing a towel and washcloth that he realized he was flashing his butt at Todd. *Shit! Have I lost all sense of decorum?*

He turned slowly, feeling the heat of a growing blush on his face, and saw Todd's was the same. "Sorry," he said, holding out the stuff for Todd.

Todd visibly gulped. "N-No problem. It's not like I haven't seen a guy's ass before. Gym class, right?" He turned redder.

Once again they stood there and looked at each other, neither saying a word. Todd's head was slightly cocked back, and the muscles in his neck stood out clearly. What would that skin feel like under his lips? Gabe's gaze was drawn to Todd's mouth. Wide and soft, with stubble on his upper lip. What a kissable, kissable mouth. *Gosh, what is this kid doing to me? You'd think I was fifteen with a runaway libido.*

"Um...." Gabe noticed the stubble across Todd's cheeks as well. He had wide sideburns, which Gabe didn't usually like, but somehow they worked for Todd. He had a patch of hair on his chin as well, this fuller and obviously something the young man had elected, at least recently, to let grow. But Gabe would still bet Todd would like to shave. The growth down his neck had to be itchy. Gabe turned, started to bend over at the sink, thought better of it—giving the boy another view of his ass and possibly some dangly bits might not be a good idea—and turned back. "There's a package of disposable razors in the bottom drawer if you want to shave," he said. "And an extra toothbrush or two."

"For all those hot guys you have coming over?" Todd asked.

Gabe couldn't believe it, but he was blushing all the more, despite how long it had been since he'd been with a man. No time for the most part, and tricks and one-night stands didn't hold much interest for him. The fact that he'd invited Todd up for sex was not his usual modus operandi.

Liar. You know exactly why.

Fine. He knew.

Brett. He reminds you of Brett.

They're nothing alike!

"No men. I just have a dentist who gives out a new brush every time I go in. I like to get an extra appointment in every year. They stack up."

Todd nodded. "Thanks. A lot. My mouth tastes like crap and my body feels like I've rolled in it. I needed this more than I can say."

"No problem." Another pause. For a second there, it felt like Todd was going to kiss him. Had he actually risen up on his toes...? He noticed Todd's toes and damn, even they were sexy. A man's feet. Wide, a scattering of hair across their tops, with strong-looking toes that lined up the way Gabe liked them and not with the second toe being longer than....

And then Todd did kiss him. Rose up and gave him a little chaste kiss that hit Gabe like a wrecking ball. He might have even moaned. *Please, God, no. Tell me I didn't moan.*

"Thank you," Todd said, his face totally pink. "Thank you for everything."

Gabe nodded, not trusting his voice. He turned to leave the bathroom.

"Night," said Todd.

"Night," Gabe managed. He shut the door behind him and went straight to his room and closed his own, turned off the light, and headed right to the bed. His nightshirt was up, over, off, and on the floor faster than a magician could have done. Gabe was on the bed and had barely touched himself when his semi-erection, heavy and thick, arched up and filled into an almost painfully hard pillar. He took his cock, already leaking, in his fist, the fingers of his other hand just grazing his nipples, and in record time he was splashing his chest and belly with his semen. He groaned in pleasure, biting down on his lower lip to try and suppress the shout he wanted to release. Shower running or not, he didn't want Todd to hear.

Surprisingly, after that he was able to slip off to sleep.

TODD climbed in the shower and caught a glimpse of himself in the mirror on the back of the bathroom door, saw his lightly furry butt and thought of Gabe's. The abrupt view of the man's ass had startled him. And what an ass. Big, but solid and muscular, and smooth as marble. He'd felt a strange compulsion to touch it, but hadn't, of course, thank God. What would that have started? The thought made his cock rear up, tall and proud, with a suddenness that made Todd's eyes widen. A wave of arousal hit him, unexpected and strong.

Shit. I'm hard thinking about a man's ass.

Not gay. I can't be. Just freaked out is all. Tired.

Weak.

He started the water, found a temperature just south of scalding, turned on the shower head and discovered heaven. It felt good. So damned good. It hadn't even been quite twenty-four hours since his last shower, yet it seemed like a century. He found a bar of soap and a bottle of shampoo as well, sniffed both, and found he loved the scent of the bar. Something herbal and country smelling about it. It lathered quickly, and he was soon covered in suds, and the sight and feel and smell was more heaven.

Why in the hell did I kiss him?

He froze at the thought.

I kissed him. I really did. I kissed a man. "And I liked it" came a familiar song in his head.

No!

Why didn't it feel like it did when he kissed Joan? Kissing her had been like putting his mouth on that CPR dummy at school when they were teaching lifesaving techniques.

No. Gabe's mouth was strong and warm and alive and real and *God!* Todd's cock throbbed and showed no sign of going down. He was almost afraid to touch it. It felt like it wouldn't take anything and he'd shoot. Why was he so fucking horny? *Should I just do it?* God, wouldn't it be tacky to masturbate in someone else's bathroom?

Well you can't very well do it on the couch!

Gabe's face came to his mind then, and that chest, and that bare butt. Gabe's butt was so smooth while his was furry. Would Gabe like that? A hairy butt?

Todd thought of Gabe's mouth. His smile. His tongue wet and demanding against Todd's own.

No! No no no!

Todd focused instead on Joan and grabbed himself. He pictured her, with her round pale face and her wild explosion of dark hair. He thought of holding her close. Began to stroke the long yet slender length of himself.

Weird. It didn't feel all that good. The thought of Joan wasn't doing anything for him. Immediately, her whiney voice came to mind, and how she called him "Toddy," even though he'd asked her not to a million times. He shook away her voice, focused instead on her body. But when he pictured her large breasts and that triangle of hair below— the slitted opening—he felt his semi-erection grow limper. Her private place just wasn't attractive to him. Why did boys make such a big deal about vaginas? He was sure it was all bullshit. No one could really like that, could they? There was nothing there. What was all the foofaraw about? Now a guy on the other hand... a guy had something to get excited about. A guy had something to play with. And a girl's butt. He'd never liked Joan's bottom either. Nothing like the hard muscular asses of the guys in the locker room at school.

Unbidden, Gabe's beautiful, hard, muscular bottom crept into Todd's visionings again, took over the picture of Joan and—Oh! his dick felt good. Slick and—*Oh oh oh!* His legs started to tremble, and *Christ!* He was cumming hard, shooting in jets so strong he could feel it through the surface of his cock. He bit down on his lower lip, afraid he'd scream, because shower going or not, surely Gabe would be knocking on the door and asking if he was all right. Spots swirled before his eyes, and he marveled at the pleasure that rocked through him. Only when he finally came down, somehow not falling down while doing it, did Todd realize how he'd been thinking about Gabe's butt.

God. God, no.

Am I a fag after all?

It just wasn't fair. Not with everything else. Not fair at all.

Sleep didn't come easy. All he could think about was that he was lying on this couch and a man who *wanted* him was just down the hall. The thought scared the shit out of him. And yet in no time, he was hard again thinking about it.

("You a faggot or something?")

Am I? Am I queer?

("The word is 'gay'.")

Gay.

Todd tossed and turned, and after a while, he finally fell asleep.

In his dream, he was walking silently down the hall. It seemed as long as a football field. On the way, he was passing other doors he recognized. Doors that shouldn't be in that hall. The door to his mom's room. The door to his stepfather's. Joan's bedroom door. Christ, was that Austin's basement? There was the door to his own room at home. And the door to his apartment, 6-B. Finally, it was Gabe's door. He felt a huge surge of relief and pushed it ever so quietly open. There was an enormous bed, and sprawled across it, nightshirt hiked up so his smooth muscular bottom was clearly visible, as well as a hint of large hairless balls, was Gabe.

Todd crept up to the bed, its surface vast and wide, and climbed up onto it, crawled across to Gabe on hands and knees. When he finally, finally, got to Gabe, he reached out and touched the man's butt. It was so hard and so sleek. Like suede, but as smooth as glass. Then, startling Todd, Gabe's hand came back and around, took hold of Todd's own hand and pulled him up against his back.

They snapped together like two pieces of Lego. *Click.*

After that, Todd remembered no more.

CHAPTER FIVE

TODD woke to a silent apartment. He sat up, looked around. It was true. He had spent the night in a strange man's apartment. In the bright light of morning, which crept through the balcony doors, the place looked different. More functional than lived in?

Todd looked down and saw his jeans on the floor, listened for any movement, and then scrambled into them. He pulled on his sweater, made his way down the hall, and saw Gabe's bedroom door was open.

If he peeked in, he would see the big man sprawled across a king-size mattress. His shirt would be pulled up, and his ass and part of his balls would be right there on display.

Todd turned away. Then thought—*who are you fooling?*—and looked.

The bed was empty, and made. Todd felt a little ripple of disappointment.

(*"You a faggot or something?"*)

Gabe was gone? He went to the bathroom, and peeked in the other rooms as well, all with their doors open and all empty. Was he really gone? That didn't make any sense. How did Gabe know he could trust his apartment and everything in it to Todd? Why, he could steal the man blind. Hock Gabe's shit and turn around and get all his own junk back.

Of course, "junk" was the word.

A twin bed, the same one he'd had all his life. Shelves made of boards and cinder blocks. A dresser he'd found on the curb after a garage sale, missing the front of one drawer plus another drawer entirely. A couple of rugs, one torn, the other with a few cigarette burns. Two ugly, mismatching lamps (also from garage sales—one actually in the trash), his childhood desk (in good condition), a couch (where you didn't want to sit on one end—ouch!), a badly scarred coffee table, a small TV (where everyone appeared green), and two matching chairs (wow!). Then his clothes, of course. All his clothes. And his laptop—piece of shit that it was. His laptop that had everything on it. His dreams. Pictures that represented his dreams. His recipes: those found online or transcribed from magazines, and of course, those he'd come up with on his own.

Finally, a few *Star Wars* toys he just couldn't bring himself to leave behind. His stepfather would have just thrown them away. That was his legacy. *Star Wars* toys. Pathetic.

But pathetic or not, it was *his* legacy, and he wanted his stuff back. Especially one more thing hidden in a rolled-up sock in the back of the second drawer on the right-hand side of his dresser. He had to have that. His real and final backup plan, as piteous as it was.

The other rooms in Gabe's apartment were just as amazing as the living room. The office held a big, gorgeous, darkly stained wooden desk, a large comfortable chair, and a stunning computer setup. Why, just the monitor was larger than Todd's television. Everything looked expensive, even the throw rug and curtains. There were several bookcases, all filled with books. Gabe sure was a reader. Todd had been known to get lost in a Stephen King book or something by Michael Crichton—and of course, his vast collection of *Star Wars* books—but this was something else again. There were also a few photographs. A woman. One look and Todd knew she had to be Gabe's mother; the resemblance was striking. No way could she deny him. Another of her and… shit! Gabe in a tank top with a trophy. Young. Not much older than Todd's own age, maybe a year or two younger. But that same dazzling, almost goofy (cute) smile, same (country sky) blue eyes, sparkling. Cute. Very cute. Every girl in his school must have wanted him.

But he wanted other boys.

Todd reached out, almost picked up the picture, stopped himself. What if Gabe noticed? How weird would that look?

Todd turned away and went to the next room.

The workout room astonished him, especially the Bowflex. He'd called the 800 number on one of those commercials late at night once and been shocked at the price. This was another room where a lot of money had been spent.

And of course, there was that bedroom. The bed was an immense four-poster affair, all dark wood, and when he couldn't stand the temptation anymore, he checked it out and wasn't surprised in the least to realize the mattress was some kind of memory foam, or whatever it was called. The kind you could supposedly bounce on and not spill a glass of wine. The rest of the bedroom furniture continued to bear out the fact that Gabe did nothing cheaply. The whole apartment spoke of money. Why the hell did the man live here instead of a loft or a luxury apartment building?

There was no doubt about it. If Todd wanted, he could call some friend—what friend? Maybe the hustlers from the park—and clear the place down to nothing but some hooks and some wire. That and a speck of food too small for a mouse, as Dr. Seuss might say. He could do it in a few hours, and what would Gabe be able to say? Do? Tell the cops he'd let a hustler spend the night and left him to his own devices the next day? Would an insurance company even pay up on that? (And was there any doubt that Gabe had insurance on everything?)

But of course Todd wouldn't steal from Gabe. Todd could no more steal so much as a fork from the man who had let him in from the cold as he could haul the huge treadmill out on his shoulders.

Why do I have to be such a nice guy?

Todd went back to the living room and then headed to the kitchen. Surely it would be okay to get a soda or juice or something. To his surprise, after finding a pitcher of orange juice and going to a cabinet to look for a glass, he found a note addressed to him.

Morning Todd.

Wanted to let you sleep in—you needed it.

There is bacon in the sink thawing, and eggs in the fridge. Feel free to make yourself breakfast—and make it a big one, OK? You won't break me if you do. If you drink coffee, just turn on the coffee maker and press the brew button. It's all set up.

I pulled out the crock pot and if you don't mind, please dump the frozen chicken in it, spice it to your tastes—I certainly trust a man who knows how to cook—and set it on low. You'll find the chicken in the freezer. It should be perfect by the time I get home which will be anywhere between 4 and 6. I hope you'll be joining me for dinner.

Please take it easy today. You have nowhere to go and I have no reason to run you off.

Weather forecast said it snowed 8 inches last night and we could get another six today. Stay. Rest. Nap. Watch TV.

Get your shit together.

There is always tomorrow.

Hoping I'll see you tonight,

Gabe

Tears began to gather in Todd's eyes. Apparently they had replenished themselves in the night. Gabe—a man who didn't know him from any other stranger on the street—not only trusted Todd in his home, but was giving him another day.

How could this be happening after all the horrible shit that had gone on in just the previous twenty-four hours?

Maybe Gabe was right. Maybe the only way was up.

"WHAT? A hustler?" Tracy Creighton had almost shouted the words, and Gabe looked over her shoulder and out the door to see if anyone was looking. "Mother skeeter, please tell me he wasn't a hustler."

"He's not a hustler," Gabe answered, fighting the annoyance that was threatening him. She was looking at him as if he'd announced he had suddenly decided to go straight and asked her to marry him. Why was Tracy acting like this? She was his co-worker, friend, and confidante of several years, second only to Peter Wagner.

"Gabriel, have you lost your mind?"

"No, I haven't lost my mind. Damn, Tracy. You think you could lower your voice a few decibels? At least close the door."

"You must have," she said, placing her hands on her shapely hips. "Letting a stranger spend the night in your apartment."

"Oh, please. It's not like either one of us has never had a one-night stand or two," Gabe replied.

"At least those were people we knew. Name one time I ever took someone home that I met that night...." She paused, blushed, and looked away. "Never mind, don't answer that."

Gabe tried to hide a grin. He remembered a business trip the two of them had gone on a couple of years back and the devilishly handsome man Tracy had met in a bar.

She turned back and must have seen the amusement on Gabe's face. "Okay, so I'm no Mother Theresa. But at least that was a hotel room. What was the guy going to steal? My makeup? A dress?"

Tracy—who was wearing red (of course) and whose dark-lined eyes were wide in drama-shock—held her hands out to her sides, fingers drawn into claws, and let out a muted scream. "I can't believe this. You left a whore-boy in your apartment? *Your* apartment? You get in your car and you head the heck home right now! Get there before he cleans you out."

"Tracy," Gabe said as he got out of his chair and went to close his office door. "It's okay. He's not going to steal anything."

Tracy fell back in a chair, leaned her head back so her long luxurious hair fell down in a wave, and gave another silent mock scream. "I will never understand you, Gabriel. Never. Unless you really are an angel. You know, maybe all this time I've been working with an angel unaware?"

Gabe laughed. "Only you could get prostitutes and the Bible in one conversation."

She hunched her shoulder and rolled her eyes. "Nonsense. The Bible is full of prostitutes. The whore of Babylon, Jezebel, Mary Magdalene."

"Except Mary Magdalene wasn't a prostitute," Gabe said.

"Of course she was," Tracy returned.

"Nope. Look it up. Same chapter. Two different women. Common mistake."

Tracy shook her head yet again. "And only an angel would know that. Gabriel! The point is you need to get out of here and get home while you still have a home to get to."

Gabe sighed. "Tracy, my only worry is that he won't be there when I *get* home."

Tracy smiled. "Oh. So that's it. You got laid. You got laid at least, right? And please tell me you wore at least *two* condoms."

"There was no getting laid. He slept on the couch. And like Mary Magdalene, you're getting it wrong. I said I *thought* he was a hustler, but he wasn't. He's just a poor, down-on-his-luck kid from Smallville."

Tracy groaned. "Gabriel. You are too trusting. It's your worst fault."

"I am not too trusting. I would rather be too trusting than be as cynical as you, my dear one." This conversation needed to stop before he said something he couldn't take back. "When have I ever been screwed over? Tell me. Tell me one time."

Tracy's eyes narrowed. He could see the wheels turning, trying to decide which man to throw in his face. Daniel? Brett?

Why had he been so wrong about those two? Especially Brett? What had he been thinking? He was usually so good about his assessments of people, and he had been sure he'd had something special with the kid.

Peter Wagner—the owner of the company he and Tracy worked for—had discovered his talent for reading people, for feeling out clients. Gabe's almost sixth sense for when it was okay or not okay to trust someone. It was why he was so successful at his job. Gabe knew when a client was being honest, when investing in them was a good idea, when they were withholding information. He couldn't read minds. Gabe didn't believe in that. He, as well as Peter, maintained he had some kind of instinct for reading faces. They said dogs could do that, and most humans had just lost the ability.

Yet he sure had fucked up with the men in his life, hadn't he? Except for Peter, that is.

But no. Todd was no Brett. Gabe believed in Todd. He *knew* he could trust him.

Tracy was not going to be able to find a single—

"What about when you found out Daniel took your Logan McCree videos? You said he'd never steal from you. Those were your DVDs. I bought one of them for you. An autographed copy!"

Gabe burst into laughter. How disconcerting it must have been for her to arrange that for him. She was no prude, but overt sexuality did embarrass her. "You're reaching, Tracy. You are really, really reaching."

"And the buffet?" Tracy asked, jumping to her high-heeled feet.

"I let Daniel have it."

"He was still stealing. You bought that. He didn't pitch in a dime."

"Daniel picked it out and I hated it. It was a win-win situation."

Tracy sighed, and at least it wasn't an overly dramatic one. And at least she wasn't going for the jugular, which she could. "Your funeral, buster." She started to reach for the door, then stopped. She turned back. "Is he at least cute?"

A slow smile crept across Gabe's face. "Yes," he replied without even needing to stop and think about it. He closed his eyes and imagined the kid. A good head shorter than him, had looked stocky until Gabe had seen him with his shirt off. While Todd had no cut abs, there wasn't any fat on him. That creamy, smooth skin, except for the dark patch of hair on his chest. And on his face. Scruffy. Dark hair. Thick brows. Eyes so deep you could fall into them—and he almost had several times. "Yes, Tracy. He is god-awful cute."

He opened his eyes and saw Tracy biting her lip. "So at least a little bit of this is your little head doing the thinking?"

Gabe grinned. Little head. Tracy would no more say "dick" than she would "hell" or "shit." Loud she might be, crass she wasn't.

"Maybe," he admitted. "Tracy. I look at him and…." He paused, trying to think of what it was. Peter would know. He'd listen to Gabe and know. Peter. Gabe gave a little sigh. "Todd reminds me of me not that long ago. Todd has big dreams, and they've all been crushed. He came from this little town—I can't remember the name. And sure I came from a big one. St. Louis is much bigger than… Buckman. That's the name. But big or small, that was me. Then Peter came along—"

"Who I still wonder if you shtupped."

"No you don't. You know I didn't." *I actually offered*, he remembered. "Tracy, look, Todd has lost it all. He has the clothes he's wearing and nothing else. His landlord took everything. If there's some way I can help him out, then maybe—just maybe—I can pay forward just a little bit for what's been done for me."

Tracy came to him then, reached out a hand and placed it on Gabe's arm. "Oh, sweetie." She sighed. "That's all you do. That's who you *are*." She leaned in and hugged him. "I don't mean to be a B-I-T-C-H. I'm just worried that—"

"I know what you're worried about." *You're worried Todd is another Brett.*

"Gabriel, it's your turn. All you do is help people. It's time for someone to do something for you again."

Gabe shrugged. "I know it's hard for you to believe, but I'm happy. I've got everything I want." *Almost everything.*

Tracy stepped back.

"I leave you on your own, then, dear one. I hope you know what you're doing." She left him there alone, and good, she closed the door.

Gabe looked at the time. Ten thirty. It was going to be a long day. He usually loved work, but today he found all he wanted to do was go home.

TODD found the chicken right where Gabe said it would be. It wasn't shrink-wrapped, like the ones he'd seen since moving to the city, but was contained in a paper bag instead. A label proclaimed it was a "Carlisle Free Range Chicken." All natural. "Raised and grown as a chicken should be."

In other words, raised on a country farm. And raised at the edge of the universe as he was, local farm chickens were all Todd had known. There was a difference. He could taste it. He hadn't had a chicken that didn't taste "wrong" since he'd moved to Kansas City. This would be a delight.

He noticed the price and winced. Shit. But should he be surprised? Gabe would be interested in his health—witness his body and the expensive work-out equipment he owned. The man wouldn't be worried about cost.

Todd put the chicken in the sink to thaw. He saw where Gabe was going with the Crock-Pot thing; Todd's mom had used them his whole life, hers too. Stick a frozen something in the Crock-Pot, put it on low, go to work, and *voila!* dinner was ready when you got home. But that was not going to happen today. Nuh-uh, no way.

A quick inspection of the kitchen showed—to Todd's delight— some fresh fruits and vegetables (and what would he bet they were organic?) and the hanging tiered basket by the sink included onions and some new potatoes, as well as some ginger and cloves of garlic. He got an idea. He wasn't sure where they came from, he never was. But somehow they worked…

(*"What the fuck is this? Can't you just make a goddamn burger or a friggin' meatloaf? What is this supposed to be?"*)

… no matter what his stepfather said.

The spices in the cabinet were obviously, while dried, fresh considering most of them were in little baggies instead of grocery store bottles. Who knew how old the spices were in those little bottles? He started to open a bag, but even before he did, he could smell the fresh scent of the rosemary he held. Oooh, he could come up with something all right.

First though, the weather. Another peek out the balcony doors showed a world covered in white, dazzlingly bright in the morning sun. While there were clouds, there was blue sky as well. In other circumstances, he would have been enchanted. Today he could only shiver thinking about actually being out there.

He found the remote and turned on the TV, only to discover, to his amusement, a DVD had been left in the player. *The Avengers*! Who would have thought it? Gabe watching *The Avengers*? Todd found the case and, yes, it wasn't even a rental. Gabe owned it. It made Todd curious, and he quickly found the armoire in the corner held a stash of movies, many of them a geek's delight. And, *ohmygod*, a set of all six *Star Wars* movies! So even though Gabe hadn't caught his little joke the night before about where he came from, or made the connection with the name of Todd's cat, the man wasn't a sci-fi hater. For some reason, that pleased Todd immensely.

He turned the DVD off long enough to check the weather—it didn't take long, it was already set on The Weather Channel—and found out that, yes, indeed, there was another six inches in the forecast for late afternoon, early evening. Crap. Would Gabe let him stay another night? The note seemed to say so. Todd looked outside, saw all the snow, even there on the balcony, and wondered about that blowjob.

No. Don't go there.

Todd turned the player back on, ejected *The Avengers*, and put in the first *Star Wars* movie. Born into a whole new generation, he didn't have the prejudice against the prequels and knew the whole series nearly by heart. It would make good background noise anyway.

Then he was back in the kitchen and was soon dicing up a couple of apples, as well as a few oranges. He would have gone with some pineapple, but he didn't find any in any of the cabinets. The search did reveal some walnuts, which made him quite happy—especially since they were English walnuts and not the black, which he always found too bitter. He shredded some ginger, then mixed everything together, along with cloves, nutmeg, cinnamon, and some very fresh raisins (again in a baggie and not a box). He placed the mixture in a glass bowl, covered it with cellophane. He put it in the refrigerator and then sat to watch *The Phantom Menace* while the chicken thawed.

Bacon grease, he thought. *I could do something with the bacon grease.* He hadn't had a clue what Gabe wanted done with it after Todd made breakfast. His mother saved it in a grease pot—although it wasn't really a pot, just a little aluminum container kept at the back of the stove—but Gabe hadn't appeared to have anything like that, not even an empty jar. Todd's neighbor in Buckman had poured grease down the sink while running hot water, but Todd hadn't thought that would be a good idea in a building as old as this one. It killed him that this meant he couldn't wash the frying pan, but now his thoughts were percolating. *Bacon grease instead of butter. Mmmm....*

Despite his love of the movie, Todd dozed off. The last few day's events—everything over the last few months—had been far more exhausting than even *he* had realized.

He dreamed of a dark cellar and his friend Austin and a porn video his buddy had snitched from the collection his older cousin had brought back from college. Quite a collection, in fact, and a very varied selection. They'd kept the volume way down despite the fact that no one had been home. Austin didn't want to take a chance someone would catch them.

To Todd's surprise, he'd been hard as a rock during the video, despite the profusion of breasts, and pubic hair shaved into a dozen different styles. The dream was so real, so like that night months ago, except this time the erection straining Austin's underwear—his pants were unzipped and opened wide—was frighteningly huge. Bigger than any of the men on the television screen. Much bigger than he remembered Austin being. Austin's TV was hardly better than Todd's, except that everything was orange and red instead of green, the actors leaving ghostly images behind them as they moved. Todd barely noticed, though. He couldn't stop staring at Austin's lap and the growing wet spot in his underwear.

Then Austin turned, looked at him, and smiled a Cheshire grin. "It's big, isn't it?"

Todd blanched, drew back.

Austin began to grope himself. "Come on, Todd. Tell me you want it. Tell me you want to suck it. It tastes really good."

Todd woke up with a start, as well as a rigid erection, aching in need.

CHAPTER SIX

A WORKOUT. And where better than in Gabe's workout room?

Todd had no idea how to even attempt to use the Bowflex, and he didn't want to try. Not really. What if Gabe had it on some kind of favorite setting? And how did he even use it? The thing was a mystery.

But the Nordic? That was something else again, and he wanted to give it a try. Todd hadn't exercised, not really, since he'd left home months ago. He missed it. He didn't think Gabe would mind.

Any kind of long time running in jeans would be a little uncomfortable, though. He supposed he could strip to his underwear. He shrugged. They were a little ragged, but they weren't his worst pair.

Of course, these days they might very well be his only pair.

Jeez.

It didn't take long to figure the piece of equipment out, but before he started his run, he went ahead and shucked down to his boxer briefs. That's when he found the iPod. Gabe must use it when he worked out.

"I wonder what he likes?" Todd wondered aloud.

It turned out to be Lady Gaga.

"Well, I'll be dammed," Todd said with a grin. Maybe he wasn't the only Little Monster around.

With a small amount of guilt he pulled one of Gabe's T-shirts from a clothes hamper, put it on, and, music blasting in his skull, began to run. Common sense dictated he should start out slow, but he found himself running full tilt, letting his feet pound and his heart race and the music pour through him like the demons of hell were after him. After all, it had felt like that lately.

In no time, he was drenched in sweat, his eyes stinging, his lungs burning, and a stitch beginning in his side. He knew he should stop, but he couldn't. He wanted it to hurt. He wanted it to hurt on the outside like it did on the inside, and that was a lot.

Lady Gaga sang about how she was going to marry the night, and he ran. He ran from all the things he'd cried about the night before. Cried! He'd cried like a kid. Worse, he'd cried in the arms of a man. A gay man. Todd couldn't remember crying like that in his life, at least not in the presence of another living soul. Sometimes he would go into the woods behind his house, to a secret little place he'd found when he was a kid, and there he could cry or read or do whatever he wanted. It was there and only there he'd felt free. One day he'd even dared to take off all his clothes and sit in the sun. Where the idea had come from he had no idea, but it was one of the most liberating experiences of his life. Soon he found himself naked in that clearing more and more often. He would stand and spread his arms and let his head fall back, eyes closed, bathing in the sunlight. Not long before he moved to Kansas City, he thought about inviting Austin to join him in the woods. The idea had really taken him over those last few days. About how maybe they could repeat what happened in his friend's basement, but this time with no porn tape to ruin things. What would that be like? Maybe more would happen.

And did it make him a faggot?

No. He wasn't in love with Austin. It was just friendship. Hadn't he read in that book from the school library it was normal for young men to play around together? Something natural because they had all those hormones raging and no way to release that sexual energy with someone of the opposite sex?

(Although of course, Todd had been doing that for months.)

The feelings would go away. He would get interested in Joan. He was just a late bloomer. Soon—any day he was sure—his desire for vaginas would begin and the thoughts of what he might do with Austin would just fade away.

Todd had found the little clearing in the woods the day his mother told him she was getting married. He'd been stunned. She was remarrying? And worse, it was to that creepy guy Urston, the one that always looked at him funny? The guy with the black eyes and the pockmarks all over his face who worked on cars down at the gas station on the edge of town. The guy who came into the diner where his mother worked nights and drank endless cups of coffee and always ate a couple slices of apple pie, the first with a big wedge of cheddar cheese and the second with a heaping scoop of vanilla ice cream. And hadn't that just been weird?

When Todd's mother had broken the news to Todd, he'd run out of the house and deep into the woods, and that's when he'd found what would become his secret spot by the creek. That first time, he'd come to a complete stop, the air whooshing in and out of his lungs (like now!), and stood there in awe. It looked like a magic place, where elves or fairies would be at home. There was even a ring of mushrooms. Somehow he'd run right into the circle and not damaged even one of the little lovely orange umbrellas.

It had been his secret place from that day forward and was the only thing he missed about Buckman. There were no good woods anywhere near him except the trees near Liberty Memorial, and he'd heard fags went there for sex. There was no way he was going to a place where some queer tried to get at his dick.

(*"The word is 'gay', and yes I am."*)

God. How could Gabe be gay? It seemed impossible. The only gay man Todd had known before he moved to Kansas City was Mr. Tanson, who ran the town library, such as it was. He was short and balding and spoke in an effeminate voice, and people were nice enough to his face but said mean things behind his back. Really mean things.

"Cocksucker is what he is," Todd's stepfather would snarl. "He has no place running a place where kids go. Frigging fudge packer. Homos are all degenerates. Perverts. They like little boys. They kidnap them and they cut them."

"Cut them?" Todd had asked in shock, his eyes wide.

His stepfather nodded. "They fuck little kids in the ass."

Todd had actually staggered back. "What?"

"And if their assholes are too tight, then those fags cut them to make them big enough."

The words had made Todd want to vomit. He thought of Mr. Tanson and just couldn't imagine the man doing such a thing. Couldn't imagine anyone doing anything like that. The very idea horrified him. Todd didn't know whether to believe his stepfather or not, but it was months before he could look at the quiet little man without thinking about blood. The damage had been done.

Running became a thing for Todd. Running let him get away from stuff. From a mom who remarried half a year after her husband died. From a stepfather who said horrible things.

Today Todd ran from memories as well. He ran from homelessness and snow and boys who told him he should sell himself for money. He ran again from his stepfather and those hurtful hands. He ran from a mother that stood aside and only offered platitudes, and over time, a host of ugly words as well. What had happened? How had a sweet childhood turned so dark and horrible?

Todd ran, and when Lady Gaga began to sing about being as free as her hair, he knew just what she was singing about. How he wanted to be left alone. To be able to be who he was, without small-town—or a stepfather's—expectations. And in that moment, screaming pain in his side or not, he was free.

He hurt. The pain felt good. He wasn't nude under the sun in his clearing in the woods in Buckman, but he was nearly naked. And strangely turned on by the shirt, Gabe's shirt, which was stuck to him by sweat, and by the scent that rose from it and mixed together as one with his own. Something told him that had he allowed himself to be with Gabe the night before, it would have been nothing like that night in Austin's basement. Oh, no. It would be something altogether different.

He opened his eyes to belt out the final lyrics.

And that was when he saw Gabe, standing in the doorway staring at him.

GABE'S mouth dropped open. He'd come home for lunch, bringing sandwiches from Quiznos (terribly unhealthy prime rib sandwiches with tons of cheese and sautéed onions and peppercorn sauce), because after all, a growing boy needed to eat. Gabe had walked in the door and called out, but there hadn't been an answer. His stomach dropped as he wondered if Todd had left. There was no smell of cooking chicken, and when he went into the kitchen, he found it thawing in the sink. Why hadn't Todd put it in the Crock-Pot? Had Todd not been able to find it? Gabe turned to look for it, and sure enough, there it was. What the hell?

That's when Gabe heard the singing. A young man's voice. Todd. He was singing about being free as his hair. Lady Gaga.

Gabe walked down the hall, calling out so as not to startle Todd. He followed the singing to his work-out room and froze when he got there. He rocked back, totally taken aback by what he saw: Todd, in nothing but black underwear and one of Gabe's own T-shirts, soaked with sweat and running hell bent for leather, voice booming like a rock star. The wet clothes clung to the young man, an erection straining the front of his briefs, leaving little to the imagination. And while there was a certain desperation pouring off Todd that was almost alarming, Gabe found himself witness to one of the sexiest things he'd ever seen.

Gabe knew he should back off—this time he really was being a voyeur—but he was paralyzed, unable to move. He felt as if he had stumbled on some animal in the wild, was witness to something one rarely got to see. Like coming across a deer in a clearing or an immense flight of butterflies, or a cougar making a kill.

Todd was sexy and scary and beautiful all at once, and Gabe felt himself grow hard at the sight.

Of course, that's when Todd opened his eyes.

"Fuck," Todd cried, and stopped running, which sent him flying backward and onto the floor.

"Todd!" Gabe leapt forward, reaching for the young man. "Todd, are you okay?" He fell to one knee where Todd lay in a heap. He placed a hand on Todd's sweaty shoulder. The smell of the young man nearly boiled off of him, all musk and flesh and pits and balls. It did nothing to reduce Gabe's erection.

Todd looked up through wet bangs, rubbing his head, face going red. "Jeez," he said. He pulled the iPod plug from his ear and Lady Gaga's voice boomed out in German. "You scared the shit out of me." He glanced down at himself, then hunched tighter, putting his arms around knees. "Damn. I-I'm so embarrassed."

"Todd, don't be. I'm sorry. I brought us some lunch and heard you singing…."

"Could you give me a minute?" Todd refused to meet Gabe's eyes.

"Sure. Of-of course." Gabe stood, started to turn. "Do you need a hand?"

"Gabe. Please!"

"Sorry." Gabe found he was blushing as well. "I'll be in the living room." He turned and left Todd alone.

TODD couldn't remember the last time he'd been so embarrassed. Not even when he'd been staring at his classmate's dick in the high school locker room. That time he'd been able to pull off a snarky comment to throw off suspicion. But what must Gabe be thinking, catching him running in his underwear and Gabe's own T-shirt? What had it looked like? He glanced down and saw the wet cloth that clung to his hard-on. Jeez. He might as well have been naked. How the hell did he go back down that hall and face the man?

You gotta, he realized. There was no way out except through the front door and the kitchen.

Maybe if I stay here long enough he'll just leave.

Todd ran fingers through wet hair and sat up straight.

(*"I brought us some lunch and heard you singing…."*)

Lunch. Gabe had brought home lunch. He wasn't going anywhere. Shit!

Todd stood, looked at himself again, and knew he couldn't pull his jeans on over his soaked underwear. Jeez. Even his socks were sopping. He peeked down the hall, and seeing no sign of his host, quickly scrambled out of his clothes, or lack thereof, and into his jeans and sweater. Then, barefoot, he went to face the music.

He found Gabe in the kitchen, back to him, sitting at the table. There were two plates set out and a wrapped sandwich at the empty setting. Lunch.

"There's some sodas in the fridge. I didn't know what you liked. A couple Cokes, Diet Cokes, some Mountain Dew. Don't guys your age like Mountain Dew?"

Todd went to the refrigerator and pulled out a Coke. It gave him another second not to face Gabe.

He saw me running in my underwear. With a hard-on.

Jeez. He heard me singing.

Todd sat down. "Did I break your eardrums?" he asked, trying to make light.

"Huh?" Gabe asked.

"My singing."

"Actually," Gabe said, eyes focused on his own sandwich. "Considering you were running at the time, you sounded pretty good."

Yeah. Right.

(*"Hey, Todd! Don't give up your day job, okay?"*)

"I think my stepdad would disagree."

"Yeah," said Gabe, then eyed him over the top of his meal. "Fuck your stepdad."

Todd gave a mock shudder. "I doubt you'd want to. He's pretty gross."

Gabe laughed. "At least you don't think I'd screw just anybody."

Todd stared at the wrapped sandwich in front of him.

"Go on," Gabe said through a mouthful. "Eat."

Todd nodded and pulled the paper open. What he saw looked good. He didn't know if he could eat it all. He had made a big breakfast, one bigger than he'd planned. But everything had just been so damned good. "I-I'm sorry about using your treadmill."

Now he'll tease me about my underwear.

Gabe didn't. Instead he shrugged. "Why?" He took a bite. "You're my guest. *Mi casa es su casa.*"

"I-I…. And your shirt…." Todd played with his food.

"All you had was your sweater. You couldn't run in that. You could have gotten a clean one, though. Sorry you felt you had to use one of my dirty ones."

"It-It's okay," Todd mumbled. "I didn't want to go through your stuff." Besides, wearing Gabe's shirt had made him feel…. What? Kind of what it felt like to have the man hug him.

Todd reached out, picked up the sandwich, and took a bite. The flavor exploded over his tongue and it was all he could do not to moan. When was the last time he'd had something so good? Once more he had to stop himself from shoving the food down. What would Gabe think? That he had no table manners at all?

"Let me see if I have anything you can wear," Gabe said.

"Yeah, right," Todd said and gave a laugh. "I'll swim in your clothes, and your pants will fall down around my feet."

"I don't know," Gabe replied. "They might be a little long, but you can cuff them up. I bet our waists aren't all that different." He stood up. "You want the rest of my sandwich?"

Todd eyed the remains of Gabe's lunch, looked up into his eyes and then back down. He did. But he also wanted to save room for the dinner he had planned. "Later?" he asked. "That is, if you really don't want it."

Gabe shook his head. "I don't. Wrap it up." He turned and left the room and came back a few minutes later with a couple of pairs of old jeans, a few shirts, and God, underwear. Was the man lending him underwear? "Here," he said, handing the clothes to Todd. "Go try these on. It'll give you something for the next few days."

Next few days? Todd wondered. Next few days here or on the street? Could he really stay here any longer?

Well, maybe at least one more night?

He reached for the sandwich, started to wrap it, and Gabe offered to take care of it instead. "You go change."

Todd sighed, grabbed the clothes, and headed back down the hall to the bathroom. To his surprise, he found the jeans did indeed fit almost perfectly. A little loose maybe, and of course, the legs were too long. But after cuffing them up a few turns, they actually worked. He pulled on a shirt that said, "The Other Team" (whatever that meant), and headed back to show Gabe. *Interesting*, he thought. *A great advantage for gay couples. They could wear each other's clothes.* Joan had worn a few of his shirts, but he'd never—of course—worn anything of hers and had no interest in doing so.

"Well, you are swimming in the shirt, but the pants aren't bad at all."

Todd noticed Gabe staring at his feet and he shrugged. "I don't think your shoes will fit me," he said. Gabe's feet looked huge.

"No. Probably not. But we'll figure that out."

"My shoes are okay," Todd said.

"No, they aren't. They're falling apart."

The comment stung for some reason. "Why do you care?" he snapped.

Gabe looked him in the face. "It's a pair of shoes, Todd. Not a Mercedes. You'll need new shoes."

When I'm back on the street, Todd thought. *That's what you're not saying.*

"There's a thrift store near here. Or we can go to the Mall."

Todd shook his head. No. No more trouble. With all the food and the couch and showers and not teasing him about being in his underwear, Gabe had done more than enough. "Shouldn't you be heading back to work?" he asked. He needed to be alone for a bit. This guy... he was just too... present. He couldn't think with the big (beautiful) man here.

"Yeah. Yeah, I should. Look, go into my bedroom and you'll find a dish full of change. Take some and go downstairs to the laundry room and wash your clothes, okay? And you'll find some of my flip-flops. They'll be big, of course, but you got to wash those shoes too."

Todd blushed. "Stinking up the place?"

"Todd, there is *nothing* that stinks about you, okay?"

For some reason the comment brought Todd up short. He looked up at Gabe, thinking of all the times his stepdad had called him a stinking deadbeat, or a stinking idiot, or worst of all, a stinking faggot. Gabe looked at him curiously, those light-blue eyes seeming to grow darker as the man studied him.

"You all right, Todd?"

Todd tried to put on a brave face, but before he could answer, Gabe did.

"Of course you're not. Stupid question. Todd, you wash those clothes and take it easy. You can use anything here you want. I see you watched a movie. Good. And the treadmill was no problem. Use whatever you want. Please. You are staying the night?"

Todd's heart skipped a beat. "You... you don't mind?"

Gabe smiled and Todd felt his heart miss another beat. "Not at all. It's nice to have the company."

Todd couldn't help but smile back.

"There's an extra key in that dish too, okay? So you don't lock yourself out."

"I can use your key?" Todd said in surprise. How did Gabe know he wouldn't make a copy?

"Well it's not like I think you're going to run down to the True Value and get a copy," Gabe said, as if reading his mind." He turned, then stopped. "You better get that chicken in the Crock-Pot. At least it'll cook faster now that it's thawing."

This time Todd really did smile. "You let *me* worry about the chicken, okay?"

Gabe raised a brow, then dropped it. "Okay. I trust you."

I trust you. Wow. Todd smiled even more. Imagine three little words making him feel so good. Could there be three better words?

Gabe had turned again and headed toward the door, when he glanced over at the TV. He stopped. Laughed. Faced Todd. "Leia," he said. "Your cat. And that comment about your town. Something about how if there's a shining center to the universe, your town is the farthest one. I'm messing it up, I know, but that's from *Star Wars*."

Now Todd felt his head would split in half from his smile.

"Duh." Gabe shook his head and grinned in return. "I'm an idiot. I love those movies."

"Me too," Todd replied.

"Maybe we'll watch one tonight," Gabe said. "Just not the first one, okay? I hate Jar Jar."

"Awww," cried Todd. "Jar Jar really gets the short end of the stick. It's not fair."

Gabe was grinning and shook his head. "You're fighting a losing battle with that one. Don't even go there. Besides, who said life was fair?" He winked at Todd. "See you tonight."

Gabe left Todd standing there, in his clothes, and his words hung in the air.

Who said life was fair?

Indeed. Who?

CHAPTER SEVEN

WHEN Gabe got back to work, Tracy grabbed him and pulled him into his office. "Wagner is here!"

"Really?" he asked, surprised. Peter rarely showed up without calling first. And in this weather? Peter wasn't too fond of cold weather.

"He came to take you to lunch, but you were off with your little boyfriend," she said with a huff.

"He's not my boyfriend!"

"Alas" came a melodic and wonderfully familiar voice. "I was hoping you had run off for... what do they call it? A nooner?"

Gabe looked over his shoulder and sure enough, it was Peter Wagner: his boss, friend, confidante, and sponsor. Looking almost impossibly tall, the man was leaning against the threshold, holding a cane in one hand, the other resting comfortably on his hip. Despite the silver hair with just a hint of chestnut brown and the deep lines in his face, his blue eyes twinkled like a child's, and he looked more like a buccaneer than one of the richest men in the country. Maybe it was the cravat he wore instead of a tie? Of course, pirates didn't wear anything designed by William Fioravanti or Brioni.

"Peter," Gabe exclaimed, delighted to see the man. He crossed the office and held out his hand. Peter took it and they shook, then pulled each other into a gentle hug.

"Gabriel," said his old friend in his unique inflection that was not quite any known accent, not Midwest, not British, not European, but perhaps a combination of all of them. "I was in town and decided to stop by. You were gone, so I took your boss out instead—the cranky old poop. He wasn't nearly as entertaining as you would have been."

"Sorry, Peter. I had no idea you'd be coming. Especially in this weather."

"Bad weather always looks worse through a window," Peter replied in that tone that said he was quoting someone. He was always quoting someone. This time Gabe had no idea who. He'd have to look it up. Thank God for Google.

"So what's this about a boyfriend?" Peter asked.

Gabe shot Tracy a look and she gave a fake grin—almost a grimace—in return. "No boyfriend, Peter," Gabe replied.

"Then I will repeat myself," he said. "Alas, alas. You need someone special in your life."

"Well, I have work to do," Tracy said, her voice tinged with a bit of helium. "Mr. Wagner." She nodded.

"Ms. Newman." Peter nodded back.

Tracy all but curtsied and then fled the room. Peter closed the door behind her, then sat down, crossing one lanky and incredibly long leg elegantly over the other.

"Drink, Peter?"

"I think I will," Peter replied and placed overlapping hands on the silver head of his cane. "As long as it's the Lagavulin."

"I wouldn't give you anything else." He opened the armoire in the corner of the office and pulled out the crystal decanter half-full of a light tea-colored liquid. "And besides, you bought me this."

Peter raised an arched silver brow and gave Gabe an amused smile. He had a wide mouth, full of big white teeth that at one turn could be as cheerful as could be, and at another sharklike and deadly. Luckily Gabe had never had the latter look trained in his direction. "You expect me to believe you have some of that left from your birthday?"

"I don't drink much at work, Peter." He poured two short glasses. "This is the stuff you got me. Older than what I usually buy as well, if I remember right." Gabe handed Peter his Scotch.

"To surprise visits," Peter said and held up his glass.

"To any visit from you," Gabe said, and tapped his glass against Peter's. They both brought their drinks to their mouths, and both paused to breathe in a scent of fireplaces on a cold day. Appropriate. Then they sipped.

"This is how I *know* there is a God," Peter said, a hint of Scottish slipping into his voice. Again, appropriate.

Gabe couldn't help but chuckle at the comment. Who knew if Peter believed in God? He seemed to be disposed either way. One day Peter would curse a school system that refused to teach evolution and made its students pray, and another he would lean in and softly say something like: "Science without religion is lame, religion without science is blind."

That was Albert Einstein.

"So you *braved* the snow," said Peter. "I knew you would. All work and no play. I figured you would get one of those dreadful sandwiches from downstairs, though, instead of going out for lunch. You sure you don't have a boyfriend?"

Gabe pulled up a chair and sat beside his friend. There was no way he was sitting behind the desk. That would feel like sitting on a throne when meeting the Queen of England, and be maybe just as disrespectful. "Not a boyfriend," Gabe said again.

Peter gave an almost smirk and raised both brows this time.

"I'm just helping a kid out," Gabe explained, wishing they would change the subject. He knew Peter Wagner didn't come into the city in eight inches of snow—with more promised—to talk about boys.

"I understand he is in your apartment right now."

"I think Tracy has a big mouth."

Peter laughed his melodic laugh and waved a hand through the air. "I think simply that your compatriot cares, my boy. She worries. At times I do as well."

Gabe took a deep breath and somehow kept himself from sighing. "Neither of you need worry. I trust him."

"And I trust your judgment implicitly," Peter replied.

Gabe nodded. Now perhaps they could talk about something else. Like business and why Peter was out in such weather.

"Except when it comes to your heart," Peter added.

Shitfire. This time Gabe did sigh. "Peter. He's a young man who got evicted from his apartment. On the first day of the year in a blizzard. The apartment manager threw him out in the snow. What was I supposed to do?"

Peter's eyes sparkled and he cocked his head to one side. "Indeed. You would do what angels do, Gabriel. You helped."

Gabe smiled. "I learned from the best." He nodded at Peter.

"Nonsense. You had it in your heart from birth. Why else do you think I invited *you* in?"

After that, it was business. Big business indeed.

IT WAS funny wearing Gabe's clothes. Not as in "ha-ha!" funny, but odd and weird and dammit, kind of sexy. For some damned reason, Todd couldn't help but think about how his body was surrounded by clothing that usually held Gabe's. The underwear were especially— what? He couldn't identify just what the feeling was. Unnerving?

They're washed, Todd thought. *It's not like his ball sweat is in them.*

Todd shivered. Felt gooseflesh at the thought. *My dick is right where Gabe's has been. Of course, I'm about a tenth of his size, from what I saw through those sweats of his.*

Don't think about it. Dinner. Work on dinner.

No. Laundry first.

That made him think about why he was doing it. Not only because the few clothes he had were dirty, but Gabe had seen him running in his underwear on the treadmill.

With a hard-on.

The thought made him almost need to sit down. So embarrassing. How would he ever face the man again? The look that had been on Gabe's face. Concern, yes. But more. Lust? Had he seen lust? He thought maybe he had.

Jeez. What did I look like, running like that? And in my fucking underwear.

With a hard-on!

Don't think about it. Do the damned laundry.

Todd found detergent in the bathroom, grabbed a handful of change from Gabe's bedroom like he'd been told, and then grabbing the key, went looking for the laundry room. It was pretty easy to find, right in the basement as in most apartment buildings.

There was a little girl there, maybe ten years old, and she was pulling clothes out of a dryer. She looked up. "Hi," she said. She was a lovely girl, with long brown hair, olive skin, and huge Disney-like brown eyes.

"Hi," he said.

"I don't know you," she replied. "I'm Bianca. Are you new in the building?" She tossed her head, flipping her hair back.

"I-I'm staying with someone for a few days." How did he explain it? Especially to a little girl?

"With who?" she asked and began to fold clothes.

Todd swallowed. Nosy thing, wasn't she? "Gabe," he replied and dumped the bag of laundry he'd brought down on one of the two long tables in the middle of the room. His jeans, sweater, socks, shoes, and briefs (the pair Gabe had seen him in, and he felt his face heat up). And in what had been a last minute thought, he'd grabbed the clothes in Gabe's hamper. That turned out to be a pair of jeans, some sweats, two T-shirts, a hoodie, and socks and underwear. No dress slacks or shirts.

Dry cleaned probably. Of course.

"Really? Gabe is nice. I think he liked my daddy, but he took too long. He's with Curtis now."

Gabe was with Curtis? Wait. What? "Who is Curtis? Gabe has a boyfriend named Curtis?" The thought made his stomach drop.

She laughed. "No. Curtis is my *daddy's* boyfriend." She winked. "I got them together."

"Your dad's gay?" Todd asked.

She smiled. "Sure!"

Had he woken up in *The Twilight Zone*? A little girl who didn't care that her dad was gay? What did she mean about...? "What do you mean you got them together?"

"I'm good," she said. "Course they already liked each other. I just had to help them see it. Now I have two daddies." She giggled. "You gonna do your clothes, or what?"

"What? Oh." He cleared his throat, shook his head. He began to separate the clothes. There wasn't a lot here, but he certainly didn't want to mix whites with anything else. But then whites turned out to be nothing more than several pairs of socks and a pair of Hugo Boss boxer briefs. The pouch was pretty stretched out. *God.* Why was he even noticing something like that? He felt a shifting in his own underwear— except even those belonged to Gabe.

What was happening to him?

"Do you like Gabe?" the little girl asked.

Todd jerked his gaze away from the underwear. "What do you mean by that?"

She gave him a curious look. "Do you like him?"

"He's nice," Todd managed.

She waggled her eyebrows. "But do you *like* him?"

"I'm not a faaa...." He stopped. "I'm not gay," he said.

She looked at him askance. "You're not? You *seem* gay."

"What do you mean?" He bristled.

She shrugged. "I don't know. I just can tell. Well, usually. Maybe you're bi?"

"What?" He really had fallen into *The Twilight Zone*!

"Bi. You know, you like boys and girls."

"I like girls," he cried, his stomach clenching.

She looked at him funny. "What's your name again?"

"I didn't say," Todd answered and felt a trickle of sweat run down his side. He looked away and began shoving the clothes into two different washers.

"So are you an escaped criminal or something?" she asked.

He laughed and turned back to her. "No!"

"Then tell me your name. I'll find out anyway."

He looked at her, eyes wide, mouth wanting to fall open. "Fine," he said. "I'm Todd."

"You don't have to be so touchy," she said with a harrumph. "I'm just being friendly." She folded one last shirt and put her clothes in a basket.

"Why aren't you in school?" he snapped.

"Well, duh." She rolled her eyes. "Snow day. You gonna put those underwear in there or just stare at it all day?" She turned on her heel, the toss of her hair surely no accident, and walked out.

"Sorry?" he called out. Then looked down at the underwear in his hand. A pair of Emporio Armani boxers. Didn't Gabe have *anything* that came from Walmart? God. What a stupid question. He looked back in the washer and found a blue-striped pair of C-IN2s. Then a blue pair with a boxed pattern from Papi. All sexy, like the kinds Todd used to look at on the Internet. He stared at the pair in his hand, so bright and colorful. Had he thought the pouch was stretched out on the other pair? How frigging hung was Gabe?

Then, not even knowing he was doing it, he brought the briefs up to his face, closed his eyes, and inhaled deeply. *God. Gabe's scent.*

His ball scent. A lot like Austin's.

Dammit.

He threw them into the washer, slammed it, and quickly added the coins to start it up. Remembering the detergent, he added that as well, and then started the other machine.

With that he dashed up out of the basement as if he were escaping a dungeon.

I—am—going—crazy!

TODD found the chicken thawed to his satisfaction, so he rubbed the inside with the bacon grease, added the fruit he'd prepared, rubbed the outside the same way. Then he wrapped it up in foil and popped it in the refrigerator.

He wasn't sure just when to put it in the oven. Gabe had given him a fairly big window of when he'd be home. The chicken was a little over three pounds, so he figured it would take about an hour and a half to cook, two hours maybe.

Maybe you're bi?

Shit.

Where had *that* come from?

Busy. He needed to keep busy.

So now what? Another movie?

The balcony. He could do something about the balcony.

A little thinking brought about a plan. There was a broom in the kitchen closet, as well as a dustpan. It would take a little doing, but thankfully there wasn't all that much snow out there. At least not on the balcony itself. Interesting that it seemed to be the only balcony on this side of the building. Of course, it was the narrow side, and probably not all the apartments in the building were as big as Gabe's.

So using the dustpan first as a makeshift shovel, he applied it and the broom and in less than an hour had everything looking good. Just in time too. It was starting to snow again, with big heavy flakes drifting down out of a sky that had turned silver. Probably everything would have melted and drained away through the slots in the brick near the floor, but why not do something to help?

After that he went back downstairs to switch the laundry to the dryers. He found himself with a weird sense of dread wondering if he would bump into that little girl. It was the last thing he wanted.

Maybe you're bi?

Why wouldn't that thought leave his head?

The thought of Austin and that night in his friend's basement came to his mind.

You liked it.

I was horny. That's it.

You liked it.

The basement elevator doors opened, and once more he found people who wanted to know who he was. This time a couple by the names of Harry and Cody. They were all grins when they found out he was staying with Gabe, and this time he just let them think what they wanted to think. They were nice. It was interesting to watch them. They were obviously a couple. They knew each other well, worked well together, did the whole complete-each-other's-sentences kind of thing and more. They touched each other, but nothing overt or over the top. Just a couple.

A healthier couple than his mother and stepfather, that was for sure.

Why did that seem so weird?

Todd realized this was the closest he'd been to a gay couple. He'd seen gays since coming to Kansas City. He had seen what must be couples. But he'd never been right there, in the presence of two men who were obviously a couple. They were so... normal. What had he expected? Had he really thought one of them would be wearing a dress or something? Maybe he had. Or metal-studded leather maybe? Rubber suits?

Nice. They were nice.

"Christmas was our second anniversary," Harry, the huskier of the two, said.

"Of course, it could have been more than that," Cody said. He was slim, with a face made up of all angles. Not unattractive, just different. "But he was blind."

Harry rolled his eyes. "He loves to tell people that."

"Well, it's true," Cody replied. "We were best friends forever, and he finally let himself see how much he liked me."

"How long?" Todd asked with a gulp.

"Too long," Cody answered. "I mean, come on. How did he resist all this?" Cody did a spin and then flexed his muscles.

Harry laughed and pulled Cody into his arms and gave him a quick peck on the lips. "I was stupid is what I was."

Cody pulled away and went back to their laundry. Their laundry. Two men's stuff all in the same washing machine.

Like mine and Gabe's.

"How long have you been seeing Gabe?"

"What?" Todd asked, pulled from his thoughts.

"How long have you been seeing Gabe? Pretty new, huh?"

"I...." What did he say? He'd already let them think he was in fact seeing the man. "We're really new," he said, and felt a little flip in his stomach. Imagine, pretending he was dating a man. His stepfather would have a stroke.

"Well, there must be something going on, or he wouldn't trust you in his place," Harry said.

Todd felt a smile flicker across his face. "I guess he does." Wow. Imagine. But maybe that was just Gabe. Maybe he was naturally trusting. "So he doesn't have many guys around?" Now what made him ask that?

Harry and Cody looked at each other, then him.

"Sorry. Guess I was being nosy," Todd apologized.

Harry shrugged. "I haven't seen him with anyone in a couple years." He and Cody looked at each other again.

God. What were they thinking? "Look, I really am sorry. I wasn't trying to get into his business."

Harry smiled. It was the kind of smile that lit up his whole face. "No. It's okay. You like him then?"

Todd sucked in his breath, and then was immediately set upon by a fit of coughing.

Cody jumped forward and began to slap his back. "You okay? Something go down the wrong pipe?"

Todd tried to answer, but all he could do was cough. *Like Gabe?* Did he like Gabe?

And of course, the answer was yes. He hadn't even known the man for a day. Had only spent one evening and one lunch with him. But the plain and simple truth was he did.

"Y-yes," he said with a gasp. He liked Gabe.

A lot.

CHAPTER EIGHT

GABE came home to a wonderful smell. Chicken and spices and something more; he wasn't sure what. All he knew was it set his stomach growling and his salivary glands flowing.

"Todd?" he called when he didn't see the young man in either the kitchen or living room.

"Your timing is perfect," Todd cried as he came down the hall. "I can't believe how perfect. Dinner will be done in just a bit. You want to shower first?"

Gabe saw Todd's hair was damp, telling Gabe that Todd had just taken one. He was also wearing Gabe's "The Other Team" T-shirt, and Gabe bet Todd had no idea what it meant. Should he tell him? Gay shirt or not, he couldn't help but feel a little thrill at seeing Todd wear his shirt.

Now don't go getting possessive. Todd is straight.

He says he is.

He could almost imagine what Tracy would say.

"Jiminy Cricket! Haven't you learned your lesson? What did bringing out a kid do for you the last time?"

Heartache. Tons of heartache.

"Look at you," Todd said. "All covered in snow."

Gabe glanced at his shoulders, seemingly covered in white downy feathers. He started to shrug off his coat, and Todd darted behind him.

"Let me get that," Todd said and helped him take it off. He dashed off to the bathroom and returned less than a moment later, the coat free of snow. A big smile spread across his face and he laughed. "Your hair!" Todd reached up and patted at Gabe's hair and let out another laugh. "Just call me 'Head and Shoulders'."

Gabe felt a wonderful little lurch in his heart. He'd been touched so rarely in the last year or so that even Todd's small gesture felt wonderful. The kid was standing so close Gabe could smell the shampoo and herbal soap he liked to buy at The Village Herbal. Todd had shaved, except for his chin and those wide sideburns that worked for him. Gabe could even see the slight impression of Todd's nipples through the thin fabric of the shirt.

God! I gotta get laid. Todd's killing me. This is ridiculous.

Do you even know his last name?

Shitfire. He didn't, did he? And now seemed an awfully strange time to ask.

"Go on," Todd instructed him. "Get showered. Get out of that monkey suit. Dinner in about a half hour, okay?"

Gabe nodded. "Sure," he said. "Sure."

He went down the hall to his room and found his folded laundry on the bed. *Todd washed my clothes? Daniel didn't wash my clothes.*

But then, Daniel didn't wash his own clothes.

The laundry was folded neatly—underwear too—and Gabe wondered if that had made Todd feel weird.

Of course, he's wearing your underwear right now, he realized. And damn, did the thought turn him on? Thinking about the fact that Todd's body was clothed in a shirt, jeans, and underwear—oh, especially the underwear—that until today had never been worn by anyone but himself? Thinking that Todd's most private parts were where his own usually were?

Gabe realized he was hard. He shook himself.

Shower. Yes. Showering always did the trick.

Usually, he exercised first—and that thought made him think of walking in on Todd earlier that day.

God, it had been sexy. Did that make him a total shit? Todd had obviously been going through some big mental thing. How embarrassing must it have been to have someone walk in on him like that? Especially when he had a hard-on?

Skip the workout today. Skipping two days in a row wasn't a good idea, but hell. *I won't die.*

Shower!

Gabe wasn't sure why, but instead of putting everything away, he decided to wear some of the clothes Todd had washed—touched, folded. Once again he was being schoolgirl silly, but hell. Todd would be gone soon, why not indulge a little fantasy? It wasn't like anything was going to happen between them.

So it was the jeans, the blue Papi underwear, and his Chief's shirt. Finally, socks and his most beat-up pair of Nikes.

Speaking of which, what about Todd's dreadful Converse sneakers? Had he washed them? Gabe hoped so. They'd been filthy. Worse, they were falling apart. Why wasn't there a cheap place to get shoes around here? There was J. Crew and ALDO on the Plaza, of course, stores where he bought his own shoes. A new pair of Converse sneakers wouldn't be more than about sixty, seventy bucks. Yet something told him Todd wouldn't let him—that he would have country-boy, I-won't-accept-charity ideals. But the closest Walmart, where they could find something for twenty bucks, was thirty minutes away. And with the hour and the snow, it just wasn't a viable option tonight. Maybe this weekend?

Weekend? You're going to let him stay until the weekend?

Why not? he thought. He liked having someone around. It made the big apartment less empty.

He made his way to the kitchen and found Todd bent over, taking the chicken out of the oven, and *What a butt!* It was broad and strong and round and downright breathtaking.

Got to get laid. Got to get laid. Got to get laid!

And how you gonna do that?

I've gotten laid before.

There were all kinds of possibilities. Craigslist. E-MaleConnect. He could go to one of the gay bars in town.

I'm not exactly chopped liver. When I set my... mind to it, I usually find someone.

Then you only wind up feeling even lonelier after. Besides, you're gonna bring someone home with Todd here?

Gabe sighed and Todd spun around with a start. "Oh! You surprised me."

"Sorry," Gabe said sheepishly.

"How can a guy as big as you be so quiet?" Todd was holding a large casserole dish in front of him with a pair of oven mitts. The chicken, which was half wrapped in foil, was beautiful. It smelled even better.

"That looks amazing, Todd."

A pleased look came over Todd's face. "Thank you." He turned and crossed into the small dining room and set it on the table. It had already been set for two. Then he returned to the oven and pulled out a pan of twice-baked potatoes. Gabe practically drooled. They looked even better than the chicken. "I hope they're okay," Todd said. "I did something a little weird, but I wanted them to complement the stuffing."

"Stuffing?" Gabe asked.

"Sure." Todd grinned and winked. "You'll see. Sit down."

Gabe did as bid, almost asked if Todd wanted to eat by candlelight, and realized that would certainly be pushing things. But this felt so right. It felt like what he'd always wanted. As Todd bustled about, it was so easy to imagine them eating, then cuddling, then going off to bed.

But dinner was all he was getting tonight.

And as Todd took Gabe's plate, cut off a large breast and wing portion, scooped out some fruity-looking concoction from inside, and then added a potato, Gabe suddenly felt more content than he had in ages.

That was when the apartment buzzer went off, startling them both.

Now who the hell could that be?

"Sorry," said Gabe, and he rose and went to the threshold and pressed the intercom button. "Hello?" he said.

"Gabe, my boy! You're home." *Peter? What was he doing here?* "How fortuitous! I was hoping you'd be there. Ring me up?"

ONE minute they were about to sit down to dinner, where Todd hoped Gabe would be impressed, and then everything had changed.

Minutes after that damned buzzer had gone off—"I am so sorry," Gabe had told Todd as he pressed the button that would let Peter in. "He's my boss."—and their solitude was broken by a character right out of *A Christmas Carol*.

The man seemed impossibly tall, but when Todd got up to meet him, he saw the older man wasn't any taller than Gabe. He was thin, though, almost gangly, with a narrow chest and what looked like disproportionately long arms and legs, all clothed in a suit that looked like it cost a million bucks. The man had to be sixty if he was a day— his face had begun to take on the creases of age, his great mop of hair almost silver—and yet, oh how his eyes danced!

"Greetings, greetings!" cried the man, holding his cane before him as if he were ready to part the Red Sea.

"Hello, Peter," said Gabe.

"Peter" gave Gabe a big hug, and then spun to face Todd. "And you must be Gabriel's houseguest. Charmed! *Charmed*, I'm sure."

He held out his hand and Todd took it carefully, and then was surprised at the strength in the grip.

"I am Peter Wagner," he said, his voice musical and vaguely British. "And you?"

"Todd Burton."

"I'm sorry, Peter. I should have introduced you. I was just so surprised to see you."

"Not disappointed, I hope?"

"Of course not. We were just... ah... sitting down to eat."

"Ye gods! And I've already told my driver to go to see that movie he's been wanting to see...."

Todd cleared his throat. "There's plenty, Mr. Wagner," he said, biting back reluctance. He had so wanted to impress Gabe. Now this odd, spiderlike man had invaded their time together. "There are two thighs, or I'll give you my breast if...."

"No! No! I will go for a walk and come back in an hour when you are both done with your repast."

Todd glanced through the balcony doors. Snow was falling thickly again. He thought of how just this time yesterday, he'd been in that himself and how Gabe had let him in from the cold. Suddenly, he felt like a selfish jerk. "No, Mr. Wagner. Please sit down."

"Well...." Peter looked him in the eyes and Todd felt like the man was looking inside his brain.

"I mean it, Mr. Wagner. Please." And he did mean it. After all, it wasn't like he'd been on a date with Gabe.

"Well then, *if* you insist." The old man did a sort of twirl and like a magician, he was—presto change-o—out of his long dark winter coat and scarf. Suddenly a bottle of wine seemed to appear out of nowhere. Where had it come from? Under his arm? A pocket of that coat? "I hope this will serve. It's a grenache by Chateau Rayas Chateauneuf du Pape. It goes well with chicken."

Todd had no idea what the man had just said. He didn't know wines as well as he wished; there just wasn't a market for them in Buckman, and he was too young to buy any wines in the first place. All he could do was say, "Thank you."

Before he could take it, Gabe swept in. "I'll open this right away," he said.

Todd turned and got another place setting, and Peter folded himself into one of the other dining room chairs. "And the dark meat will do, young Todd. I prefer it actually. I love a thigh." He winked and smiled wickedly. Then; "My God, it smells like heaven. Is that a fruit stuffing you've made?"

Todd smiled and nodded.

"You're a cook then?"

"I'd like to be."

"My dear young man, you either *are*, or you are not. What does your *soul* say?"

Todd plopped down in his chair. Who the hell was this guy? He swallowed hard. What did his soul say? What did that mean?

"Todd, is it something fun? Like watching a cartoon or playing cards? Or is it more? When you cook, does it come from your heart? Do you feel connected to something beyond and within? When you are done and you take that first bite, does a thrill race through you? Do you say, 'My God! I made that?'"

Todd's mouth fell open. Yes. That was exactly what it felt like. From pancakes with white chocolate chips made on a Mother's Day a lifetime ago to chickens haphazardly stuffed with fruit and nuts this very afternoon. It *was* like some inner part of him knew just what to do. "Yes, Mr. Wagner," he whispered. "Yes." That really was just exactly what it felt like.

"There shall be none of that Mr. Wagner stuff. At least not here in this humble abode. I shall be Peter to you or nothing at all. Am I clear?"

Todd let out a laugh. "Okay… Pe-Peter."

"Single P, my boy. Although two pee-pees have their place." He turned toward Gabe. "Wouldn't you agree, Gabriel?"

Todd watched Gabe's eyes go wide and a blush color his cheeks. It was all Todd could do not to burst into laughter.

God. Did Peter think the same thing as Harry and Cody, the couple he'd met in the laundry room, thought? That he and Gabe were together? Todd looked around him, looked at the clothes he was wearing. He looked at the meal before them. Hell, all the table was missing was candles. Of course Peter thought something romantic was going on.

Gabe brought the wine and an extra glass. He filled them, and when Todd looked at him, he saw Gabe's face had an unreadable expression. Gabe was looking at neither him nor Peter Wagner. He sat down, sighed, and then smiled broadly, the emotions coming back. Now what was that about?

"Shall we toast?" Gabe asked, as if everything were normal.

Peter snatched up his glass. "We shall. I say we drink to new friends and warm hearths."

Todd smiled. He couldn't help it. This man was crazy. But so was everything else that had happened in the last day or two. Why not just ride it out and enjoy? Who knew how soon he might be heartless again? He raised his glass. So did Gabe. They clinked glasses and then drank.

Todd was sure to sip this time. And take in the scent of it, of course.

He was glad he did.

It was aromatic, and as the wine settled over his taste buds, he thought of rose petals and raspberries.

"Yes! Exactly," Peter cried and Todd blushed. He didn't know he'd spoken aloud again. "And kirsch and violets. Can you taste the white pepper?"

White pepper? In wine? Todd sipped, closed his eyes the way Gabe had done the night before, and waited. Then, to his surprise: "Wow," he said with a quiet gasp. "I do."

"It's sexy, is it not? Don't you agree, Gabriel?" Peter asked.

Gabe coughed, his eyes widened slightly, and then he smiled, wiped his mouth. "Maybe…."

"Yes," Peter decreed. "Sexily aromatic, like linen sheets after making love on an island in Greece." Peter took another sip. "It is superb. And now if I might?" Peter lifted a fork as if it were a conductor's baton, then a knife, cut into the thigh Todd had placed on his plate and sliced it quickly and masterfully. He brought the morsel to his mouth, stopped, inhaled. Then popped it into his mouth.

Todd held his breath.

A corner of Peter's mouth slowly tipped upward. He opened his eyes. "Heaven," he whispered.

Todd felt a rush. He had no idea why. He had no idea who this strange man was with his flourishes and declarations, his nimble swagger, and the graceful way he moved his hands and arms and lanky body. Yet, the compliment Peter had given him might have been the best in his entire life.

Peter sat up, took a forkful of the fruit stuffing, ate. His smile broadened. "It is Florida. It is Washington. It is Asia and the last days of fall. Delightful."

Todd blushed again. The man had to be pulling his leg. Or he was crazy. Or both. Silly for sure. He was downright silly.

Last Peter tasted the potatoes, and this was where Todd really did hold his breath. Would they be horrible? His idea really had been crazy.

"I'll be damned," said the man. "The perfect touch. The absolutely *perfect* touch. My Lord, Gabriel. Taste this. You're sitting there like a bump on a log, and you have been served a meal by a chef!"

Todd laughed. He couldn't help it. A chef? He looked at Gabe, whose face was suddenly glowing. He looked beautiful. Gabe turned and looked at Todd, and he felt gravity cease. Those eyes. Looking at him. So blue—but light. Unreal.

Todd felt the shiver of gooseflesh run down his back and arms. How was it he was here? How was he here with this man? With this man and his insane boss?

Gabe took his fork and reached for the chicken but Peter let out a cry. "Wait. Try the potatoes. See what he's done."

Gabe nodded and did as he was told. He paused, then smiled sweetly. "Is that orange, Todd?"

"Yes," he answered. "It's not too weird? I squeezed just a little orange into them while I was mashing them. I thought it might complement the fruit in the chicken."

"But there is more," sang Peter. "Walnut. You've added tiny, infinitesimal bits of walnut, haven't you?"

Todd nodded. "I was afraid I might have made the potatoes too sweet."

"You did not. Todd, this is wondrous, I tell you. You are right. You—are a cook!"

GABE thought the look on Todd's face was beatific. This was the same boy who just last night looked so miserable? And a simple compliment on his meal from a stranger could make him smile so beautifully?

For some reason, Gabe beamed with pride. He knew he had nothing to do with the meal, nothing to do with any of it, really. It was all Todd's doing. But he felt proud all the same. He looked at Todd and wanted to jump up from the table and hug him.

That would probably not be the thing to do, though, would it?

The meal went well. For a while, there were few words. Compliments on the meal—Gabe had to tell Todd how good it all was. And he had wanted Todd to stick the chicken in a Crock-Pot.

"Todd came to town with dreams of learning from Izar Goya, but she doesn't take students."

"Izar Goya?" Peter asked. "She owns the Basque restaurant, Izar's Jatetxea. Fascinating food. Fascinating that you want to learn from her. There are chefs with far more approachable and common specialties, Toddy."

"If I wanted common, I'd learn from Burger King," Todd snapped, then covered his mouth. His outburst only made Peter laugh.

There were compliments on the wine, of course. Then there was a discussion on the weather. Would the damned snow last? Peter hoped so. It was an excuse to light a fire and read a book, or be with one's loved ones.

"And why don't you light a fire, Gabriel?"

A fire? Why not? "Is that all right with you, Todd?"

Todd gave a nod. "Sure, Gabe," he said.

"The light won't bother you later? When you try to go to sleep?"

Todd shook his head. "No. Not at all."

"Why would the light bother his sleep?" Peter asked.

"Because, Peter. He's sleeping on the couch." Gabe rose to get some logs from the caddy and arranged them in the fireplace.

Peter raised a great silver brow and gazed at Todd.

Oh, Peter. Stop it! You're going to send him running out of here.

Which was the last thing Gabe wanted.

Peter was a lot to handle on first meeting. Or could be. Their first meeting had been pretty wild. Of course, it had turned out to be a meeting that had changed his whole life. But then he hadn't been quite as naïve as Todd. St. Louis had been a whole different way to grow up than Buckman, surely.

Peter gave a slight shrug and tossed back the last of his wine. He picked up the bottle, held it up to the light. "There might be one last swallow," he decreed.

"Go for it," said Todd.

"Are you sure?"

"I'm sure," Todd said and stood to gather the dishes.

Peter poured just the amount of wine he'd predicted into his glass. Swirled it around. Breathed it in one last time. Swallowed. "A miracle, don't you think? That God's grapes can be squished and bottled and finally turned to such an elixir?"

Todd gave a shrug. "I haven't had much wine. I sure like this, though."

"Of course you do!"

Gabe just shook his head. How was Todd taking all this? He hoped Peter wasn't scaring him. He lit the paper he'd twisted under the kindling and logs and watched it take.

At least Peter had asked Todd his last name. He felt a little less lascivious lusting after the kid now that he knew his last name.

"Ah, yes," Peter said with a sigh. "There is no place more delightful than one's own fireplace. So says a great Roman statesman and so say I." He stood and joined Gabe. "I shall have to call ahead and have a fire waiting for me at home. This would be a perfect time for the Lagavulin, but you've left the bloody stuff at your office."

"Laga… viewland?" Todd asked, coming from the kitchen.

"Lagavulin," Peter corrected.

"It's a Scotch whisky," Gabe explained.

"There's the Schwartzbeeren," Todd said, then grinned in a way that made Gabe's stomach all fluttery. "Sit down! Both of you." He turned and practically scampered back into the kitchen.

They sat on the couch and Peter turned and regarded Gabe, his brow raised once again. "He's lovely."

Gabe gulped. "He's straight, Peter."

"Preposterous. If that boy is heterosexual, then so am I."

What? Gabe looked toward the kitchen. "Do you think so?" Peter thought Todd was gay? Not that it made a difference. Todd was a young man in trouble. That was all. He was helping Todd out. Helping him survive. He wasn't going to help Todd in any other way. The last time he'd done anything more, his life had gone to hell. The last thing he needed was another Brett in his life.

"You are thinking of Brett, aren't you?"

There went Peter again, reading his mind. Gabe started to deny it, then thought better of it. He sighed. "Yes, Peter. I am."

"You're afraid."

"I'm not afraid, Peter. Just getting wiser. I won't make that same mistake again."

"What mistake did you make?"

"You know damned well what."

"But he who dares not grasp the thorn, should never crave the rose."

Another quote? It sounded like one. Gabe turned and looked at his friend. "*I* dare not, Peter."

"You dare not what?" Todd asked, entering the room with two bowls.

"Nothing," said Gabe and looked to see what Todd had brought. When he saw what it was, he couldn't help but smile.

"What is that?" Peter asked.

"It's ice cream with Schwartzbeeren over the top," Todd answered. "Dessert."

Gabe laughed. "Where did you get the ice cream? You didn't make it out of snow, did you?"

Todd rolled his eyes. "No. I borrowed it from these two guys in the laundry room."

"They had ice cream in the *laundry* room?" Peter took the offered bowl.

"No!" Todd giggled. "This... well... couple. Cody and—Harry, I think? They let me have it." Todd handed Gabe his bowl and ran back to the kitchen, only to return a second later with a third bowl.

"That was nice of them," Gabe said. "They're a great couple of guys."

"Oh, and this is wonderful," cried Peter.

Todd stood over them, scooped up a spoonful, and popped it in his mouth. Gabe followed the spoon with his eyes, watched Todd's mouth open and close, his throat work as he swallowed.

"Those sweet lips. My, oh my, I could kiss those lips all night long," Peter whispered.

"Hush, Peter."

"What are you two talking about?" Todd sat down on the corner of the coffee table.

"We talk of many things: Of shoes—and ships—and sealing-wax," Peter replied and had another bite of ice cream.

"What?" Todd asked.

"It's not important," Gabe said. "Don't worry about it."

CHAPTER NINE

THEY all loved the ice cream. The Schwartzbeeren, the wine that had been almost too sweet the night before, really had been wonderful as part of a dessert. Todd was glad he'd thought of it, and glad there had been a little left.

He took the bowls, rinsed them in the sink, and came back to sit with his friends.

Friends? Are they really? God. The way they smiled at him he could almost believe it.

Don't let it get to your head; in another day or two, it will all be over. They are the ones who are friends. Just look at them. Sitting there, not touching, and almost touching. Lovers? God. Could they be? Or maybe once? Wasn't Peter too old?

"How did you two meet?" he asked them.

The two of them looked at each other and Peter bobbed his head to the side, like a bird. His mouth opened, then half closed, as if he were about to say something and then thought better of it. He gave a strange smile. "Ten years ago, this young man saved my life."

"Your life?" Todd leaned in, his curiosity aroused. "How?"

"I hardly saved his life," Gabe said with a groan.

"Ah, but mayhap you did." Peter turned to Todd and waved his hand through the air in that curious way of his. "I was shopping—"

"Drinking," Gabe said.

"Was I?" Peter's eyes twinkled and he winked at Todd. "Perhaps I was."

"He was," Gabe affirmed.

"Ah, yes. This awful little hole in the wall. I had wandered in earlier, on a lash...."

There was a long pause, his eyes shining like mad—a time during which Todd could only wonder what "lash" meant.

Peter rolled his hand, stirring the air and the thoughts of his audience. "It means to imbibe."

"Too much," Gabe added.

"Nonsense," Peter said, cocking his head toward Gabe in that birdlike manner. "I *never* drink 'too' much. I always drink *exactly* how much I was meant to." He swiveled his head back and focused on Todd. "Relax and understand, boy, whether or not it is clear to you, no doubt the universe is unfolding as it should."

Todd shook his head. He wanted to giggle again. What was it about this man? Suddenly he felt good. Really good. What's more, he realized he'd been feeling good all evening. He looked at Gabe and saw Gabe looking at him (with those country-blue-sky eyes). He felt his breath catch.

My God. He's gorgeous.

(*"You a faggot or something?"*)

Maybe you're bi?

Dear God.

For a brief instant, looking at the man all sprawled back and comfortable on the big leather couch, he wondered what it would be like to climb up into his lap.

Maybe I am bi? My God. Could I be?

(*"Perverts. They like little boys. They kidnap them and they cut them...."*)

But looking at Gabe, Todd knew this man wasn't capable of such an act. The idea was hideous.

Of course it is. Why would you believe anything your stepfather told you?

"Have I lost you, Todd?"

Todd jerked, Peter's words bringing him back. "Sorry," he said. "I was just thinking."

"I could see that." Peter's eyes went from mischievous to an abrupt depth. It was like staring into space. And space was staring back.

He's inside my head again!

Peter broke the contact and tossed his head, that great mop of silver bouncing like a child's. "Where was I?"

"Lashing," Gabe replied cynically.

"Ah yes. I had dropped into this little bar, and when it came time to leave, I was seized upon by brigands."

"What?" Todd said with a gasp.

"Mugged. I was mugged. Or they attempted to mug me, that is. That is when yon hero"—he waved toward Gabe—"sprang to my aid!"

Todd looked at his host. "You did?"

Gabe shook his head. "I was sitting in this alley—"

"An alley?" Todd furrowed his brow.

Gabe nodded. "I was going to sleep there."

"In an alley?" Todd said, surprised. "You were sleeping in an alley? But why?"

"Because I didn't have a place to stay, Todd!"

There was another silence. Then Gabe went on, "I'm sorry. I didn't mean to say it like that. I *had* a place. I *had* a boyfriend. And I came home and caught him in bed with some guy he'd picked up at a bar."

Todd twitched. Cheater. Was the world made of cheaters?

"So I packed a bag," Gabe continued, "and just ran out of there. Left without making sure I had a place to stay first. I'd only lived in the city for a few months and realized pretty quick I didn't have any place to go."

"And that," Peter said, breaking in, "is when he saw the scoundrels attack me. He gave out such a cry that wolves would have stopped to listen, and then he fell upon my assailants."

"What I didn't know," said Gabe, "was that Peter is an expert swordsman."

"Swordsman?" Todd goggled at them both. This story was just getting more and more interesting.

Gabe nodded. Peter gave a single nod and grinned his big toothy grin. He then pointed. "Would you get that for me, Toddy?"

Todd looked and saw the man was pointing at his cane. He got up, retrieved it, and brought it back to its owner. Peter reached out in his quick and graceful way, took the cane, and tugged on its silver head. It began to pull out, and when it did so, Todd gave a gasp. It was a blade!

"I didn't carve them up too badly," Peter said.

"He was like Zorro." Gabe held out his hand and pretended to use an invisible sword.

"*W*'s," Peter rejoined. "Not *Z*'s. Quick and shallow *W*'s. For Wagner. I may not even have left a scar."

"It was a good thing too," Gabe said. "'Cause it wasn't until I jumped in that I saw I'd taken on more than I could have handled otherwise."

"No, no, no! You were Ares. Gilgamesh. Heracles fighting off the Hydra."

"More likely it was Peter here who was Errol Flynn. You could hardly see him move. And he was toasted."

"Cabbaged," Peter said nodding.

"Three sheets to the wind," returned Gabe.

"Full as a tick," Peter added matter-of-factly.

"Hammered."

"Drunk." Peter rose from the couch. He stepped away from his companions and raised his sword high. "I was pissed!" He whipped the blade through the air. "Plastered, blitzed, gassed, pickled!" The blade began to make whickering sounds as his wrist flickered effortlessly this way and that. "Schnookered, stuck like chuck, *shit*-canned." He leapt into a classic *en guarde* position and stabbed an imaginary foe through and through. "I was off my tits," he shouted.

Todd exploded into laughter.

Peter whirled around, the blade disappearing into the cane as if it had never been there. "Thank the Lord I was not driving," he said, voice dropping to barely a whisper.

Todd doubled over laughing, afraid he would fall off the coffee table.

"It was *glorious*," Peter declared.

Gabe joined the laughter. "It was pretty awesome."

"Those who were not on the ground crying for mercy had run like the wind, base cowards that they were."

Todd wiped at his eyes. "That's how you two met? Really?"

"Really," Peter replied. "And then upon making sure my hero was not too badly harmed, we went back into the bar for another drink."

"Oh, my God!" Todd began to snicker anew.

"That is when I discovered Gabriel's name—an angel you must know—"

Gabriel. Peter called Gabe that every time he said his name. Gabriel? Silly, but it hadn't occurred to Todd that was Gabe's real name.

"And that is also when I discovered he was homeless. He slept that night in one of my guest bedrooms."

"I stayed more than one night. He wouldn't let me leave!"

"And soon a companionship had been born. I hired him for one of my companies."

"I started as an assistant to an assistant," Gabe explained. "Kind of a glorified mailboy."

"He tells not the story right. I was watching him. I knew not yet of what he was capable. I would have let him sit around my pool, but he insisted on earning his keep," Peter clarified. "So I gave him a job as

an assistant to one of the investment officers. Now he is one of my two
Chief Business Development Officers. He practically runs the place.
We changed the name and its mission and everything about it. When it
comes to Symmetry Innovations, Gabriel is my right arm."

"Wow," said Todd.

Peter nodded. "I watched him metamorphose to a lovely butterfly
right before my eyes."

THEY sat before the fire, Peter and Gabe on the couch and Todd on the
floor, and talked. Gabe talked about how he would never have dreamed
growing up in St. Louis that one day he would be living the life he was
living. He seemed so happy, yet Todd thought he detected a note of
sadness. Maybe life wasn't quite as perfect as he said? What had Harry
and Cody said? That they hadn't seen Gabe with anyone in a couple of
years?

Peter told tales of his travels and adventures around the world.
Some were crazy, some outlandish and unbelievable. Peter had a
delightful way of telling the stories of his exploits. Todd hung on every
word.

Then Todd found himself slipping into his own story. Sharing
with the men his dreams of cooking, of getting away from a small town
and people and parents and a girlfriend who didn't understand him. He
let it all come out. How he'd lost his van, his money, his apartment.

Then he fell silent, exhausted. After a long pause he looked up
into Gabe's eyes—they were so deep and filled with mystery—and
Peter's—they sparkled with mischief and wisdom and more. Energy.
How did the man have so much energy? How old was he?

Peter cocked an eyebrow. "How old am I?" Peter raised a hand
before him, stared even higher. "'A man's age is something impressive,
it sums up his life: maturity reached slowly and against many obstacles,
illnesses cured, griefs and despairs overcome, and unconscious risks
taken; maturity formed through so many desires, hopes, regrets,
forgotten things, loves. A man's age represents a fine cargo of

experiences and memories.' So said Antoine de Saint-Exupéry, and so say I."

Shit! He'd done it again. Spoken aloud without thinking. That was his out-loud voice. "I'm sorry. Sometimes I wish I had a backspace for my mouth."

"How old do you think I am, young squire?" Peter asked.

Oh no. There was no way he was stepping into that! He could only get into trouble.

"Please," Peter said, placing his hands on his hips and thrusting out his chest. "Be quick about it—make a guess!"

"I-I... I don't know. Sixty?" Todd clenched his jaw.

Both of Peter's brows shot up and vanished in his great hanging bangs. "I am sixty-eight. Excellent. You chose to shave off a few years from your actual estimate. I recommend you always do this, especially in guessing the age of women and old queens. I also recommend you do not get yourself into a situation where age-guessing is required."

Todd didn't know whether to laugh or cry. Eyes wide, he said, "But I didn't think you were that old."

"Old? You have heard the words of de Saint-Exupéry, now hear Douglas MacArthur. 'You are as young as your faith, as old as your doubt; as young as your self-confidence, as old as your fear; as young as your hope, as old as your despair.' Remember that, my boy."

Todd let the words sink in. *Young as my faith... my hope... my self-confidence....* Wow. "Do you believe that?" he asked.

"I do." Peter stood up. "And as I totter into antiquity, I vow always to surround myself with youth, from whom I gather great handfuls of energy." Peter reached out with one of those hands, long fingers grasping Todd's shoulder. "I know times are tough for you now, Toddy. I know things look bleak. The days are cold and you have been thrown into the streets."

Todd froze.

"But please remember this also, if nothing else. Remember the words of Albert Einstein: 'There are two ways to live your life. One is as though nothing is a miracle. The other is as though *every*thing is a miracle.'"

His eyes bored into Todd once again. It was like Peter was right there, inside his head, looking through files, touching here and there. And yet.... Todd wasn't afraid. There was no harm coming from this tall spider of a man. It was like he was gently settling things into place. Todd felt a strange peace come over him.

"Live life as if it were a miracle, Toddy, and surely you will find miracles just beyond the next bend in the road, over the next rise of a hill. *Great* things await you. I see it in you. I saw it in Gabriel here. Trust my words."

Peter whirled away from him and raised his hand high again. "And on that note, I bid you adieu. This time is right. I know that my chariot dost await."

"Are you sure, Peter?" Gabe asked, rising as well.

Peter glanced down at his watch. "Yes. My driver has probably been waiting, although not long." He then turned to Todd. "Until we meet again, Toddy. You don't mind if I call you 'Toddy', do you?"

Todd smiled. Wasn't that funny? Peter had been calling him Toddy all evening. He hated "Toddy." Had hated it so much when Joan called him that he wanted to scream. But from this man? Peter made him feel warm and safe and a part of something. But what? "I don't mind."

Peter reached out once more, grabbed Todd's shoulders, and pulled him into a hug. Pressed up against him, Todd was surprised to feel the iron in that body. This was no sagging old man and no skeleton either.

Then Peter hugged Gabe while Todd ran to grab his coat and scarf. When Peter was done, Todd helped him into both. Peter smiled at them both as if he had one last thing to say, then winking, spun about and threw open the door.

Todd saw it then. Peter tried to leave them with those words, but he couldn't help it. He would say something more....

"Parting is such sweet sorrow…. Thank you for the lovely dinner. Thank you for the lovely company. Merry meet, merry part, and merry meet again."

And then he was gone.

CHAPTER TEN

"Wow," said Todd, staring at the door.

"Wow is right," Gabe said.

"He's unbelievable," Todd replied.

"He is."

Todd turned to face Gabe, who seemed to stand over him like a giant. Like a miracle.

"I'm sorry about dinner," Gabe said. "I wasn't expecting Peter to drop in like—"

Todd shook his head. "No. Don't. He's amazing. I don't mind at all." And interestingly, he didn't. It was hard to remember his disappointment a few hours before when the man had first shown up.

"What's it like to have a man like that in your life?" Todd asked.

Gabe propped his chin in his hand on the arm of the couch. "Well… pretty amazing actually."

"You know what I think?" Todd said. "I think from the minute he walked in here, he looked like a man who just finished causing trouble and was waiting to be caught for it. I want to live my life that way."

"He makes me want the same thing," Gabe replied. "I don't know where I would be today if he hadn't helped me when he did."

"Well, you helped him first." Todd sat on the chair next to Gabe. "And something tells me you would have been okay."

"Maybe," Gabe replied.

Todd took a deep breath, then let it out slowly. "What would I have done if you hadn't helped me?" It was true. What would have happened? He might have died.

Gabe sat up and reached out and laid his hand on Todd's. "Something tells me you would have been okay."

Todd swallowed hard. He hoped so. "Maybe," he said. "Maybe not."

"Todd. Anything can happen if you set your mind to it."

Looking at this handsome man, he thought that might be true. Imagine, ten years ago Gabe was going to spend the night in an alley, and today he had this apartment and a high-paying job and a man like Peter Wagner as his boss.

Todd looked down at the hand lying across his. So big. So masculine. Gabe's hand almost dwarfed his own; even his fingers were manly. Their hands looked so different from when he held Joan's. Her hand was so small. Todd's gaze traveled up the length of Gabe's arm, the light dusting of hair across its back, then the huge bicep and the sleeve of the red T-shirt stretched to encompass it. Then that chest. Massive. The word "Chiefs" was almost strained out of proportion over the man's pectorals. Just one of them looked as big as Todd's whole head. He remembered resting his face against it. Hard and soft at the same time. Nothing like Joan's breasts.

His eyes moved up that huge chest and up Gabe's neck—even it was corded with muscles. What must it be like to have a body like that? He would never be built like Gabe.

Finally he looked at Gabe's face. So handsome. Gabe's short dark-blond hair looked so soft, and Todd found himself wondering just what it would feel like. When he'd patted the snow off Gabe's head the hair had seemed soft. But it was wet then. Todd almost leaned forward to touch it, but stopped himself.

They locked eyes and Todd trembled. That look. Those eyes.

What's happening to me?

("*Maybe you're bi?*")

God. Could I be?

It would explain a lot. How excited he'd been in the basement with Austin.

And it was hot. Admit it.

Todd felt his cock stir.

He remembered when Peter was here and how he'd looked at Gabe and how he'd suddenly wanted to crawl up into the man's lap. Why not? It was the least he could do for this man who had helped him so much.

His cock stiffened, began to shift uncomfortably in his—Gabe's——jeans. A slight moan escaped his lips.

"Are you okay, Todd?" his friend asked.

Todd stood, took a few steps until he stood between Gabe's legs. His heart was pounding in his ears and he felt just a little light-headed. His erection filled and throbbed. Had Gabe seen it?

What are you doing?

What I want to do.

What about your stepdad calling you a faggot?

Fuck him.

Todd lifted a knee and then brought it to rest on the couch between Gabe's open legs.

"Todd?"

Then he climbed up into the man's lap.

"Todd?" Gabe's eyes grew alarmed. "What are you doing?"

Todd settled down, then pressed forward, his hard cock against Gabe's abs. He moaned again.

"Todd!" Gabe sat up, and if Todd hadn't reached out and grabbed Gabe's shoulders, he might have been dumped on the floor. The move instead spread his legs wide, and then Gabe did see his erection. He saw Gabe's eyes drop down and stop. *He's looking.* Todd felt his cock throb again and yes, Gabe saw it.

"Todd…." Gabe looked up into his face. "What are you doing?"

"Thanking you," Todd said. He leaned in and kissed Gabe.

Todd's heart exploded. The kiss lasted only an instant, because before he could even attempt to open his mouth, Gabe was pushing him back. But in that minute Todd knew. He liked it. Liked it in a way he'd never, ever, liked kissing Joan.

Suddenly Gabe was standing, his muscles easily lifting Todd and then setting him on his feet. "No! I won't have you do this."

"But...."

"No! I can't."

Todd was confused. He glanced down and—yes!—he could see. Gabe was getting hard as well, and was there ever a more sexy sight? He looked back into Gabe's face. He knew the man wanted him. Why was he resisting? "Gabe. I—"

"No. You don't understand. Todd—I-I can't." And with that he ran out of the room.

GABE couldn't remember being so hard in his life. Not even when he was a teenager and he'd discovered his best friend's mother's stash of *Playgirl* magazines. God. What had just happened? How had it happened?

They'd been eating dinner, he and Todd and Peter, and it had been so nice. But sexual? Had he missed something? When had things turned sexual? Had he misled Todd? Made him feel he had to pay to be able to stay?

They'd just been sitting there, and before he knew what was happening, Todd was climbing into his lap. He'd had a hard-on, and it had looked so hot pushing against the front of his—or rather, Gabe's—jeans. Then Todd had kissed him, and—Christ!

A month or so ago, Curtis—one of his co-workers—had brought a friend to the holiday party at the office. It was a man Gabe had known was gay. In fact, he and nearly everyone else in the office had thought Curtis and his friend were a couple and just wouldn't admit it. But when he'd talked to Curtis's friend—Gavin—he'd been shocked to find out they weren't. It explained a lot. The last time he'd seen Gavin had been at a summer company picnic. He'd thought there had been sparks between the two of them back then, but he'd kept his distance since he thought the man was his co-worker's lover. But at the holiday party, he'd discovered differently. Then the punch—liberally spiked by who knew how many partygoers and with how many different types of alcohol—plus the looks Gavin had seemed to be giving him made him act like a fool. He'd kissed the man right there in the office, under the mistletoe.

It had been a nice kiss. And it had been so long since he'd kissed anyone. Ever since the fiasco with Daniel and Brett. It was a kiss that had ended messily when the supposedly straight Curtis had admitted he did want to be with Gavin after all. Apparently the two had been together ever since. Gabe had wondered what might have happened if he'd made a move on Gavin at the picnic instead. Would it have made a difference?

Or maybe Gavin was meant to be with Curtis, and it would have been nothing but another disaster?

The kiss had been nice. But that kiss was nothing like the kiss he'd just shared with Todd. It had lasted only a second but this time his good sense had kicked in and he'd stopped it. No. He would not have another Brett on his hands. He couldn't.

Another Brett?

Gabe closed his eyes and punched his bedroom wall but immediately regretted it. Surely Todd had heard that?

Todd.

Oh, my God.

I've done it again.

I'm falling for this kid!

As stupid as that sounded… it was true. Ridiculous. He'd only known the young man for twenty-four hours, but it was true.

No. You're just horny. Lonely.

Then he saw an image of Todd in the lobby downstairs. Scared. Cold. How he'd felt compelled to help the kid. How he'd brought him food. How his heart had leapt in his throat at just the sight of him.

That was followed by the memory of Todd running on the treadmill. How beautiful and wild and sexy he'd looked.

Then the smile on his face when Peter had complimented him on his meal.

And finally, the look on Todd's face when climbing up into his lap minutes ago. His eyes all heavy and sexy, and his jeans tented with an erection. The kiss the boy had given him. Seconds. Not even that long. How close he'd come to melting into it and then, suddenly realizing what he was doing, how he'd pushed Todd back.

My God. The kiss had felt like love.

Shitfire!

Impossible. He couldn't feel anything for Todd. He'd just found out his last name a few hours ago. Not love. Hormones. He'd read about this. What did they call it? Limerence? Yes. He read all about it after everything that had happened with Brett. Peter had given him a book about it. He dashed out of his bedroom and into his office, scanned the bookshelves quickly. Hadn't it had a pink spine? Yes! There it was.

He pulled it off the shelf. *Love and Limerence: The Experience of Being in Love.*

I am not in love with Todd. That would imply love at first sight, and that was ridiculous. It was just some involuntary state of mind caused by lust and loneliness and a lack of being laid.

There was a tap and Gabe spun to see Todd standing there. The look on his face cut into Gabe's heart. Anguish.

"Did I do something wrong?" Todd asked. "I thought... I thought you wanted...."

A shudder passed through Gabe. "Todd...."

"Was I wrong? I mean you... you offered to pay me, and I thought I could...."

Gabe shook his head. *God, no.*

"I figured it was the least I could do. You've been so good to me."

Gabe stepped forward. Then stopped himself. Shook his head again. "Todd, no. You don't... I don't want you to pay for what I've done for you. I'm paying it forward, don't you see? Like Peter did for me. He didn't ask me for sex—"

"He didn't?"

"No! We've never slept together. It's not like that. We were never attracted to each other. He helped me because he could. That's who he is. Peter helps people. I'm helping you."

Todd trembled, looked away. Looked back. "Because that is who you are. You help people."

Tracy's words came back in a flash: *"That's all you do. That's who you are."*

Todd took a step, held out his hand. "Then let me do this for you. You want me, don't you? I think you do!"

"Gabriel, it's your turn. All you do is help people. It's time for someone to do something for you again."

No! Not this way.

"Thank you, Todd," Gabe said, nearly shaking. "But I couldn't live with myself if I used you that way. Please. Let's not ruin a perfect evening, okay?"

Todd gave a little gasp, his voice hitched. "Okay."

You've hurt his feelings.

It's better than using him.

Todd turned away, then back. "You're sure?"

I've never been more unsure of anything in my life, Gabe thought. But instead he said, "I'm sure."

Todd nodded. Turned away again. And left the room.

CHAPTER ELEVEN

THE day was shit. Gabe had slept like shit, he'd woken with a strange hangover (and he never got hangovers), and the day had gotten even worse. One disaster after another. All he'd been able to do was answer one call after another, solve (or try to) one problem after another.

There was the continued problem with AbledRides, something he'd been working on for days. AbledRides rigged and repaired cars so the disabled and paraplegics could drive them. The company had been doing quite well on their own. They had more work than they could handle as a matter of fact. They now faced a problem that often popped up with growing businesses. They'd run out of space and had nowhere to expand. That was a major problem because it would cost them too much to move and far too much to buy out any neighbors. They were doing well, but not that kind of well.

The solution Gabe was working on had to do with the unit backing onto theirs. However, it was in legal contention due to a bankruptcy. So Gabe had done the only thing he could do for now. He'd introduced Sal Davidson, the owner of the business, to Wilfred Cooper, one of Peter's up-and-coming young lawyers.

Now all Gabe could do was sit and wait to see if Cooper could resolve the bankruptcy agreement, making the unit available for rental. Then AbledRides would be able to expand into the property and take on new staff. Everyone would be happy. AbledRides would survive.

New jobs would be provided. And Wagner Enterprises, via Symmetry Innovations, would own a share in another promising venture.

Waiting was something Gabe wasn't good at. That's why he'd called Cooper and asked for a favor. Controlling what he could always helped.

Next there was the kid who needed a little capital to keep his no-kill animal shelter from being shut down. Was there any way the business was viable? Was it a waste of time?

But then that inner voice had somehow managed to make itself heard through the maelstrom of Gabe's emotions. All he had to do was think of the dachshund he'd had as a kid, of Leia, Todd's cat, and he knew the answer.

The biggest problem of the day was that all he could think of was Todd. No-kill animal shelters made him think of Leia, and that made him think of Todd. Not that he needed a cat for that.

Gabe had gone to bed last night and done nothing but stare at the ceiling. He wanted Todd. He wanted him so fucking bad, and it didn't make any sense. He hardly knew the boy.

It's Brett. He reminds you of Brett. It is Brett all over again.

But it wasn't. Brett was so different from Todd. The situation was completely different.

Tell yourself that.

If there was anything in his whole life he regretted, it was Brett. It had started so innocently and then gone to hell. Hell in a handbasket.

Things seemed to suddenly calm at lunch. The calls just ceased, or at least the ones to Gabe did.

Which only gave him more time to think of Todd. *I could go home and join him for lunch.* But then he thought of how the evening had ended and how it could just be more confusing for him to suddenly show up. He needed to work. Let Todd have the day to himself.

There was a knock, and Gabe turned to see Tracy standing in the doorway. She had a big smile plastered on her face. She wasn't wearing red or purple. "Hey Gabriel," she said through clenched teeth.

"Come in, Tracy."

Tracy scuttled in sideways like a crab and quickly sat in one of the chairs in front of the desk. "Do you hate me?"

Gabe looked at her through slitted eyes.

"For what...?"

Tracy coughed, looked this way and that, then looked back. "I just heard Mr. Wagner dropped by your apartment last night."

Gabe furrowed his brow. "Yes...?"

Tracy jumped up. "I know what you're thinking."

"What am I thinking, Tracy?" What was she acting so weird about now?

"You're thinking I told Mr. Wagner to stop by your place and check out your rent boy," she cried.

"Tracy! Your voice." Then—*Oh, God, she didn't.* "Tracy. You didn't."

Tracy started to close his office door and then froze. She spun. "No! I swear, Gabriel. I swear. I didn't speak to him except for yesterday morning."

Gabe leaned back in his chair. "When you *did* tell him about Todd?"

Her shoulders slumped. For a minute he thought she just might cry. "Gabriel. I'm worried. I didn't mean to interfere. I promise. I only mentioned him because I was worried about you."

Gabe sighed. "I swear to God, Tracy."

She closed the door and came back and sat down. "He asked me how you were doing, and then before I knew it, I told him about Todd. But I didn't mention the hustler part."

"Todd is not a hustler," Gabe said, gritting his teeth.

"I know! That's why I didn't tell him about that."

Gabe shook his head. "What would you say if I told you Peter liked him?"

Tracy sat upright so fast it looked like she had been goosed. "Really?"

"Yep," Gabe said. "He liked him a lot. Todd charmed the hell out of him. Peter approves." Which Peter hadn't actually officially said, but it was obvious he did. "Tracy, you know what kind of kid he is? I thought maybe he was going to cry when he was telling me about his cat. He had to leave his cat behind, and he's worried his stepfather has killed her. *That's* the kind of kid he is."

Tracy's shoulders relaxed and then a tiny smile came over her face. "That's kind of sweet. Any man who is worried about his cat can't be all bad. And if Peter likes him, that just doubles it." She nodded. "Enough said, then. I won't say another word."

Yeah. Right. "Yes you will, Tracy."

She shook her head adamantly.

Gabe leaned forward and rested his head in his upturned hand, elbow on his desk. "You trust Peter, but not me?"

Tracy shrugged and gave him a little smirk. "Your luck with men hasn't been exactly stellar recently."

Touché. "It has been almost two years since I've really had anything to do with a man, Tracy."

She sat up straight, her eyebrow cocking and smirk growing. "Except when you sucked face with Curtis's boyfriend at the holiday party."

Touché deuced. "To be fair, they weren't boyfriends at the time."

She shrugged and rose from her chair. "I'm going for Subway. Want to split?"

He smiled. "Todd made me leftovers," he replied.

"Leftovers?"

He chuckled and rose from his seat. "From last night's dinner. It was amazing." He stood and then retrieved the Tupperware container from the small refrigerator in his armoire.

She harrumphed. "What is it?"

He opened the container and showed it to her. "Chicken."

"Is that some kind of fruit stuffing?" she asked. "It looks good."

"Oh, it's real good." He left the office, Tracy trailing behind him, and went into the kitchen and popped it into the microwave.

"Your pretty boy did that?"

"Yup."

"He *is* pretty, isn't he?" Tracy asked.

"He is," Gabe said. "And I'm not sure what I'm doing, so stop asking. He offered...." He was about to say "he offered himself to me last night," and then stopped. He told Tracy almost everything, but he suddenly knew he didn't want to tell her about that. It was private. It would horrify Todd if he thought Gabe had told anyone about what had happened. It would be wrong.

The microwave sounded and he opened it, the aroma of the food immediately filled the room.

"Smells good," Tracy said. "*Really* good."

He pulled a fork from a drawer. "It is," he said. He sat down and took a bite. Damn. Even microwaved it was delicious, he thought, and made approving noises.

"Here," she said. "Let me try."

From anyone else, the request might have been rude. But this was Tracy. They did things like that all the time. Gabe made her a forkful, being sure to include both chicken and Todd's stuffing. He held it out to her, and she leaned over and took the offered food.

"Oh.... Ohmygawd," she said and Gabe almost laughed. Tracy had kind of said "God." She never did that. She considered using God's name in any way profane. "Oh, oh! That's *amazing*. And Todd did this?"

Gabe smiled, nodded. "He sure did."

"Well, girl!" Tracy laughed. "I take it back. I take it all back. When am I invited for din-din?"

This time Gabe did laugh. "You're too much, Tracy."

"You didn't answer my question," she replied and winked.

"We'll see. Let me have him to myself a little bit more, okay?" he asked. "Before he lowers the boom on me and vanishes?"

Tracy sighed, reached out, and patted his hand.

"Ah, Tracy. Don't worry about me, okay? Really. I'll be fine. I am an adult."

She shook her head again. "So you say. I still don't know what you'd do without me." She kissed his forehead and then turned on her high heels and strode from the room as if walking off a stage.

Gabe slumped back in his chair and sighed. *Oh, Tracy*, he thought. She couldn't help but get in his business. Reminded him of a Jewish mother. But Jewish she wasn't, and neither was she his mother.

Tracy would just have to accept what he was doing. He needed to help Todd. He had to. Couldn't just let the kid go out onto the street. But more than that, he had to figure out a way for the kid to help himself.

Suddenly the name of Todd's apartment building sprang to his mind. The Dove. A quick Google search showed Gabe where it was. He passed it all the time. Right next door to the glaringly ugly Red Garter gentlemen's club, just like Todd said. He snorted. *Gentlemen indeed.*

And that's when he got an idea.

WHEN Gabe got up that morning for work—moving quietly through the apartment—Todd was wide awake. The man might as well have been parading around with a marching band. Todd pretended he was asleep. He just couldn't face Gabe. Todd had humiliated himself. Thoughts of how he'd thrown himself at Gabe kept rolling through his head. Rolling? Hell, it was more like a stampede of elephants. What had gotten into him? He'd been denying he was gay all his life, and then to suddenly crawl into the man's lap like a sleazy stripper from the Red Garter? And what the fuck would he have done with Gabe had the man taken him up on it? He would have had no idea what to do. Not really. Sure, suck a cock. But fucking? And who would fuck who? And jeez, if he was the one to get fucked, wouldn't it hurt beyond anything? How or why would a man want to get fucked?

Sleep—when it did come—was fitful and restless.

At one point in the middle of the night, he'd gotten up and made Gabe lunch and written a note. A gesture of some kind. Then he worried it might be stalkerish or like he was trying to be Gabe's wife or something even worse. So he got up and tore up the note. Crazy. Only to then get up and write a second note.

I'm going crazy!

Todd finally got some deep sleep after Gabe left, but he was woken up after only a couple of hours by a knocking at the door. He panicked for a moment, afraid it was his landlord demanding the rent "Right now!", and then he calmed down when he realized how ridiculous that was.

Dreaming. I was just dreaming.

There was another knock, louder this time.

"Hold on," he called. *It's that little girl*, he thought. *She's going to ask me if I'm bisexual.* But when he peeked through the peephole, he saw it was only Cody, half of Cody and Harry, the guys from the laundry room. Hmmmm…. He opened the door and leaned around it since he hadn't bothered to put on any pants.

"Hey, Todd," said the slim young man. "Gabe called me. Asked if I would run you to the grocery store."

"The grocery store?" Todd asked.

"Yup. He said to pick up some food. He said to check *The Wizard of Oz* first."

"*The Wizard of Oz?*" *Now what the hell could that mean?* "I don't get it."

"He seemed to think you would. Can I come in?"

Todd started to open the door and then remember he was wearing only his—well, Gabe's—underwear. "Ah, hold on a minute, okay?"

Cody gave a curious, one-shoulder shrug and Todd closed the door and scrambled into his jeans. *The Wizard of Oz?* Could he mean one of his DVDs? Todd wondered, starting for the door. The though made him detour to the armoire, and upon opening it, he found the movie, right where it should be, alphabetical with the *W*'s. He looked it over, front and back, then popped it open. And there were six fifty-dollar bills. *Holy shit.* It made him think of his rolled-up sock in the back of the drawer of his dresser.

He quickly stuffed the money in his pocket and then dashed to the door. "Come in," he said.

"You gonna check what he asked you to?" Cody asked.

"Already did. He wants you to take me to get groceries?"

"Yup," Cody nodded. "A week or two's worth, he said."

A week or two's worth? For both of them? he wondered. Or just Gabe? "Well, okay," he replied and then slipped into his Converses. "You want some coffee before we leave?" he asked Cody.

"Nah, I already had some. Let's get going. I still have to go into work today."

"What do you do?" Todd asked, slipping on his jacket.

"Can't you tell?" Cody winked and patted his head. "I'm a hairstylist."

Todd tried not to react. *Hairstylist? Was there anything gayer?*

"I'm assuming we're going to Nature's Corner?"

Todd shrugged.

"Did Gabe not talk to you about this at all?" Cody asked.

Todd shook his head. "Nope." *He was too busy ignoring me after I made a horse's ass of myself.*

"Well I know Gabe likes organic, and I know he does shop for his herbs and veggies at Nature's Corner. So let's head there."

"Okay," Todd said. Nature's Corner was a little grocery store he'd stumbled on one day and then been shocked at their high prices. Everything was natural, or so they said. Everything organic. Maybe that's where Gabe got his Carlisle Free Range Chickens.

Cody turned out to have an old Country Squire station wagon— green, with fake wood paneling down the side. "Wow," Todd said. "My grandparents had one of these."

"So did mine," Cody said, raising an already arched brow. "Now I have it."

They got in and a moment later were heading south on Gilham. "Any idea what you want to get?" Cody asked.

Todd thought about it a moment. He had three hundred dollars to buy a "week or two's worth of groceries." At lease he assumed he was supposed to spend it all. Was it emergency money? What did he buy? "Just some staples," he said. "Some ground beef, I suppose. Some turkey. Hey!" He got an idea. "Maybe some lamb chops. I want to really impress him. The chicken I made was nothing."

"Boy," Cody said. "Lamb. You can cook lamb?"

"I suppose," Todd said. "I cooked it once. I thought it was pretty good, but my mom and stepdad didn't care for it. But then they're bologna-and-gravy-over-instant-biscuits kind of people."

"My parents too," Cody replied. "Lamb. You must really like Gabe a lot."

Truth to tell, Todd was beginning to suspect he liked Gabe more than he could have guessed.

(*"Maybe you're bisexual."*)

"Cody, can I ask you a question? It's pretty weird, but I don't have anybody else to ask."

Cody gave another of those one-shouldered shrugs. "Sure." They stopped at a light and Cody turned to him. "And weird is a matter of experience, trust me. I've *seen* weird. A weird you wouldn't believe."

Todd nodded then steeled himself for the question. He took a deep breath.

"Oh, go on!"

Todd took a deep breath. *Do it. Now or never.* "How can I tell if I'm bisexual?" he asked in a rush.

Cody's eyes went wide for a second then quickly relaxed. "Shit. Does Gabe know about this?"

Todd dropped his head back against the back of his seat. "Shit," he said with a groan.

"So you think you might like girls?" Cody asked.

Todd jerked up in his seat. "No! Well, I mean, yes. I mean.... Shit, I don't know what I mean."

The light changed and Cody stepped on the gas. "You must if your boyfriend is Superman and you're thinking about women."

"I'm not," Todd cried.

"You just said you were," Cody said.

"No. No, it's just... I'm... I'm wondering...." He dropped his head back again, closed his eyes, and let out a long sigh. Shit. Could he actually say it out loud? And to a virtual stranger? He lifted his head and stared out the window. "I'm wondering if I like *guys*." God! He'd done it. He'd said it.

Todd spared Cody a look with his peripheral vision.

Cody's eyes were wide but staring forward. "But I... I thought.... You aren't... you don't? But...." Cody scratched at his throat. "I though you said you and Gabe...."

"I never actually said that. I just let you think it."

"But *why?*" Cody was looking at him, obviously confused.

"It was easier than explaining the whole story."

Cody cleared his throat. "I've got time," Cody said. "In case you didn't notice, I've turned around. I don't know if Nature's Corner has lamb. We're going downtown. If we need to, we'll get that coffee too."

Todd sighed. "Okay." So he did it. He told Cody the whole story. He told Cody about moving from Buckman and coming to Kansas City with stars in his eyes...

"I'm surprised you chose KC. Why not Chicago or New York or LA?"

... and how badly he'd wanted to learn to cook from Izar Goya. How he'd lost his job at McDonald's and how surprisingly hard it was for a guy from a small town to find a new one with nothing but jobs with Pizza Hut and a yearbook company under his belt. And finally how he'd been thrown out of his apartment and into a snowstorm, and how Gabe had helped him by letting him stay the last few nights with him.

"Gosh. That totally sucks. But you were lucky in the end. Gabe is the nicest man in the world." They pulled into a parking lot and got out of the car. "And now you're wondering if you're bisexual?"

"Sssshhhh!" Todd looked around desperately. "Someone will hear you."

"So what?" Cody shrugged. "No one cares, Todd."

"I care! I've never said anything like this to anyone."

Cody's brown eyes softened. "No one?"

Todd shook his head. "Not until you."

Cody stopped walking. He looked at Todd. "Thank you for trusting me." He tilted his head to the side. "Okay. Come on."

He led Todd into the grocery store—it was huge!—and toward the back into a small coffee shop. "Sit down," he said, indicating a table off to the side by a large window. "I'll get us some coffee after all."

"What about your work?" Todd asked.

"I just bought the place," Cody said. "I can show up whenever I want. What're they going to do? Fire me?"

Todd sat while Cody got the coffees and then settled in the chair beside him. Cody gave Todd a large paper cup and placed some creamer packets—as well as sugar and sweetener—on the table. "I didn't know how you liked it."

"Thanks." Todd started to add some creamer and then stopped. *Taste it. Wouldn't that make Gabe happy? Hell. Shouldn't you know better? You want to be a chef.* Wasn't there a story about how Henry Ford used to take people out for dinner before he hired them for any key positions? And how if they salted or peppered their food before tasting it, they didn't get the job? Something about how Ford didn't trust anyone who made a decision before getting all the facts?

Todd lifted his cup, blew for a minute, and then closing his eyes—like Gabe—he sipped.

Flavors flowed over his tongue. First earth, then berries, and sweetness. Sweetness even though there wasn't any sugar. "Wow," he said. It wasn't Folger's, that was for sure.

"Kansas City is starting to get a reputation for its coffee," Cody said with a smile. "I've read top critics who put us right up there with New York and San Francisco."

"Really?"

"Really," Cody replied. "Now spill it."

"The coffee?" Todd asked, suddenly regretting opening up to Cody. Did he really want to talk about this? Talking would make it more… real. Did he want to open Pandora's box?

"You *know* what I mean," Cody answered.

"No. I don't," Todd said stubbornly. "I've told you everything."

"Except the most important part. Why you think you might be bisexual."

Todd froze a moment, looked around him to see who might have overheard, and saw Cody was right. No one was listening. And if they had overheard, they didn't care.

How could they not? he wondered. Especially about something that might just be the biggest thing in his life.

"How did you know?" Todd asked.

"About…?" Cody returned.

"Your… your sexuality. When did you know that… that… that you were…?"

Cody rolled his eyes theatrically. "Gay?"

"Well… not necessarily that," Todd said. "I mean, you probably had girlfriends, right? When did you know that…?"

"Nope," Cody replied. "Not one. Never had a girlfriend. Never wanted one. I've always known I was gay. Always."

"Oh, come on," Todd returned. "Always? What does that mean?"

"Well, since at least fourth grade," Cody said, running fingers through his brown hair.

"Fourth grade? How could you have known since fourth grade?" Todd was stunned. "I didn't know what sex *was* in fourth grade."

"Oh, please!" Cody laughed.

"No. I didn't. I barely knew about the birds and the bees. I was in fifth grade before my asshole stepdad took me into his workshop and showed me magazines with men and women fucking. I was—" Horrified, Todd almost said, and froze. *Holy shit. I was. I was horrified.*

He thought about Joan. How he'd known her since kindergarten when she had helped him tie his shoes. You weren't supposed to be able to start school until you could tie your shoes, and she helped him out. He'd learned from her that very day. They'd been inseparable from that day forward. How he had loved her (still did?), and of course, it was only logical that they become boyfriend and girlfriend. And how that had gone fine until she decided they were old enough, at seventeen, to start having sex. He'd pretty much always done what she wanted because she'd almost always been right. But something happened once they turned sexual. He suddenly found Austin was his best friend instead of her. Todd had begun preferring Austin's company over Joan's. *God. How could I have been so blind?*

"Maybe you were a late bloomer—"

Really late, Todd thought.

"—but I knew."

"How could you know that young?" Todd asked. "You actually knew you were different, that you liked men *instead* of women that young?"

"Yup. It was Al Borland from *Home Improvement*. Oh, my God. I was in love. No doubt about it. While the boys at school went on and on about *Baywatch* and the near-naked girls, for me it was Al. That beard. His hairy chest. Those eyes. And I *loved* his chunky little belly. I would dream about him hugging me."

Todd gaped at Cody. He wanted a man to hug him when he was only, what? Ten? Silly. It was silly.

"And I was pretty hot for—and don't laugh—David Hasselhoff, although not as much as I liked Al. It was the belly. That belly and that chest set up my taste for life, I think. Maybe part of why I was so hot for Harry when we met."

No. It was silly. How could Cody have been in love with a man at that age? Ridiculous.

Trip.

Todd almost gasped out loud.

Suddenly the image of Connor Trinneer, who played "Trip" Tucker on *Star Trek: Enterprise* came so clearly to his mind that he felt a tingle rush all up and down his body. How mysteriously thrilled he'd been when Trip had suddenly taken off his shirt one night when Todd had been watching the show. When had that been? He wasn't sure. But he'd been about the same age Cody was when he claimed to have fallen in love with Al Borland.

In the *Star Trek* episode, Trip had been all sweaty. His skin so smooth. How Todd wondered what that skin would feel like. Had it been the desert planet episode? Or was that later? Earlier? Sudden vivid memories hit him of Trip in his blue underwear, and how distinctive his bulge had been. How Todd had stared and how he could clearly and suddenly remember being able to see three distinct sections to the bulge, and how he had known that was the man's cock and balls. He'd called it a penis back then. Maybe a pee-pee?

Todd suddenly remembered the night clearly, and how he had gotten very hard staring at Trip's nipples and wondering if there was any way he'd get to see the man naked. How he'd been unable to look away. How he'd lain in bed that night confused and feeling all fluttery. Sweaty. Wondering why his pee-pee was so hard.

Oh, my God.

He hadn't thought of that night in years. Todd felt sweat break out across his forehead. Good God! It wasn't possible, was it? Was he looking at men even back then?

"You all right, Todd?"

Todd jerked in his seat and stared at Cody unseeing for just a moment. "Trip," he whispered.

"Excuse me?" Cody asked.

"On *Star Trek: Enterprise*. I used to stare at his crotch. I didn't know why. But now...."

Cody didn't say a word. Just sipped his coffee.

"You saying I was gay back then?" Todd barked.

"I wouldn't dare to presume." Cody took another sip.

Dare to presume. It was like something Peter would say.

My God, he thought. Was it happening even then?

Cody reached out and touched Todd's hand. He jerked it away as if burned. Then felt stupid. "Sorry," he said.

"Gosh," said Cody. "You really are just realizing all this, aren't you?"

Once more Todd felt like he was about to cry. How could this be? How could this be? How? Gay? Was he gay?

Bisexual. Maybe I'm bisexual.

"Todd. Are you okay?"

"I don't know," he said quietly. "I don't know."

CHAPTER **TWELVE**

WHEN Gabe stopped before the Dove apartment building, he all but groaned at the sight. *Dear God*, he thought, *what's holding it upright?*

He parked his silver Saturn Sky across the street and approached the old brick building. It wasn't all that easy. He wasn't exactly dressed for walking through heaps of snow, especially given how little of it had actually been shoveled here. The street was slushy and a mess, the sidewalks barely cleared. He almost fell, and when he swung out his arm, realized he had his briefcase. He hadn't realized he'd brought it. Habit? Instinct?

The front door of the building was a mess of peeling paint with what looked like a million layers underneath. It opened easily, as did the inner door. No lock? Could anyone just barge in? Gabe paused, looking at the four apartment doors before him. Which one held the building manager? Did the man even live here? Gabe hadn't even thought about that.

Gabe returned to the small foyer and looked at the mailboxes. Yes. There by the box for 1-A was the stenciled word "Manager."

He went back in and knocked on the door.

Nothing.

He knocked again.

Still nothing.

Maybe the man was out doing some kind of managing? Or maybe he was locking someone else out of their apartment? Gabe looked around him, noticed a frozen cockroach as big as his thumb in a dark and filthy corner. Gabe shuddered. He hated cockroaches. Thank God the Wilde didn't have any. Had the manager done Todd a favor by kicking him out?

Gabe sighed. Would he have considered losing his own dingy apartment a favor ten years ago? The answer, of course, was no. Even though he had walked in on his first official boyfriend fucking the bejesus out of some trick Gabe later found out was a local bartender. For a while, he'd been hopelessly in love, and in that time, the apartment had seemed like Camelot to him. A place for him and his lover. His *male* lover. How exciting it had been making house with a man. Shopping together and fixing meals together and eating by candle light. Being naked with him whenever the mood struck them. Making love. Fucking.

At least his ex and his trick were using a condom when they'd cheated.

One more time, Gabe raised his hand and knocked on the manager's door, this time a little more forcefully.

This time he got an answer.

"What the fuck?" came a bellow from behind the door.

"Hello?" Gabe called back.

The door flew open to a sight that made the Wilde's overly large manager look positively svelte. At least Gabe's building manager kept himself clean. Wore a nice shirt and slacks or jeans. This man? This man looked like a caricature of the worst of the worst. Hugely fat, a dirty gray sweatshirt stretched over an immense belly. Suspenders. Cheeks and nose fiery red. The signs of an alcoholic? Greasy black hair combed ridiculously over a balding and shiny head. A broken and missing tooth up front, the rest stained by what looked to be cigarettes. Pants half-unzipped. Gross. Disgusting even.

"What the fuck do you want?" the man shouted, foul breath rolling out of him. Then noticing Gabe, probably the way he was dressed, his scowl vanished and was replaced by an insincere smile. "Oh. Hello, Sir. Howz can I help you?"

Gabe fought to keep from shuddering. "Are you the manager of the Dove?"

"The what?" the man asked, piggy eyes blinking.

"This apartment building. Are you the manager?"

"Yessir, I am. Whatcha want?" He wiped at his nose with the back of his hand.

"And there is a Todd Burton living here?'

The man's eyes turned guarded. "Who wants to know?"

For some reason the man was pissing Gabe off already. Of course, he had been prejudiced before now. The man had kicked a near child out in a blizzard.

"I'm with Wagner Enterprises. Perhaps you've heard of it? Owned by Peter Wagner."

The man's eyes narrowed even more. "Nah. Who's he?"

"He owns, among other things, Baily, Cranston and Watch, one of the biggest legal firms in Kansas City," Gabe said.

The man stepped back, wiped his hand across his sweatshirt this time. "So?"

"So Mr. Wagner's firm has decided to represent Mr. Burton in his eviction." The lie came abruptly and completely out of Gabe's lips before he had a chance to think it through.

The man took another step back. "That little fucker hadn't paid his rent in two months. I did what I had to do. There are lots of people want to live here."

Gabe raised his brows at the words that proved the manager could lie just as easily as he could. "Oh, really? Then that apartment is already occupied?"

The man's eyes flickered back and forth. *He was deciding whether to lie again.*

"Be careful what you say," Gabe said. "I'm listening to every word and what you say can be used in court."

"Whafuck?" the man said, and ran that nasty hand through the little hair he owned.

"May we sit down?" Gabe asked.

The man looked back and forth several times, then gave a quick nod. He backed up and waved Gabe in. *As if it were a palace instead of the "roach-infested firetrap" it is*, Gabe thought.

The place was worse than Gabe had imagined. He actually saw a cockroach run away as he walked into the squalid room. There was trash, empty pizza boxes, and crushed beer cans on every surface as well as the floor. Dirty clothes lay in heaps and over furniture. The air reeked of cat urine so foul it made Gabe's eyes water. It was all he could do not to gag. Sit down? He'd asked to sit down? Was there any place to even sit down beside a recliner that was obviously the "manager's" favorite? The dent was so deep, Gabe was disinclined to even think of sitting there. But it seemed to be the only place.

The fat man leapt forward, surprisingly quickly considering his bulk, and shoved a pizza box, a huge pair of underwear, and a sock off the couch. He indicated the free spot with a wave and Gabe stood there staring at it. He spotted some relatively clean newspapers, picked them up, and placed them in the "empty" spot before sitting.

"Sorry the place is a little messy," the man said, an almost sneer on his lips. "If I'da known you was a comin', I'da baked a cake."

Ala cockroach? Gabe wondered. *No thanks.* He opened his briefcase and pretended to ruffle through it, then pulled out a file— opened it. "According to Mr. Burton's testimony"—was that the right word?—"you never gave him notice of his impending eviction."

"That's a fuc.... That's not true! I warned him bunches of times!"

"But did he get a written notice?" Gabe asked. *As if you could write*, he wanted to say.

"Sure he did."

"Be careful, Mr.... I will remember what you said if called upon to testify."

"Now waits just a damned... darned minute. Testify? As in court?"

"Yes," Gabe said. He turned pages in his file, pages concerning the small but growing company called AbledRides. "According to this copy of the legal agreement with Mr. Burton, he should have had one more month to pay his rent before you seized his assets." It was a lie. A complete and total fabrication, but just as he had surmised, he saw total confusion on the man's face. Did the manager not even know what the lease said? "What did you say your name was?"

"Bill Racine. Ah... *William*. Racine."

William. An attempt to make himself seem more important. Gabe read it on the man's face as clearly as a Dick and Jane children's book.

"Yes.... That's just what I have here," Gabe said, poker-faced.

Racine wiped sweat off his forehead.

Nerves. Interesting. "Please, Mr. Racine, tell me the fate of Mr. Burton's belongings."

"Huh?" Racine scratched his balls.

"The boy you kicked out on the street in a *blizzard*—which is against the law, and of course, you know that—"

"He ain't had paid his rent!"

"I am asking what you did to his belongings. Furniture? Clothes?"

"They're still all up there," Racine practically shouted, pointing at the ceiling. "I ain't done nothin' with any of it yet."

"Excellent!" Gabe smiled graciously, even though it took control. Control was what he was good at, part of why he got paid the big bucks. "I knew that. My associates were worried you might have done something stupid—"

"Stupid?" Racine said, sitting up straight.

"—but I told them you wouldn't be an apartment manager if you were stupid."

"Yeah! Right. I ain't stupid. You tell 'em that too!"

"They thought you might cause trouble. But I told them to let me talk to you first. We're reasonable adults here, right?"

"Uh, yeah. Reasonable." Racine's eyes darted back and forth. "Adults."

Something was up, and Gabe's instinctive distaste for the obese man intensified. He hadn't planned on lying like this, but then he often flew by the seat of his pants. Went with the intuition that Peter had encouraged and nurtured in him since they met that dreary, yet ultimately comedic, night.

Gabe smiled even wider, letting good will positively pour from his eyes. "I am here to say that the legal firm—Baily, Cranston and Watch—is willing to forget any legal action as long as Mr. Burton's belongings are released to him."

"Released? Wha' da fuck? He owes me rent!"

Gabe studied him. Could Racine be any trouble? Who knew how the legalities stood on this? He wasn't sure just how the law worked on renters and weather. Gabe wasn't a lawyer, and he was misrepresenting himself—letting this man think he was part of a law firm. Racine very well might have quite a legal leg to stand on. Who knew what Todd had signed? Why take a chance? And just what the hell was he doing here in the first place? "How much do you show Mr. Burton owes you?" he asked, plunging ahead.

"Twelve thou—."

Gabe fixed Racine with a steely gaze.

"Nine hun'ert. That should cover it." Racine gave him a look, daring Gabe to object.

Gabe didn't. He wanted this over and done with. He wanted to get away from this gross and unpleasant man. He wanted away before the troglodyte got it into his feeble mind that there was something rotten in the state of Denmark. Or in this case, Missouri.

"May I write a check?" Gabe asked.

Surely you're not writing a company check?

Of course not. I'm paying this myself.

"Ah… sure. A check'll do." Racine wiped at his upper lip.

Gabe pulled a checkbook out of his briefcase, made a great show opening it, turning to the right place, raising a pen, then.... "Naturally, I will need to actually *see* Mr. Burton's belongings," Gabe said.

Racine's eyes went wide. "Why da fuck do ya need to do that? You got my guar-un-tee all his stuff is there."

"Ah, Mr. Racine. This isn't personal. It's nothing but a formality," Gabe said, voice calm. "I trust you implicitly." He didn't, obviously. What he really wanted to do was punch the man. But that would be a bad move, wouldn't it? Totally unproductive. So far things really couldn't be moving along any better. "Why don't you take me up now?"

Racine looked away, biting his lip again, refusing to meet Gabe's eyes. "I'll have to find the key."

"Of course. I'll wait."

Racine gave Gabe a look in which hate simmered just below the surface. Gabe saw it. That was his gift.

Racine nodded and left the room.

What are you doing?

Helping out my fellow man.

You sure you're not just trying to get your wick dipped? Or get Todd's wick dipped in you?

No, he thought, denying the suggestion.

Then why pay? Haven't you helped the kid enough?

I'm paying because I can, he told himself. *Paying it forward. Like Peter did for me.*

Still, it's a lot of money.

Not really. I can afford it. And what is money? Money means nothing if it is not put into circulation. It's not real otherwise. As Peter taught me, it is nothing but pieces of paper we as a culture have agreed represents gold supposedly resting in Fort Knox. It means nothing unless it is used. And I am using it to help Todd.

That's when Racine walked back in the room.

RACINE'S ass was disgusting was all Gabe could think of as he followed the plodding figure up the stairs to the sixth (*sixth! and no elevator!*) floor. One butt cheek was easily the size of both of Gabe's.

And I've got a pretty sturdy ass! Gabe shuddered.

Some people do have problems with glands, a kinder part of Gabe reminded himself.

True. He knew that. Knew more than one friend with such problems. But somehow he knew the only gland *this* particular man had a problem with was the one that controlled his hand slinging food into his mouth.

After what seemed like a mountain climb—the man wheezing alarmingly, his face red and covered in sweat—they reached the top floor. Racine pulled out a ring of keys fixed onto a retractable wire, fumbled for a minute, found one, and pushed into the lock of the first apartment on their right. Funny how fast he found the key. Gabe imagined Racine had had it all along. Why the stonewalling? Was it a power issue, or something worse? Was Racine up to something?

Racine pushed the door open and turned to Gabe. "Go on," he said with a grunt.

Gabe nodded and entered the tiny apartment, only to face a place worse than he'd imagined. His own bedroom was almost as large as the room he stepped into. His living room certainly was. It was dreary as well, depressing. The ceiling was cracked, the wallpaper faded and ugly—one entire sheet missing—the floor a scarred disaster. He hoped Todd never walked around barefoot; it was a million splinters waiting to happen. The only thing Gabe could say was that the apartment was clean. The furniture was sad and mismatched, but not ugly. It was homey even so, Gabe thought. As he looked around the room—spotted the *Star Wars* toys on a cinder block and board shelf—he found he could imagine Todd living here. He sniffed and smelled incense (Nag Champa?) that had obviously been used to try to hide the smell of human urine in the halls—hell, from the stairs and sneaking from the apartments they'd passed as well.

Gabe walked around, as much as he could in the close quarters. A few books were lined alphabetically on the shelf below the toys. He saw a sad dresser missing a drawer. There was a tiny TV that actually had rabbit ears cocked wildly on top.

Then it hit him. He didn't see a laptop. Gabe narrowed his eyes and he turned toward the apartment manager. "Excuse me, Mr. Racine. But I don't see Mr. Burton's laptop."

The man shrugged. "Does he have one?"

He won't meet my eyes. He's lying. Part of the stonewalling? That he'd stolen Todd's laptop? He smiled a big friendly smile. "Ah, Mr. Racine. I bet if you think about it you'll remember that Mr. Burton does have one. I bet, in fact, you were worried someone might steal it and you have it for safekeeping!"

Their eyes locked and... what was that? Fear? Was Racine afraid of him? By, God, he was.

Gabe did not look away. He held Racine's eyes with ironlike force. The battle of wills lasted for less than ten seconds before the man looked at the floor. "Yeah. Now that I think about it. Shit. I do have it." He grabbed at his crotch for what seemed like the ten-dozenth time, but may have only been twice. "In safekeeping, like you said."

Gabe nodded and smiled. "You're a good man," he said and clenched a fist.

"Yeah. I am."

"Why don't we get it then?" Gabe asked.

Racine gave a quick nod and turned around and headed back down the stairs. Gabe closed the apartment door and then followed. When they reached the ground floor, Gabe went into the manager's apartment right after him. Racine went into another room and came back sliding a battered black laptop with a big sticker on top into a carrying case. "You got that check?" he asked, still barely looking into Gabe's eyes.

"I will write it now," Gabe answered, resisting the urge to snatch the little computer from the man's hands. He set his briefcase down, got the checkbook out again, and began to write in it. While he wrote, and without looking up, he very calmly said: "Of course, you will take part of this money, rent a U-Haul or something, and deliver the goods by tomorrow to Alexander Storage on Troost."

He looked up into Racine's shocked face.

"What the fuck did you say?" The man's face grew even redder.

Gabe smiled. "By *tomorrow*. If not, I will sue you for every single thing you have. I know of eight violations you could be charged with already." Which was another lie. Gabe didn't know if he could charge the man with anything. "Furthermore, I will make sure you never work another day in this city again. No. Make that Missouri or Kansas. Not only that"—and then he let his voice turn as icy as the streets outside—"I might just have a few men come over here and talk to you about it. Do I make myself clear?"

Racine grabbed at his chest and fell back into his chair.

"I can't hear you, Mr. Racine. Do you catch my drift?"

Racine didn't answer. Only gave a single nod.

"Excellent. And my partners said you would be trouble." He gave a little fake laugh. "I knew you would be a sportsman." Gabe tore off the check and handed it over, careful their fingers did not touch. Funny how fast the man's hand shot out to take it.

Then Gabe turned and left. He left quickly. The lies had been fierce and not at all how he usually did business. In fact he never lied. But this time the exception was the way to go.

He fled the building before the sights and smells finally overwhelmed him.

He couldn't wait to get home. To clear his head.

And to tell Todd the good news.

CHAPTER **THIRTEEN**

THEY were in Austin's basement, of course. It was where they always went. It was practically their clubhouse—Todd even had a key to the sloped cellar door—although a few years ago Todd's friend had moved his bedroom down there as well. They sat on the couch in the dark, the only light coming from the TV. Austin's bed was behind them, messy and unmade as usual. In fact, the room was a disaster. Dirty socks, underwear, and other pieces of clothing were everywhere. A jockstrap even hung over the bedside lamp. Todd wondered how it had gotten there but didn't ask, even though he was curious.

Behind them and to the left were some weights and workout equipment, far better than what Todd owned. But then Austin had been raised by well-to-do grandparents—his parents had died when he was very little—and he could afford better than garage sale salvage. Todd loved Austin's equipment. In fact, the two of them had just finished a pretty extensive workout, and both still wore their sweaty clothes.

"Let's wait to shower. I like the way we smell, don't you?" Austin asked, his eyelids heavy, a strange look in his dark eyes. Todd had known his best friend for practically his whole life, and he'd never seen a look like that on his face—in his eyes.

He saw Austin was waiting for an answer and Todd looked away. The honest truth was that he *did* like the way they smelled. He'd certainly liked his own masculine scent—especially after a workout. It was far better, sexier, than the way Joan smelled down there. But that was crazy! *What's wrong with me?*

(*"You a faggot or something?"*)

Lately, in the last year or so, he'd begun to notice Austin smelled good down there as well. Like when they worked out. Todd might be lying on Austin's weight bench for instance, doing presses, and Austin would be standing over him, spotting him. When that happened Todd could see right up the open leg of Austin's shorts, see his friend's underwear-clad bulge—and with it so close, he could smell the musk radiating from Austin's balls. Sometimes it would be all Todd could do not to get a hard-on, and it confused him.

Why, just this evening he'd gotten hard. He hadn't been able to help himself. It wasn't even like Austin was all that handsome or anything. More cute than anything else. But he was skinny (nothing like the men in Todd's muscle magazines), had a big mouth and a mop of long dark hair that was always a mess. Who grew their hair long anymore? Despite that, something was making Todd horny. Austin's masculine scent had been particularly strong. Fresh. Wild. And his zits.... They'd been going away lately. Not like they'd been even a year before.

Todd had been bench pressing, nothing abnormal, when he found himself looking right up that opening in Austin's shorts again and saw the mounds he knew were Austin's balls. Did they shift? Then, to his horror, he saw Austin looking right into his eyes. He winked at Todd.

Oh, God! He saw me. Todd felt his face flush. What if Austin thought he was a fag?

(*"You a faggot or something?"*)

But no! How could he be? How could he be the thing his stepfather hated so much? How could he be something so loathsome?

Maybe it's not loathsome. My stepfather is an asshole. He's a horrible excuse for a human being. Could anything he hates be so bad? Why, it only stands to reason that something that man hates might be good.

Yeah. But a faggot?

"Want to watch some porn?" Austin asked.

"Porn?" Todd's voice had come out as a squeak.

"Yeah," Austin said, his voice husky. "I snitched it from my cousin. He brought back a bunch of it from college. All kinds of shit. Want to watch?"

Todd saw the begging in his friend's eyes and didn't know what to do. It was crazy to even consider the suggestion. And yet....

He gave a single, slow nod, and a grin fired across Austin's face. "Awesome, man!"

His friend jumped up, ran to the DVD player, and pressed a button.

The movie opened without preamble on two naked women doing things to each other that Joan harped at him to do to her. Touching down there. Dipping fingers into folds of flesh. Licking. For some reason, nothing he saw turned him on. He looked at Austin, who seemed to be liking what he saw. *What is wrong with me?* There were sonnets written about women's bodies. The Song of Songs in the Bible praised women. Wasn't he supposed to feel that way about Joan's body? Did men really feel that toward what he was seeing on the screen?

Making matters worse was the fact that Austin's TV always made everyone look overly orangeish red. *How could Austin be turned on?* Todd wondered, as the camera zoomed in tighter.

After what seemed like forever, a door opened and a man walked in on the two women. For all of about ten seconds they seemed upset—apparently his girlfriend was cheating—and then he was diving in and enjoying the "fun."

Todd glanced at Austin once again and saw his buddy rubbing at his crotch. A furtive glance from Austin and their eyes were locked. "God, I'm crapping horny," Austin said with a gasp.

But why? Todd wondered. The women were awful. Too skinny, their breasts immense, bigger even than Joan's. But where Joan's breasts sagged because of their size—a size all his male buddies appreciated to no end—these women's were solid and high and impossibly firm. They barely moved.

The man was even skinnier, his face close to ugly, his hair stringy and starting to recede. The only thing that might be said about the porn star was that his cock was enormous, easily twice Todd's length. It didn't seem to get fully hard though, a phenomenon Todd had experienced when he was with Joan.

He glanced over at Austin again and to his surprise saw his friend had unzipped his pants. Austin's penis was so hard it had his fly gaping open. A small wet spot had formed right at the head. Todd could see the impression of it and his own penis, which had been like a piece of overboiled manicotti, turned almost instantly into an iron bar.

Austin absently began to touch that spot on his cock on the underside just below the head—a spot Todd knew felt good from his own experiences. It was one of the best places. *Austin too, how cool is that,* he thought. As he surreptitiously watched, Austin's underwear steadily grew wetter right at the same spot.

Todd moaned and Austin turned to look at him, and then down at Todd's obvious erection straining the front of his jeans. He gave Todd an impish smile. "I know, buddy. *Hot.*"

Todd wasn't sure what Austin meant. It couldn't be about the gross things happening on the TV, could it? But he didn't dare think Austin might be excited about the two of them sitting here, both hard as steel.

"Todd," his friend said in a rough whisper. "You horny too?"

Was he horny? Holy shit—yes, he was horny. He didn't ever remember being hornier. "I... yes."

Was that relief on Austin's face? "Wanna do it?" Austin asked.

"Do what?" he somehow asked, his voice quavering. He felt sweat break out in his pits and his stomach knotted painfully. What did Austin want to do?

"Let's jerk off, buddy."

"Jerk off?"

Austin nodded. Ran his fingers up and down his erection. "Yeah. You said you were horny."

"Together?" Todd's voice cracked. "Now?"

"Why not?" Austin asked. "We've done everything else together."

Jerk off? The two of them? What had that sex book said about this? That it was perfectly normal for boys to play around together? Experiment? Of course, they were both a little old to fit into that theory, weren't they? They hardly qualified as boys, did they?

Austin popped open the span on his jeans, staring right into Todd's face. Todd's cock throbbed and found he couldn't move. Couldn't say a single word. Austin must have taken that as an okay, because then—and Todd held his breath at what he saw coming (*my God! is he going to...?*)—Austin pushed his thumbs under the waistband of his underwear, pulled it up, down, and over, and snagged it under his balls. Todd gasped at the sight. Austin's cock was rock-hard, rigid as steel, and gave a throb of excitement. A big pearl of precum began forming at the head, and as Todd watched, completely unable to look away, it began to run slowly—like syrup—down the length of Austin's cock.

"Take yours out," Austin said, his voice gravelly.

Todd looked up into his best friend's eyes, saw the hunger and lust, and without even knowing what he was doing, he unzipped his own jeans, opened them, and with a gulp, pulled down his underwear, exposing himself to his friend.

"Fuck," Austin said. "You're bigger than me."

Todd doubted it. Austin's looked huge. The foreskin, which had always secretly fascinated Todd, had slid back, revealing the purplish head, which glistened in the light from the TV. His throat seized up and he had to concentrate to be able to swallow.

"Lean back," Austin instructed. "I want to see it."

Todd did as he was told and that allowed his cock to rear up, totally on display to his friend.

"Nice," Austin said. "I've seen it a million times, but I never thought it would get that big."

You've thought about it? Todd wondered. *You've thought about my hard-on?*

Austin grabbed the base of his own erection and gave it a stroke. Then another. "Grab yourself," he whispered.

Todd was afraid to. He thought he might shoot if he even touched his cock.

"Do it," Austin demanded.

Todd gulped, and then did what he'd been commanded. Electricity shot through his body and his ass rose up from the couch before settling slowly back down to the cushion. His cock pulsed, and like his buddy's, began to leak.

"Stroke it," Austin said.

Todd closed his eyes. *I can't believe we're doing this!* He gave his erection a long stroke and gasped at how good it felt. Had it ever felt this good? He'd jerked off about a billion times. Why was it so much better this time?

Todd opened his eyes and saw Austin's eyes were moving back and forth from his cock to the porn on the television. The girls there were both playing with the ugly man's huge penis. After a moment Austin looked up into Todd's eyes. In a voice Todd could barely hear, he said, "Want to do that?" He nodded his head toward the screen.

"Do... do that?" Todd managed.

"Help." Austin took a deep breath. "Want to help each other out?"

Todd's eyes widened. Austin not only wanted them to jerk off together, but to touch each other's cocks?

"Nobody will ever know," Austin whispered. "*You* know what it feels like to have someone else touch you. You have Joan. I don't. I want to know...."

So this was just about being horny, then, Todd saw. Austin didn't have any feelings about this. About him. Austin wasn't gay or anything. It was just like the book said. No chance to get at a girl, so Austin wanted this instead?

"Todd?" There was desperation in his friend's voice. Suddenly Todd knew it was okay. That he was going to do this…

(*"You a faggot or something?"*)

… and he didn't give a shit what his stepfather would think.

After all, it was normal. It was just hormones. Raging hormones. It didn't mean anything. He moaned, and just like that, Austin was scooting over next to him. Austin reached out with his left hand, hesitated for just a second, and then took Todd's throbbing erection into his warm, rough palm and curled his fingers around it.

Todd cried out and had to bite down on his cheeks to keep from cumming.

Fuck! All he's doing is touching me!

Austin gave Todd's cock a stroke or two and moaned himself. "Your cock is so warm," Austin said. "Hot. It feels like it's on crappin' fire." He rubbed his thumb under the head, which was slick with precum, and Todd shuddered in pleasure. His now empty hand began to flex. Did he do it? Did he touch Austin's cock?

"Please," Austin said, as if reading his mind. "Please, Todd."

Todd let out a long breath, and then slowly reached out and took another guy's penis in his hand for the first time. It was so hard! So damned warm, just like Austin had said. Alive. "God," he moaned. He trembled. Shit! He was holding a cock. He was holding onto his best friend's cock. He gripped it, stunned by how it felt. He'd touched his own cock countless times, but this one felt different as much as it felt the same. It felt sexy. Thicker than his own. He moved his hand up and down the length.

"Oh God, yes," Austin moaned.

So the two of them sat that way—Todd pretending to enjoy the porn—slowly masturbating each other. Over and over again, Todd thought he would cum, and as if sensing it, Austin would lay off or slow down at just the right moment so his orgasm was held off. God, Austin was good at this. So much better than how Joan did it. In fact, all of this was actually exciting, exciting in a way being naked and sexual had never been with his girlfriend.

What did that mean?

Gay. Is it gay? Am I gay? No! Not gay. I won't *be gay!*

Then Austin did something different. He leaned over so his face was right over Todd's cock—

Shit! Is he going to suck it?

—and then let a big drop of saliva fall down onto the head and began to stroke anew, but very slowly.

"Fuck!" Todd half shouted.

Austin shushed him, although Todd didn't know why. Austin's grandparents had surely gone to sleep hours ago.

"Do that to me," Austin said.

Todd trembled, and then did as his friend asked. It put his mouth only inches from his friend's pulsing wet cockhead, and he suddenly flashed on that afternoon in the locker room—with his classmate's penis so close to his face—and the thought: *What would it be like to take that in my mouth?* From this angle, Todd couldn't help but smell Austin's crotch scent rising up to him. Sexy. Austin was right. They did smell good. Fucking *hot* as a matter of fact. So different from the way Joan smelled. Their working out had brought out that musky man smell—and now Todd knew that was what all men must smell like. *Why is this so hot? The guys at school are always talking about how good pussy smells!* Austin's balls, unlike that boy's in the locker room, had drawn up tight in their hairy sack. They weren't loose at all.

That's cuz he's close to cumming, Todd realized, and then knew he wanted to see it. Needed to see it.

"Todd?" Austin asked, breaking Todd free from his near mesmerized state.

He opened his mouth and drooled down onto the head of Austin's cock, although as much precum was flowing, he hardly needed to do it, then leaned back and resumed stroking his friend. He couldn't believe what he was doing—what they were doing. But an orgasm was building he knew would be bigger than any he'd ever had.

Austin leaned over his cock, paused a moment, then looked up into Todd's eyes. "Don't tell, okay?" and before Todd could say, *Hell no, I'm not going to tell*, found out what Austin actually meant. To his shock, he felt the warm wetness of Austin's mouth close around his shaft.

Todd thought he would die. His ass arched off the couch again— Austin gave a slight gag but didn't pull away—and then fell back down to the cushion. Awkwardly, obviously not sure of what he was doing, Austin gave several experimental bobs. That was all it was going to take.

"Austin! Stop! I'm gonna…." But to his shock, Austin didn't pull away and then it was too late. Todd came like he never had before in his life. His eyes slammed shut, and it felt like his balls were turning inside out. The orgasm bordered on painful. Stars formed in front of his eyes, and when he finally returned somewhat to reality, finally was able to open his eyes, he looked down to see his best friend—his best friend!—gently nursing his cock. And when his buddy looked up, he saw lust in Austin's eyes.

Austin giggled. "Crap, that was hot. You really needed to blow, didn't you?"

Todd didn't answer. He couldn't. He couldn't believe what had just happened. Couldn't help but wonder, be afraid of, what this would mean.

Austin leaned back and gasped, "Now me. Finish me!"

Todd panicked. Could he?

"Do it. Please!" Austin pleaded. "I know you want to!"

Todd's eyes flew wide and he stared at his friend.

Austin nodded. "I know you do. It's okay. You're my best friend."

Todd's head turned into a cacophony of thoughts and emotions. He wasn't even thinking. Okay? They were still buds?

Austin nodded. "Please, Todd. I gotta cum. Blow me. I know you want to."

Todd was frozen. Want to? What was Austin saying? That he thought Todd *wanted* to give him a blowjob?

He looked down at the hard erection, and in total horror realized he'd never wanted anything more in his entire life.

And then...

(and then he ran out into the night)

... and then...

(and hadn't there been terrible consequences when he'd done that?)

... and then the cock suddenly looked bigger. Thicker. Longer. Where had the foreskin gone? It seemed paler as well. It was fucking huge!

He looked up and gasped. It wasn't Austin. It was Gabe. Gabe wearing that damned 2CUTE2BSTR8 shirt and nothing else—those powerful thighs spread wide. "Please, Todd. I gotta cum. Blow me. I know you want to."

And God, didn't he want to? He looked at the gigantic thing. Oh, God! As if in a movie, he reached out and took the mighty erection in his hand, so much bigger than either Austin's or his own, and again he was stunned by the heat on the flesh, and then he leaned over...

"Todd!"

... and opened his mouth wide, and...

"Todd! Wake up!"

Todd jumped, came awake as a hand landed on his shoulder gave him another shake. His eyes opened to Gabe standing over him, impossibly tall and resplendent in a suit obviously not bought at Walmart. "G-Gabe?" he asked, unprepared for the handsome man or how incredible he looked.

"Todd? Sorry to wake you, but I've got some news I think will make you happy."

CHAPTER **FOURTEEN**

TODD looked up into Gabe's face with blurry eyes. His erection ached painfully in the confines of his jeans (and they really were his jeans this time). He blinked, looked Gabe up and down. *How did you get your clothes put together so fast?*

He felt his erection throb again, glanced down. His jeans were zipped up. What the…?

Dream. You were dreaming.

"You must have been having a hell of a dream," Gabe said, eyes shining.

Todd felt the color drain from his face…

"Was it about me?" Gabe asked and winked.

… and then felt the blood rush right back, his cheeks feeling like they were suddenly sunburned.

He knows!

He doesn't know, for God's sake.

He saw my hard-on.

Who cares? He's seen it before. He doesn't know you were dreaming about him. He still thinks you like girls.

I do like girls.

Really? Really?

Gabe snapped his fingers. "Earth to Todd, Earth to Todd. Are you there, Todd?"

"I-I, uh." Todd rubbed at his eyes, then quickly sat up (once more worried about his crotch—had Gabe noticed?) and crossed his hands over his lap. "Yeah. Yeah. Uh. What did you say?"

"I said I've got some news I bet is going to make you happy."

Todd blinked again. "Good news?" He could certainly use some of that. "What news?"

Gabe grinned a big toothy smile, shifted his right arm, and what he pulled from his side made Todd's mouth fall open in surprise. It wasn't Gabe's briefcase. The big winter coat had hidden the fact that Gabe had Todd's laptop bag, and it looked like the computer just might be inside.

Todd's eyes flew wide. "Oh my God!" It was all he could do not to yank it from Gabe's hands.

Gabe laughed. "Go on. Take it."

Todd grabbed it, quickly unzipped the bag and pulled out—yes!—a large "May the Force Be With You" sticker on its surface, his beloved laptop, piece of shit that it was. With bated breath, he booted it up, worried what he might find—or not find. A message popped up informing him his computer had not been properly shut down the last time he had used it and would he want the same files to be available? He thought for a moment. What had he been working on? A recipe, he remembered. He hoped it was okay and let the computer know he indeed did want to see said "files."

What came up was not a recipe.

It was one of the pictures he had downloaded from a men's underwear site. He blanched, horrified Gabe might have seen it. He closed it quickly and then went looking for the recipe he'd been playing with in his head, even though he had no money to buy the ingredients, even the meat. It didn't matter, though; his imagination was pretty on target. He had a good idea what it would all taste like. The point was to get his ideas down so he wouldn't lose them. He shook off the worry about what Gabe might or might not have seen and checked for the recipe. Thank God. There it was. It was there.

But of course, what really counted was that he had his computer back.

When he glanced up, Gabe seemed oblivious. The man looked happy as a puppy and—poof!—just like that Todd was happy too. Nothing else mattered.

"My God, Gabe. How did you do it?" Todd asked aloud.

"Never you mind, everything's been taken care of," Gabe replied.

Everything? Todd wondered, forgetting both the underwear file and the recipe for a moment. Took care of everything? Now what did that mean? "Gabe?" he asked. "What have you done?"

"Nothing someone hasn't done for me in my life. I helped. That's all."

"But Gabe...." He started shaking his head.

"All your things are being delivered to a local storage locker tomorrow. We'll head down after lunch and see what you want brought here."

"*Here?*" Todd asked, his voice catching. What did he mean? He couldn't mean....

"We'll have to move some stuff around. Make room for the things you want. I'll bet you want your bed. Nothing like your own bed, right?"

Not necessarily, he thought, and barely stifled a gasp. Where else did he think he'd be sleeping? "My bed?" Todd asked. "But what about your office? Your workout room?"

Gabe waved his hand as if whisking Todd's words away.

How can this be happening? Todd wondered.

Two days ago he was being cast into a blizzard.

And now?

"Gabe...," he whispered.

"Todd," Gabe whispered back, and then winked.

Something happened then.

Every once in awhile in Todd's life, a moment would come that seemed to abruptly stand outside of time. It was as if the Universe had pressed a cosmic pause button and time ceased moving. The outside world would take a brief siesta. Man-made noises—car horns, lawn mowers, the shrieks of children playing, the bellowing of some parent calling for their children to stop playing and get inside—would all simply fade away. Light seemed to grow brighter, and yet somehow less harsh. Todd swore he could hear the very dust motes in the air, like the tinkling of miniature wind chimes. Then time would reassert itself and the world would become normal again.

This had only occurred a few times in his life. It happened when he found the Polaroid in the back of the drawer of the dresser in the attic. The picture of him as a baby, sitting in his father's lap on the porch swing, the man with a huge smile on his face. The photograph had almost felt alive. Warm even.

It happened when Todd found his special place in the woods.

And it was happening now. He was sitting there on the couch, computer in his lap—it seemed to hum beneath his fingertips—looking up at a man who suddenly seemed to have grown more beautiful, taller than before. The dust in the air was making those tinkling sounds and shimmering in the light coming through the balcony doors. Gabe's skin looked like it was glowing, the flecks of snow caught in his hair sparkling.

I love you. His breath caught and tears sprang to his eyes.

I... I'm in love with him. He felt lightheaded, the significance of the realization all but overwhelming. *How? He's a man. You've known him for forty-eight hours. You can't be in love with....*

Kiss him.

Todd shook his head. Gabe's lips were moving but Todd couldn't hear him.

Kiss him.

"No!" he cried, and time resumed.

"Todd! Are you okay?" Gabe asked, alarm capturing his features.

I don't know, Todd thought. *I have no fucking idea.*

Because as wrong as he'd always been told such feelings should be, his heart was telling him—singing to him—that nothing had *ever* been so right.

"I INSIST. Please, Todd. They're not that much. I'm not buying you something that costs thousands of dollars."

Todd shook his head. Couldn't Gabe see? It was the principle of the thing. His parents had taught him about charity and how only the weak accepted it.

Of course, they taught you all kinds of shit, didn't they?

The object of discussion was a pair of Converse sneakers. He'd been stunned at all the colors and styles—the choices had been almost overwhelming—but logic and practicality demanded he go with the standard style. Especially with Gabe insisting on buying them for him. Why was Gabe doing all this for him?

And in this store? On the Plaza?

Todd loved the Plaza. It was stunningly beautiful, classy, upscale, the buildings all designed architecturally in a Spanish style. He loved to walk the streets, view the dozens of gorgeous fountains—he'd discovered that Kansas City had the second most fountains in the entire world—and peer through the windows of the restaurants and high-end retail stores. He would dream of one day being able to afford a coat, a lamp, a table, even cocktails in the many establishments. He'd pretend he could, sitting on the ledge of the stunning J.C. Nichols Fountain and imagining what his life would be like if he didn't have to worry about the price of a cheeseburger at Mickey D's.

And now here he stood, actually inside one of the stores, with Gabe insisting on buying him a pair of shoes. Seventy-dollar shoes. Seventy dollars! His own sneakers—dying as they were—he'd found for thirty online and that had been an expense that had driven his stepfather into near apoplexy. How could Gabe be so casual? He hadn't even given the man any sex. In fact, Gabe had wound up rejecting him.

Was this guilt? Was that what it was?

"I can't," Todd told Gabe. "I can't."

To his surprised he saw something he wasn't expecting. Hurt. Gabe's big, beautiful, country-sky-blue eyes filled with something very close to pain.

"Gabe?"

"Todd," the man answered quietly. "I'm not worried about the price. If someone needed something, and it was something you could afford, something tells me you wouldn't hesitate to help them."

Todd thought about it. He'd never really had any money. However, he'd never hesitated to mow the lawn for neighbors back home, carry groceries upstairs for the old lady that lived next door to him in his apartment building. He even gave change to the homeless person that slept in the window well of the building next door. Perhaps it was the same thing?

"I-I'm…. No one has ever done anything like this for me," Todd said. "Since I got a job in high school my mom doesn't even buy me socks."

"Are they poor, Todd?"

Todd thought about it. Poor? Certainly not for Buckman. They always seemed to have enough for everything they needed. He shrugged. "Not poor…."

"Let me do this, Todd. It makes me happy. It's been forever since I could do something like this for someone." Then, impossibly, those big eyes seemed to grow even sadder.

Now that was interesting. It also made something click. Something had happened to Gabe. Something that had hurt him. He hadn't said anything. And yet….

Okay then.

He smiled. "Gabe, thank you. It would mean a lot to me."

Gabe's expression turned radiant. How amazing that someone could feel so good making *him* feel good. Had anyone ever felt that way about him? Except for maybe Austin, it had always felt like people only wanted things *from* Todd. To have it the other way was amazing.

Gabe walked up to the small counter and told the employee—who had discreetly backed away when Todd had begun his refusal of Gabe's offer to buy the shoes—to ring them up. Then, to Todd's surprise, he threw in a pair of those leather ones. "And the colorful ones too!"

"Gabe!" Todd cried, and then shut up when the man looked over his shoulder at him. Three pairs of shoes? He'd never had more than two in his life. Sneakers and dress shoes. Now he would have three pairs of sneakers? He thought about "the colorful" ones. God, they were fun. Black with a pattern that looked like brightly colored friendship bracelets crisscrossing them. Damn. To be able to have a pair of shoes that were just for fun would be more than he would have ever thought possible. And the brown leather high tops! God!

It all seemed impossible. The gratitude almost overwhelmed him. "Th-thank you," he muttered. Then he cleared his throat. Took a deep breath. "Gabe. Thank you."

Gabe grinned. "You're welcome." Then he winked. "And we have just begun to shop!"

YEARS later, when Todd would try and remember that evening at C.L. Miles, one of the finest restaurants on The Plaza—indeed in Kansas City—he found it hard to recall just how it all went. The memories would come in little bursts, all out of order. It was like he'd been a bit drunk that evening—and he did get tipsy on fine wine—or almost like he'd had one of his stepping-out-of-time moments. Everything was mixed up, disjointed, but in a weird and wonderful way.

Gabe had wanted to take him to Izar's Jatetxea for dinner, but Todd had reeled back in horror at the idea. "Oh, no! I can't. I couldn't. No... no."

"Why not?" Gabe asked. "I was sure you would love the idea. You said when you watch her show on TV you can't really see the food, taste it. Touch it."

"But what if she's there?" he replied.

"Izar?" asked Gabe.

"Yes." Todd trembled. "I would die! The way she threw me out...."

"Did she really? Throw you out?"

Todd closed his eyes. Shivered. "She might as well have. Asked me what gave me the nerve to walk into her restaurant... no... her *jatetxea*, and ask her to teach me."

"*Jatetxea*? Does that mean something? I thought it was part of her name or something."

Todd rolled his eyes. "It's Basque for restaurant."

"Oh. Duh." Gabe rolled his eyes as well.

"Goya wanted to know who I thought I was. She said that there were people who had gone to culinary schools for years begging for her to teach them, and I thought I could just walk in off the street? Then she told me they weren't open and I should leave and not to come back unless I was a customer."

"Shitfire," Gabe said.

"It was humiliating. We can't go. I couldn't face her."

So that's how they wound up at C.L. Miles.

The restaurant was dark, small candles at the tables providing most of the illumination except for two gorgeous fireplaces. The booths were deep, surrounded by darkly stained wooded walls to provide seclusion. Even the tables were arranged at a distance from each other so that those patrons were allowed privacy as well. People could talk without a thought of anyone overhearing them.

Todd and Gabe sat in a booth. If Gabe had looked beautiful in that strange moment in the apartment, in the subdued light from the candle on the table he looked glorious. Todd's heart pounded. *My God, my God.*

Gabe was laughing about something. Mind wandering, Todd had missed what the man was saying.

"I'm sorry?" Todd asked.

"I was just thinking about the look on your building manager's face when I told him I'd sue him. I think he near peed his pants."

"He's not my manager," Todd said with a grimace. "Not anymore." He looked into Gabe's eyes, marveling how they sparkled in the candlelight. *Beautiful, still country-sky blue, even with so little light.* His heart skipped. *I'm in love with a man!*

They were at the restaurant to celebrate the imminent return of Todd's belongings. In fact, it was that event Gabe claimed the whole afternoon had been about. The shoes had been followed by several pairs of jeans, some slacks, a few dress shirts and a warm winter coat. Todd had seen the price, and his eyes had just about popped out of his head. Two hundred dollars. For a coat! Of course, it was the most beautiful item of clothing Todd had ever seen, and it had been so wonderfully warm, especially when they'd stepped out into the lightly falling snow. Maybe the rich didn't buy things just for their price tag? Maybe there was a reason their clothes cost so much?

"It looks so good on you," Gabe said, and Todd blushed.

Had anyone complimented him so much before? Todd couldn't remember. His stepfather had certainly made enough fun of him for nearly everything he wore. Said his clothes made him look like a sissy.

("Can't you just wear a fucking flannel shirt for once?")

"I still can't believe it. You went crazy!"

"We're celebrating," Gabe explained.

"But Gabe, I didn't do anything," Todd said. "You're the one who's getting all my stuff back. Why are you taking *me* out to dinner? I should be taking you out to dinner."

And tomorrow, when I get my stuff back, I'm going to.

Gabe opened his mouth to answer, then shut it. He sighed. "I... I don't know, Todd. I want to. Just let me, okay? It's been so long since...."

"Since what?" Todd asked. *Go on,* he beamed at Gabe. *Tell me. Tell me what this is all about.*

Did Gabe's face go red? It was hard to tell in the orange glow from the candle. Gabe looked away. So long since what? "Tell me," Todd asked.

Gabe turned to him, then quickly looked away.

"Tell me."

Gabe sighed. Looked at him. His eyes were glistening. Was he...? Was he crying?

"What is it?"

Gabe shook his head. Wiped at his eyes. He smiled. "Don't worry about it."

Todd might have asked again, but that was when the waiter brought the menus. He started getting nervous when his didn't have any prices. "Ah... Gabe. Ah. I can't tell how much anything costs."

"Of course not," Gabe replied. "That would be tacky. I want you to have what you want and not worry about something like price."

It's like we're on a date. Todd felt an odd little shiver. *Are we? Are we on a date?*

How can you be? You told him in no uncertain terms that you aren't a fucking queer.

Todd's stomach clenched. Why had he ever said something so rude to Gabe? How could he have been such an ass? Gabe was good to him from the very first minute, helping him in from the cold. Feeding him. Gabe had made only one mistake.

He thought I was a hustler. And why not? I looked like one.

He thought of Chaz and Doug, the hustlers from the park. Bedraggled. Scruffy. Young.

I looked just like a hustler. Homeless at the least.

Of course, I was homeless.

Shit.

"Todd? Is everything all right?"

I did it again. My mind wandered. "I'm sorry. I don't know what's wrong with me."

I'm wondering if I've fallen in love with you.

"Have I done something wrong?" Gabe asked.

Todd's eyes went wide. "No! Oh, hell no!" He reached out and laid his hand on Gabe's, which was playing with the stem of his wine glass.

Gabe looked down at their hands and then so did Todd. Hand on hand. In public. Where anyone could see. And why not? He let his hand relax, let a finger run the length of one of Gabe's. It looked nice. It felt nice. He shivered at the texture of the hair on Gabe's hand. Hair. A man's hand. So different from Joan's. Big. Strong. The veins across the back so sexy.

Todd felt his cock stir. *My God. And all I'm doing is touching his hand.*

(*"You a faggot or something?"*)

What an ugly word. Faggot. He looked at Gabe. The last thing in the world Gabe could possibly be was ugly. Outside or in.

(*Maybe you're bi?*)

Bisexual? Am I? But the more he looked at the man across the table, his face, his eyes, even the hand beneath his own, the more he had to reject the idea. For one brief moment, the word had seemed like a life raft. Less huge than the alternative. But....

But.... God... I don't think I'm bisexual. He squeezed Gabe's hand, felt his cock shifting, lengthening in his pants.

A fag then? His stepdad had been right all along?

No. Not a faggot. "Faggot" is a word for that myth my stepdad believes in. The boogeyman. Someone who drives around looking for little boys to rape and who cuts them up. Something that doesn't exist.

Jeez. If I am anything...

... I'm gay.

Todd gasped.

God. I said it. I said the g-word. Gay. I said I'm gay.

He looked up and saw the alarm written on Gabe's face. "Todd! What's wrong?"

"Nothing," Todd said. But not quite brave enough to say the words yet, he said instead: "Nothing's wrong. Everything's just fine."

THE dinner was amazing.

The waiter, making an assumption when he brought the wine—a riesling—poured a small amount first in Gabe's glass. Gabe took his time, the waiter standing like a British guard, and slowly tasted it. When he nodded his approval, the waiter filled Todd's next and watched for Todd to taste his own.

He thinks we're on a date! Todd glanced at him and just like that realized the bearded young man, probably not more than a year his senior, was gay. Gay. No horns. No glitter. No blood. Just a regular guy. For some reason Todd felt suddenly... included. Warm. And very *not* alone. Todd smiled. It was a wonderful feeling.

Todd tasted his wine, rolling the liquid over his tongue as Peter and Gabe had taught him over the last few days. It was a joy, sparkling across the surface of his tongue. He sighed in delight, and then the waiter filled Gabe's glass.

"To transformation," Gabe said, holding out his wineglass.

"Transformation?" Todd asked.

Then, pulling a Peter, he quoted, "Life is either a daring adventure or it is nothing at all."

Wow, thought Todd. "That sounds like something Peter would say."

Gabe chuckled. "It's one of his favorite quotes. Helen Keller actually."

Helen Keller said that? A blind and deaf woman? It was hard to believe. Had she found a way in a world without sight or sound to make life an adventure?

Then what fucking excuse do I have? he wondered.

They had fresh oysters on the half shell for an appetizer—which Todd had eyed suspiciously when they arrived at the table. Raw, weren't they? He had hungered for adventure when it came to food. But raw? Then he tried one; Gabe had lifted a shell as if making a toast, so what choice did he have?

To his shock, they were amazing. They slid out of the shell, landed on his tongue, and seemed to melt, almost sizzle away. Todd's eyes rolled up in their sockets at the experience. The only time he'd ever tried them was when Austin had snuck a can from his grandparents' pantry. They'd been chewy and nasty and rubbery and tasted like fish gone bad. But these?

Heaven. Truly. They were heaven.

"You like?" Gabe asked, eyes as bright as a child's.

"Heaven," Todd said, voicing his thoughts, and Gabe's smile broadened to a Cheshire Cat grin's width.

The soup was next, a tomato-basil bisque that Todd thought might send him to Olympus. He laughed.

"What?" Gabe asked.

"Olympus," Todd said. "First heaven and now Olympus."

Once again a childlike grin spread across Gabe's face.

Gabe insisted they get the prime porterhouse steak and ordered lyonnaise potatoes—thinly sliced and pan fried along with onions, and sautéed in butter with parsley and mushrooms. The meat was so tender, Todd realized he could have cut it with the dull side of a butter knife. It had been cooked medium rare and hardly needed to be chewed. Todd had never experienced food like it. Like any of it.

Meanwhile, the waiter was wonderful. At times Todd wondered if the young man had any other tables. A cloth napkin dropped on the floor was replaced instantly. They had only to let a water glass become slightly empty and it was filled, as well as the wine. With only a nod from Gabe, a second bottle arrived.

"I'm getting tipsy," Todd said, trying to stifle a giggle.

"Good," Gabe responded and their eyes locked briefly. Todd felt like he was lifting up into them, into a lovely country sky. His heart fluttered.

God. Is this what it feels like? Love? Is this what I've been missing?

"You going to take advantage of me?" he said, letting the wine give him words.

For an instant Gabe's smile wavered. "You don't think I would, do you?"

Todd's eyes widened. *Shit!* Maybe he better stop drinking. "No," he said.

Gabe's smile returned full force.

But what if I wanted you to? Todd wondered. Then knew he did want Gabe to do just that. Not take advantage really. But to take things in hand. *If he does, I'll do whatever he wants.*

Wow. Two days ago I'm thinking of him as "queer," and here I am wanting him. How does this happen?

He didn't say any of that, but he found he really wanted to say something, didn't know what to say. He knew so little about this man. Only that he'd had a hard beginning, that he made a lot of money, that his first boyfriend had cheated on him and....

Cheating.

Do I tell him about that? Do I tell him about...? No. Maybe later. It would certainly ruin the mood.

So instead....

CHAPTER FIFTEEN

As Gabe gazed at Todd across the table, he couldn't help but wonder when he'd last seen anyone, anything, so beautiful. At first he'd only seen the sad and desperate side of the kid. He'd looked so vulnerable standing in that lobby a few days ago. When Todd had come up to his apartment, he'd seen that Todd was sexy under the scruffy.

Then, after Todd had cleaned himself up, Gabe saw the young man was better looking than he'd imagined. Stocky, but not fat. Truly big-boned. Nothing like the thin and effeminate Brett. When Gabe had seen Todd in that darkened living room, his shirt off and nipples erect, he'd gotten an almost immediate erection. Gotten? Hadn't he already had one?

Then there had been that wild, impossible moment when he'd walked in on Todd on his Nordic, wearing those threadbare underwear and sporting a boner that stopped Gabe in his tracks. He remembered how it had felt when he'd once come upon some wild animal in a forest somewhere. When he was a kid, Gabe had gone with a friend's family on a camping trip and happened on a deer with its baby. The doe had stared at him, all three of them frozen, for what seemed forever before she had sprinted off with her fawn.

With each passing hour, Todd had cast a spell on him. He was falling in love, he knew that. He knew he should stop this. He could get hurt. Badly. What if Todd were another Brett? He could be. He was sure now that Todd was gay, that the realization was coming. When it did, Todd would probably even turn to him to be his first. And in that way, there be dragons.

"Gabe? Why do you live in that building?"

"What?" Gabe asked, brought out of his thoughts.

"Now *you're* doing it," Todd said with a sweet smile.

"Doing what?" Gabe asked, trying to catch up.

"Your mind is wandering."

Gave felt himself blush. "Sorry. What were you saying?"

"I was asking why you live where you do. It's not in the best neighborhood. There are much better buildings. It's kind of run down. Not your apartment, of course. It's frippin' amazing. But the rest?"

"The Oscar Wilde?" Gabe shrugged. *You too?* he wondered. *Why did people always ask him that?*

"You could afford so much better. Is it because there are so many gay people there?"

Gabe gave a slight nod. "Well. That's part of it."

"Why don't you get your own house?"

Gabe nodded again. "Tracy is always asking me that. But she doesn't get it."

"Then tell me," Todd said.

"It's because...." Gabe took a deep breath. "I don't want to find a house until I find *him*," he said quietly.

"Him?" Todd asked.

"Him," Gabe repeated. "The *one*."

"The one?" Then Gabe saw the light dawn on Todd's face. "Oh. *Him*."

"I've seen people get together. Try to decide where to live. Which place to give up. Do they sell a house? If they both have one, do they both sell? What if one guy is really attached to his house? What if the other guy hates it? I don't want that. When I find him, I want us to find a house together. So it's more than a building made of wood or stone or brick. So it's a home. *Our* home." Gabe felt his eyes grow wet. "God.

There I go again. Getting all romantic. I'm just a big overgrown schoolgirl, aren't I?"

But to his surprise he saw that Todd's eyes seemed to have grown misty as well. "I think it's wonderful."

"You do?" Gabe asked.

"I've heard buying a house is one of the most stressful things a couple can do. Worse than having a baby, even. But somehow, I bet it's wonderful too. Finding that place where you both walk in and— wow!—you both know, just *know*, that this is it. This is that place."

Gabe gave an excited nod. "Yes! Exactly. Stress or not, it's got to be worth it. And it's not like I gotta worry about the stress of a child."

Todd laughed. "Do you want one? A child?"

"You know, I don't. I know a lot of gay couples that do. Then again I know a lot that would rather jump off the Empire State Building. I love other people's kids, but I've never had that desire. I just want to take care of one person. And that is *him*." He propped his chin on one upraised hand, elbow on the table. "What about you?"

He'll still have that fantasy about having children. A lot of young gay men do. Still caught up in what our culture tells him he needs to do. Spread his seed.

"Not really," Todd said, surprising him. "I thought about it, of course. When Joan and I played house as a kid, there were pretend babies. But, no. Maybe it's my stepfather, you know? He always treated me like shit. And after graduation, I saw a bunch of the kids getting married. Most of them because they had to. Surprising how many of them had a baby nine months after prom. And I saw Joan watching me, and I realized that that was who I was going to marry. My childhood sweetheart. And the idea made me feel sick. And I don't know why. She was one of my two best friends in the world. We grew up together. I loved her, you know? She was fun and silly and I loved her. But something changed when we started having sex. I don't know. It wasn't all it was supposed to be, and suddenly, we weren't what we'd always been. Friends. There was this... I don't know—Weight? Obligation? Something!—hanging over us. We'd started down a new path, and I would look where we were headed and I'd panic. I'd think about being trapped in that little town for the rest of my fucking life, married to her, never able to do what I really wanted to do." Todd shook his head. "And then... then...."

"Then what?" Gabe asked.

Todd looked into his eyes, and Gabe all but fell into Todd's. Eyes like the eyes of that doe in the woods. He saw something battling there. Todd was trying to make a decision.

"Todd," he said, "you don't have to say anything. But you can. You can tell me anything." He reached out and placed his hand on Todd's. Why not? Hadn't Todd done the same thing to him? To his pleasure, Todd didn't flinch in the least.

Todd let out a long shuddering sigh. "She cheated. With my best friend."

Gabe froze. Gulped. Oh, God. Cheating. Did it ever stop?

Todd looked up. "With my best friend! I had a key to his place. His grandparents' place. His room. He lived in the basement and I had a key. Something happened, and I freaked and ran out on him. But then a few days later, I realized I had to talk it out with him. So I went over and let myself in, and there he was in bed with my girlfriend."

"Shitfire," Gabe said and closed his eyes. He opened them the instant an image began to form behind his lids.

Todd looked away, then turned back. "I... me and Austin. He was my best friend. We... we fooled around one night...."

Todd looked down, obviously embarrassed. Fooled around? Todd had fooled around with his straight best friend. God. As the world turns. He opened his mouth to tell Todd it was okay. That it was a story as old as time. Gay boys often fell for their straight best friends. But then he would be calling Todd gay, wouldn't he? Maybe it was one of those times to just listen?

"Gabe... I... it was hot." He started to look away again, and then with great effort (Gabe could see it almost bursting from his pores), Todd kept his eyes on Gabe's face. "It wasn't much. We... we were jerking off." Gabe could see Todd's face turn red, even in the light of the candle. He looked like he had a sunburn. "Helping each other.

Then...." He gulped again. Snatched up the wine glass, started to upend it, and then stopped. Took a swallow. Placed the glass on the table.

You're transforming every day, every minute, Gabe thought.

Then quietly—Gabe had to lean in to hear—Todd said, "He went down on me."

Interesting, Gabe thought. Usually it was the other way around. Gay boy goes down on straight boy. Maybe Austin wasn't so straight?

"I was cumming"—Todd's voice dropped even more on that word—"in about five seconds. I'd never felt anything like.... It was so amazing and...." He paused again, wiped at his face. "Then he wanted me to do the same to him. And I freaked. I ran out."

Gabe opened his mouth to tell Todd it was okay and once again decided to just listen. Todd would say what he wanted to say. What Gabe knew was that this was a big deal. Todd was sharing something very big and very important, and it was probably something he hadn't told anyone else. Who could he tell? William Racine?

"I couldn't sleep that night. Just thinking about how much better he was than Joan. How much hotter it was. He swallowed and didn't bitch about it, and it was frigging amazing. And that made me panic. I dreamed about doing it back. Over and over again. But all I could think of was my stepdad telling me I was a faggot. I didn't know what to do. I...."

Todd looked deeply into Gabe's eyes. Todd's were filled with so many emotions, Gabe found them hard to read. Pain? Confusion? Anguish? Anger? What? All of the above? *It's okay, Todd.*

"Thing is, this was my best friend. I loved him, you know? Despite how silly he could be."

A smile crept over Todd's face, and Gabe marveled again at how sweet it was.

"We had such big dreams. He liked to act. He was always in the school plays. He was the star of our senior musical *Little Shop of Horrors*. And then he stared in the Community Theatre show about Huckleberry Finn?"

"*Big River*?" Gabe asked.

"Yeah. That's it." Todd chuckled. "He was so funny. We would laugh so much." Then, on the tail of that, Todd sighed again. "I knew we had to work it out. Me and Austin. The last thing he said to me kept ringing through my head. He asked me to do what he did to me. He said he knew I wanted to." Todd looked into Gabe's eyes once more. "He actually said that. He said he knew it. I didn't know it! How could he know such a thing? What had I done that made him think that? I asked myself that a thousand times." Todd gave a laugh. A single "Ha!" that held no cheer.

"The thing is, Gabe, no matter what way I turned it over in my head, I realized I couldn't deny it. I wanted to deny it. I wanted to deny it so bad." Todd's eyes turned huge then, wet. "But I couldn't. So I finally got the courage to go over there and talk to him about it. I went over there figuring that before the evening was over, I was probably going to give my best friend a blow job."

Gabe still didn't say a word. There was nothing to say. Todd was saying it all. He wanted to assure the boy. *It's okay*, he wanted to say. *It's a part of that shitty thing called growing up.* Instead, he listened. Besides, he had to know what happened.

Todd's eyes grew wetter. *This is when the waiter will come*, Gabe thought. *God, please don't let him come. Let him know this isn't the time. Please, let him know not to come.*

"I didn't, though," Todd said. "Suck his cock?" He trembled. "I walked in to see Austin's bare ass bobbing up and down as he humped my girlfriend. They didn't even hear me, they were going at it so hard. I stood right there and watched until they came, shouting like monkeys. Then they finally saw me. You should have seen their faces. That's when I ran. I mean if I ran before, I really ran then."

Shitfire, Gabe thought. *It never ever stops. The cheating.*

Todd dropped his face into his upturned palms. Screwed them into his eyes.

"Joan kept calling, but I wouldn't talk to her. Got my stepdad really pissed off, too, but I didn't care. He hit me over my head, and I still wouldn't talk to her. I wouldn't read her notes. I never did. I don't know if she was trying to tell me to fuck off, that she was happier with Austin. Or that she was sorry. I don't know...."

Todd looked up through wet eyes and gave another strange laugh. "Because the thing was, I didn't really care. All I felt was relief. It meant I wasn't trapped. I had a way out! I could get away from her. I had the perfect excuse." Todd took a drink of his wine, finished it, stared at the empty glass, placed it on the table. Then, as if teleporting, the waiter was there, filled the glass well past the level etiquette dictated, and was gone—as if vanishing into thin air.

Big tip. That guy was getting a big *tip.*

Todd really did give a laugh that time and took a swallow *way* bigger than etiquette dictated. "Sorry," he said with a silly grin.

Despite himself, Gabe gave a laugh as well. What else could he do? "Don't worry about it."

"The bitch is, Austin didn't call once. Not once. And that was it. I did a lot more than run away from his house. I ran period. When a week passed and he didn't call once, I left. I finally left it all. Cleared out my bank, loaded up my van, and despite my stepdad telling me that if I left I couldn't come back—like I wanted to, right?—I left. I even deleted my email account. Cut every tie I had to that hell hole I came from. I came to Kansas City. Only to have every dream I had not come true."

Todd shook his head. "How's that? I frigging ruined dinner."

"You didn't ruin dinner," Gabe said, his heart filling with compassion. And more. Todd had shared something huge. Despite it all, all he could feel was closer to the boy. Not a boy. A man.

"Well, follow that with something if you dare," Todd cried.

"How about dessert?" Gabe asked and waved for the waiter. "Sugar always helps about this time, don't you think?"

WHEN Todd told him he didn't have room for anything, Gabe opted on one dessert to share—*Like two high school kids on a date*, thought Gabe. Then he berated himself for it.

Dessert was a huge scoop of white-chocolate ice cream, rolled in little broken chunks of white chocolate and then drenched in a hot fudge sauce that had surely been made by magical fairies. Todd told Gabe he thought he'd have an orgasm, it was so good, and then they both laughed uncomfortably, considering the previous conversation.

He's shared something really, really important, thought Gabe. *He's done everything but admit he's gay. He's done everything but say (or understand?) why he's yet to come out.* He was dealing with so much. This boy—no, man!—had had a year from hell.

"I really am sorry for ruining everything with the big story," Todd said, wiping his mouth of the last vestiges of ice cream.

"No, Todd. You didn't ruin anything. And I'm not sorry at all. I feel…." He took a deep breath. "I feel closer to you. I bet it took a lot to tell that story."

A look of gratitude took over Todd's face. "Me too," he said. "Feel closer to you. In fact… I'm feeling all kinds of things," he said, his voice cracking on the last word. He blushed. "I also feel like a million pounds has been lifted off my shoulders. Keeping that inside was like… it was like a cancer inside me."

Gabe looked away. *Shit. Shitfire.*

"What?" Todd asked.

Gabe looked into those huge brown eyes and felt his heart turn inside out. *Shitfire!*

"Gabe?"

Gabe felt Todd's hand come to a rest on his. Again. It squeezed. Then using his own words against him, Todd said, "You don't have to say anything if you don't want to, Gabe. But I'm here for you. You can tell me. Anything."

But could he? What would Todd think?

"Let's go for a walk," he said.

Todd nodded and Gabe asked for the check. He did indeed give a big tip. The waiter was marvelous. Maybe he had a boyfriend he could spend the money on.

So they left the restaurant and headed east. Gabe wasn't even sure how they wound up holding hands. Only that it surprised him when he realized it. He looked down—*how long has it been since I've done this? Why, two years and counting! Isn't that what this drama is about?*—and then smiled. Looked at Todd, who was obviously nervous about what they were doing. Gave him a nod of encouragement.

They didn't talk for a while. They walked several blocks to where the street ended at J.C. Nichols Parkway and then turned left, toward the Memorial Fountain—where else? He should have known that was where they were heading. Didn't he love the fountain more than just about any other place in Kansas City? It was huge and dominated by sculptures of horses that were supposed to represent the world's great rivers—at least, that is what he'd read. Thought he'd read. Funny that he loved it so much but knew so little about it. Especially considering it was Kansas City's most famous fountain, and one of its most known landmarks. A pretty special claim considering Kansas City was known as America's "City of Fountains."

How native, he thought. Isn't that the way? Tourists knew more about a city's attractions than the people who saw them every day.

Once on a visit to San Francisco, he'd gone on a tour and saw that the best place to catch his bus was at a place called the Pioneer Monument. He'd found a huge set of statues right between the Public Library and the Asian Art Museum (as described in the brochure), but he wasn't sure if it was the right place or not. It just about had to be because, while he thought that was Hera at its summit, what with her shield with the Medusa, there were also some figures that looked like pioneers. The funny thing was, when he asked a cop—a cop *obviously* on her beat—she didn't know!

What Gabe knew was that he loved the statues of the horses in the J.C. Nichols fountain and their huge masculine riders, the frolicking dolphins, all of it bombarded by jets of water. Of course, there was no water today. Sadly, Kansas City's fountains were turned off during the winter months to keep them from freezing and being damaged. But it was still gorgeous. How often had he wound up here? Sometimes he would stop and rest while on a particularly long run. He'd passed it every year during AIDS Walk. Sometimes he drove here specifically just to look up into the faces that dominated it, human and animal alike.

He'd never held hands with a man here before, though. He'd tried it with Daniel, but he'd jerked his hand away as if scalded. His flamboyant boyfriend had worried that people would think they were gay. The thought made him laugh out loud.

"What?" asked Todd as they arrived at the giant fountain, still holding hands.

He gave Todd's hand a slight squeeze. "You okay with this?" he asked.

Todd cleared his throat. Bit his lip. Looked around nervously. "I think," he said. "It's not like anyone I know is going to see me." He looked up into Gabe's eyes.

He's the perfect height, Gabe thought. He loved to be just a bit taller than a lover—not that they were that. But he liked the feeling of caretaking it gave him. He had no interest in being with a woman, never had. Not once. But he always seemed to wind up with effeminate men. Ignorant people would ask if he was the "man," and if his boyfriends were the "woman," and he had to bite his tongue to keep from telling them that since he loved taking it up the ass, did that still make him the man?

Todd isn't the least bit effeminate.

He's also not my boyfriend.

You want him to be.

Oh, God, he thought, looking down into—*falling* into—Todd's eyes. *Yes. Yes yes yes, I do. How? I barely know him? No such thing as falling in love this fast!*

Todd was looking around again, although Gabe could tell Todd was trying to do it circumspectly. *I'm not looking*, Todd's subtle movements and furtive glances told Gabe. *See me not looking?* Too bad Gabe could read him. Part of his gift. His fucking gift.

But then Todd's face lit up, and Gabe followed his gaze to see where he was looking. And there, about a third of the way around the fountain, were two men, holding hands.

Todd looked up again into Gabe's eyes, and his smile was radiant. *It's okay. We're not the only ones*, was what Todd's eyes said. *He's beginning to admit it. Right before my eyes.*

It was all Gabe could do not to kiss him.

And it's Brett all over again? Isn't that what you liked so much? Watching him accept himself. Wanting to be his first?

Shitfire. This was not going to work. He would not let Todd be another Brett. He couldn't. Wouldn't. And the first step was to tell Todd all about it. Then the ghost of Brett would lose its power.

"Okay. I'll tell you now," Gabe said.

"I'm listening," Todd said, his voice hopeful.

Gabe sighed, then sat down on the ledge of the fountain.

"Okay," he said finally. "I had a boyfriend named Daniel...."

CHAPTER SIXTEEN

"WE MET at Peter's New Year's party, believe it or not. Four years ago. Daniel caught my attention right away, leaning against a counter in this huge kitchen. He was beautiful, with this tight curly dark-brown hair and big dark-brown eyes, and he was drinking a glass of wine, and he was practically touching foreheads with this guy, and right away I was jealous. Isn't that stupid? Jealous!"

Todd wasn't sure if it was stupid or not. He'd never really had an opportunity to be jealous before. He gave a half shrug and nodded for Gabe to continue.

"They were talking real intimate, you know? And then I somehow, from across that crowded room, heard him say something about graduating, and before I even knew I'd done it, I shouted, 'Graduated from where?' He sorta jerked, and he and his friend stopped talking and stared at me, and I was so embarrassed I almost hightailed it out of there."

Gabe smiled, then crossed his leg, leaned on his knee. "Then he walked up to me and told me he'd just gotten his bachelor's degree from the Kansas City Art Institute. I thought that was pretty cool. Then he told me the degree was in graphic design. Sadly, everybody and their foot doctor had one as well, and it wasn't likely to score him a job. I guess it's like an English degree when I went to school, what everyone was doing. But I didn't care. I was smitten. Totally smitten. I just kept staring at his mouth and wanting to kiss him."

No. Wait. He did know what jealousy was. And for some frigging reason, he was feeling it now. All Gabe had wanted to do was kiss this guy? He'd been staring at his mouth? Todd could almost picture it, and ridiculous or not, he was feeling this shimmer of jealousy! Stupid was the word.

Todd shook himself. *Step back, silly boy, and just listen.*

"So I asked him on a date. I wanted to ask him home, but I wanted to be romantic."

Romantic? So it could be romantic with two guys? Todd felt his pulse quicken. It wasn't just sex?

"Of course not," said Gabe, and once more Todd realized he'd spoken aloud without realizing it. He blushed.

"Oh, Todd. Don't you see? That's what 'gay' is all about." He gave Todd a lopsided grin. "I was born homosexual. That I can't fight. I can ignore it, pretend it isn't real, but I'll always be homosexual."

Born homosexual. Todd's stomach clenched. "You really think that? That we're…." He stopped. "That people are born that way?"

Gabe laughed. "Just like the song. Sung by a lady that you have a pretty big liking for, right?"

Todd could hear the words in his head: "Gay, straight, bi, lesbian. Born that way."

"Now what I had a choice to do was embrace what I was or deny it. For me there was never any thinking about it. I had no interest in females. Never did. It didn't even occur to me until my buddies started stealing their daddies' *Playboys*. I took one look, was appalled, and knew I would never want anything to do with women. Knew it. Always did. And when I started getting crushes, it was always boys. Just like you, I fell for my best friend."

"You know," Todd said, stopping him, even though he had told himself to just listen. "I don't think I ever was. I know I wasn't. Austin was too much like… I don't know. A brother, you know? It would have been like incest."

Gabe nodded. "Okay. I get that—"

It was only then that Todd realized he had done it. He'd… what did they say? Outted himself?

"—but my point is, homosexual is genetic. 'Gay' is a choice. 'Gay' is the admitting to yourself that you are not only homosexual, but you embrace it. You find joy in it. You're thankful for it!"

"Thankful for it?" Todd asked, incredulous. "Thankful for being something everyone hates?"

Gabe nodded. "I wouldn't be straight for all the tea in China."

"Really?" asked Todd. "It would be so much easier. You'd fit in. Don't you feel weird at work functions where everybody has a wife and kids and you don't?"

Gabe shook his head. "I only felt weird when I was alone. And with Daniel, I wasn't alone. I was happy as could be. He moved in with me in a week. Not officially. He still had this apartment way out in Terra's Gate, about an hour from here. But he was spending every night at my place. We made it official a month later. We went everywhere together. People accused us of being Velcroed together. I was on cloud nine!"

"Wow," Todd muttered. Tried to imagine Gabe with this Daniel person. All dark-haired and brown-eyed with a pretty mouth. A man. "You were in love?"

Gabe's smile melted away. "I thought I was. At first. Now? Now I see lots of things. I see that maybe what I was… was that I was in love with the *idea* of being in love. Of having a mate. Of having a man on my arm wherever I went. Now I know that I was too controlling. I wanted everything my way. Here I preached that I didn't want to buy a house until I found "him," and there I had someone and never thought about actually looking for a house. And Daniel asked. I kept putting him off. And the apartment. I wanted it all my way. I put Daniel's stuff in storage. I barely let him move anything in. I was a total shit."

Gabe? A shit? Todd found that hard to imagine. "I don't believe it," Todd said. "You're not a shit."

Gabe shrugged. "I don't know. But maybe a part of me knew all along that I wasn't in love with Daniel. Not really. Why else would I have fallen for Brett?"

Brett? Who was Brett?

Gabe stood up. Rubbed his arms. "I'm getting cold. How about you? You want to get some coffee?"

"Okay," Todd said. It would keep him up all night. It always did when he had much caffeine after one or two in the afternoon. But Gabe wanted it, so the answer was yes.

They went to Gabe's car. The beautiful little silver thing still amazed Todd. He wondered just how much the car cost. He could look it up, now, but didn't really want to. It felt nosy. Invasive. But still. How they'd gotten their purchases—well, Gabe's purchases for him—in the tiny trunk, Todd wasn't sure. The little sports car didn't have a back seat.

It was a short drive to The Shepherd's Bean. "It's my favorite place for coffee," Gabe said. "I used to go to The Radiant Cup, but I like giving my money to a gay business."

Gay business? Todd wondered. "It's gay?" Todd asked.

They walked across a little red-brick patio with several trees surrounded by tables and chairs, and when they got to the door, Gabe pointed to the rainbow sticker just below where a sign showed what credit cards they took. *Ah. Gay.*

"Gay owned. Whenever I can, I use my dollars to support gay businesses."

"Is that a part of the being 'gay' thing?"

Gabe nodded. "Exactly. Embracing who I am. My community. Sharing my money with other people who are proud of their gayness."

"Proud? Really?" Todd asked.

Gabe paused "It's why I don't like words like faggot or queer," he said.

And I used those words. I use them!

Gabe sighed. "Sit down. I'll get the coffee. I'll get something that will knock your socks off."

Todd chose a table away from the window and sat down. Then thought better of it. *I held hands with a man on the Plaza! What am I afraid of? That someone will think I'm... gay? Am I?* He looked across the small room toward Gabe, who was talking to a nice-looking man behind the counter. He didn't hold Todd's attention long. He found himself staring at Gabe. Such a big man. So tall, his shoulders impossibly wide. He couldn't see more since Gabe was wearing that coat. But he knew what it hid: those wide shoulders tapered into a narrow waist and a round, muscular ass. A smooth one too. He'd seen it bare. Not at all like Joan's, which was bigger, so much softer. Who knew men and women had such different bottoms? No. Gabe's looked solid. Todd would be willing to bet it was as hard as his chest—which he'd had his face up against. Then Todd felt something. *Wow. Again. I'm getting a hard-on just looking at him.*

He closed his eyes. *I'm homosexual. I've fought it all my life, but it's true. My stepdad was right. I'm a faggot. How did he know?*

"Todd?"

He looked up into Gabe's face, those lovely eyes looking down into his. Proud of who he is. Gabe sat down, took a sip, held his paper cup up in salute. Todd took a sip of his own, blowing first and remembering to close his eyes. And God he was glad he did. What wonderful coffee. The aroma was somewhere between herbal and floral—*and would I have thought to make a comparison like that even a week ago?* Gabe was teaching him about taste and how to treasure flavor. What was really powerful was that Todd realized he'd always known this, always appreciated it. Something he knew that he knew, but had rarely had the opportunity to indulge. The coffee was heavy bodied, with simply tons of cherry and lemonade sweetness coming through. And again, would he have ever thought an unflavored coffee would taste of cherry and lemonade? His stepfather would have said such comparisons were snooty, that coffee was coffee. Now Todd saw Gabe was educating his palate. It was exciting.

"Wow," he said. "That's some damned fine coffee."

"Roasted yesterday," Gabe said, smiling. "Ground minutes before it was made. It's grown on a small cooperative from the Mukurweini District of Kenya."

He's stalling, avoiding telling me the rest of his story, thought Todd. He took another sip.

Gabe didn't say much for quite a while. Just drank his coffee and talked about the guy who ran the shop. The man used to work for one of the big coffee monsters, traveled the world, made friends on more plantations than could be believed. Finally he didn't want to work for "the man" anymore and moved to Kansas City to start The Shepherd's Bean.

Todd let him blab. He knew Gabe was only delaying what he had to say. Maybe he'd changed his mind. Or maybe it was something bad? Something really bad?

ONCE more Gabe found himself reading Todd's face. *He's starting to worry. Starting to think that my story is something bad.*

Isn't it? It's pretty bad.

But not the kind of bad Todd's beginning to think about.

"I met Brett by the Liberty Memorial," he said. "A bunch of us were hanging out that day in protest of Gay Pride."

Todd's brows came together. "You were protesting Gay Pride?"

Gabe nodded. "It had been amazing for years. It was huge, and thousands of people showed up and there were all these booths and vendors and grass. The kind you lay on," Gabe quickly added. "Hundreds of us would lay out our blankets and watch the acts—Chaka Khan, RuPaul, Crystal Waters, Martha Wash—and it was free. Then some ass got a hold of it and took it downtown to the Power & Light District and started bringing in acts no one had ever heard of and charging an arm and a leg as well. It was horrible. So a bunch of us decided to have our own day of it at the park where Gay Pride used to be. That's when I met Brett."

He could remember the day so well. He and Daniel were having a nice day. Several of their friends had joined them; they were sharing with each other, passing around cocktails. Tommy was there, and that meant his wonderful cosmos. Harry and Cody—were they there as buddies or new lovers? Gabe couldn't remember. They got together right around then. In fact it had been their volleyball net that had been set up, hadn't it? And it was the volleyball that had made him notice Brett the first time. Pink tank top and black shorts with little pink stripes down the side. Somehow he'd gotten away with the look.

"He was cute as can be, and young. Younger than you. Mixed. He had this beautiful café au lait skin and big pretty eyes. He was playing volleyball. Was good at it too. Then when everyone took a break, he started to wander off. Somehow I just knew he didn't have anything to eat, and I called out to him and asked him to sit down with me and Daniel, and we shared our lunch with him."

Like I did with you, Gabe thought. *Just like that.*

And had it been just generosity that made him call out to Brett? Or had he just been wanting to get a closer look at him?

"He'd run away from home. His dad.... Well, his father had been molesting him for years, and he couldn't take it anymore, so he ran away. He found out about Gay Pride, and that's where he ran to. Kid was sad. Broke my heart."

"YOU like him, don't you?" Daniel had asked him after they'd eaten and Brett got back up to play some more volleyball.

"Sure," he'd answered. "Don't you?"

Daniel was giving him a mischievous grin. "Honey. You know what I mean. You *like* him. I've been watching your crotch. You rolled right over on your tummy when you started to get really hard."

Gabe had been shocked and embarrassed at his lover's words. Had he been attracted to Brett? Had he gotten a hard-on? And of course, he had. "He's seventeen, Daniel."

Daniel had leaned back, laid a hand over his own crotch. "So what? I think that boy knows what he wants."

Daniel's words had stunned Gabe.

"Oh for God's sake," Daniel had replied, obviously seeing Gabe's shock. "He's close to legal. There are states where he *is* legal. Fuck. There are countries where he's a man at thirteen. If we were in Denmark today, instead of here, would you take him to bed? He'd be legal at fifteen."

Gabe shook his head. "Dammit, Daniel. It's not the same and you know it. He's still in high school. And we are *way* older than him."

"Speak for yourself, schnookums." Which was true. Daniel and Brett were only five years apart in age while he was a good ten years older than Brett.

"Anyway," Daniel continued, "I do think that my man is finally ready to admit he's hot for other men."

Gabe had gulped and looked away. Yes, damn it. He was noticing other men. He had for some time. And why? He had a lover. They'd been together for two years. Why would he possibly need to look at other men? But as he had turned to say something, he realized Daniel was certainly looking. There was downright lust in his eyes as he watched the men around him. For some reason, it really didn't bother him like he felt it should. As he watched that day, he came to see that what bothered him was that Daniel's wandering eyes didn't bother him.

"DANIEL and I talked about it and let him come stay with us a few days. On the couch by the way!"

Just like you. Sleeping on the couch when I want you in my bed.

"He wasn't legal, you know? Close, but not quite. We had to be careful so no one accused us of taking advantage of him. But we tried to help him. Showed him that being gay was a good thing. He'd been having unsafe sex and we got him tested. Thank God, he was negative, at least as far as we could tell. He had read on the Internet that AIDS was as easy to deal with as diabetes. Bullshit spread by people who don't want to use condoms." He rubbed his eyes. It wasn't easy, telling the story. It was something he'd tried not to think about and had put behind him. Now he was dredging it all back up.

"The three of us got close fast. At first it was sweet. He called us Daddy One and Daddy Two, and we started calling him Son. We were like a family in a lot of ways."

GABE was in the kitchen that day when he heard the door open. "I is home!" Brett called out. Of course, he wasn't really. They'd found him a place to stay through Passages, the local youth center. But he might as well have been for as much time as he spent at their apartment.

"I'm in here," Gabe called back. He'd been making spaghetti—the cheap and easy way as he really wasn't a cook. Ragu was just so much quicker.

Brett came in, running his hand over his closely cropped head, all sweaty. He'd obviously been running. He leaned up for a kiss and Gabe gave him as platonic a one as he could—on the cheek. "Daddy!" Brett protested. "I wants a kiss on mah lips. My momma used to kiss me on mah lips."

And so did your father, he'd wanted to say. But true or not, it just wasn't the thing to say. "Be a good son and stop whining," Gabe said, stirring the boiling noodles.

"Is Daddy Two home yet?"

Gabe nodded. "He's in the shower. He'll be out in a second."

"Think maybe he needs me ta dry his back?"

"He's been drying his own back for a long time. He's fine," Gabe said and checked a noodle to see if it was ready.

As if on cue, Daniel stepped into the room. He was wearing his jeans, but nothing else, and drying his hair. "Hey, Son," he said with a grin.

"Hey, Daddy." Brett stepped into him and Gabe saw that Daniel didn't hesitate to kiss the boy on the mouth. At least it was just a peck. He would have to remind his lover of the legalities of their situation. And it wasn't that he didn't want to kiss Brett. He did. He knew that more every day. But weren't they trying to be an example for the kid? This wasn't supposed to be about sex. It was supposed to be about friendship. Showing Brett that being gay didn't mean you had to be a slut. You could find a lover, settle down, make a home, fall in love.

Fall in love…?

"BUT then Brett started pushing us for sex. We couldn't, of course. But God, Todd…." Gabe looked away. "I wanted to," he whispered. "I was falling for him. Hard."

He turned back to look at Todd. Afraid of what he would see. But to his relief there was no judgment there. None that he could see. "I had to get him out of our apartment, you know? Before I slipped. I knew I only had to wait a few months and he'd be legal." He watched Todd's face. *Still no judgment? All right then, Todd. How about this!* "Todd, I was thinking about sleeping with Brett, and I was with Daniel. I was living with a boyfriend and fantasizing about someone else. I was falling in love with a kid and realizing every day I wasn't in love with my lover. It was terrible. I hated it. I hated myself!"

To his surprise, Todd's eyes filled with tears. And more. Was that compassion? Could it be?

"Oh, Gabe. You can't help that you weren't in love with Daniel."

"But I let him *think* I was." Gabe felt his own eyes fill with tears. "I cheated him and I wasn't even cheating *on* him."

Todd reached out and surprised Gabe again. He laid his hand on Gabe's cheek, cupped it, then ran his fingers down his jaw before dropping his hand to his lap. "Oh, sweet Gabe."

The look in Todd's eyes! No judgment. None. Sadness maybe. There was more, but he couldn't tell what. *Damn. This is what I'm good at. Why can't I read you all of a sudden?*

He started to look away but Todd reached up with a finger and pulled him back. "Go on," he said. "You're not done. I can tell."

Shit. Shitfire!

THE day Brett turned eighteen was a big one for Gabe. He'd gotten his friend several gifts to help celebrate, but the truth was, there was something else he wanted to give Brett. He had finally decided not to fight it. Tonight, when Brett inevitably came on to him and Daniel, he would take him up on it.

Daniel had made it very clear he wanted them to try some three-ways. Gabe had been way against it in the beginning. But now? Hell, now was as confusing as shitfire. All he'd wanted was a monogamous relationship, but now that he had it, he wasn't enjoying it. Not at all. Maybe monogamy was unnatural?

No. The idea just didn't sit well in his heart. In his gut. What he really thought was going on was the plain and simple fact that he wasn't in love with Daniel. He wasn't sure he ever had been.

Brett, on the other hand? He could no longer argue with himself about it. He was in love with the boy-man. And today Brett was officially a *man*. Legal and everything. And when he asked for a kiss, Gabe was going to give it to him.

The biggest problem so far had been juggling the bag of gifts, the half-dozen balloons, and the cake and opening doors. Luckily someone had opened the lobby doors for him. His elbow had called the elevator and three floors instead of just his own. When he reached the apartment door, he just put the bag down, switched hands with the cake, and unlocked it. Leaving work early had meant he could get home and get everything ready before Brett got there. It wasn't like it was a big surprise. The kid knew something was up, but he still wanted everything ready.

Gabe let himself in, set the cake and weighted balloons on the dining room table, and went back for the bag he'd left in the hall. Shrugging out of his coat, he began to look around the room for where he wanted to leave the packages. Around the cake on the table? On the coffee table? He shrugged. He'd ask Daniel. Right now he'd distribute the balloons. He'd wanted more, but the six had already filled up the front seat of his Saturn and made it almost impossible to drive. Maybe he should have just gotten one of those little tanks and then he could have filled up a shitload of them?

One on the dining room table, one on the coffee table. There by the TV. The end table. Sure. And…. He grinned. One smack dab in the middle of the bed.

That's where he found Brett and Daniel. Tangled in the sheets, cuddled together, asleep. Gabe had been moving so fast he was halfway in the room before his confused mind understood what it was seeing. He stopped. Froze. He couldn't move. His face went slack. His shoulders slumped. The tears came.

They're in bed.

They've had sex.

The room was filled with the smell of it. Sex. A glance showed a used condom on the bedside table. At least they were safe, and the thought made him laugh outright. The noise made Brett stir. He snuggled closer, buried his nose in Daniel's armpit and made a happy sound.

A happy sound.

The tears were running down Gabe's face now. It felt like his heart had stopped. No pain. No, he was numb. It felt like he was dead or something. What he was seeing couldn't be real. Couldn't be. They couldn't have done it.

You wanted to.

Yes. But I wasn't going to cheat on Daniel.

Some inner part of him laughed. *You've been cheating for months.*

No. No I haven't.

You have with your heart.

Not the same thing!

No. It's worse.

The alarm clock went off and Gabe jumped with a shout.

Daniel's eyes slowly opened, saw Gabe standing there—stupid balloon still in his hand—and then went wide.

"Fuck," Daniel muttered. He closed his eyes, let out a sigh, then opened them again and sat up. The alarm still sounded. *Waaaaaaah! Waaaaaaah! Waaaaaaah! Waaaaaaah!*

"Turn it off," Gabe somehow heard Brett saying. "Want to sleep a few more minutes before Gabe gets home."

Daniel reached across the boy—no, man now—and switched it off. "Gabe is home, baby."

Baby?

"What?" Brett asked and rolled onto his back. His eyes cracked open. Then opened wider. "Oh."

Oh. Oh? What a brilliant thing to say. Oh.

"Can you give us a minute?" Daniel asked calmly.

It took another moment for the words to sink in. When they did, Gabe couldn't answer. He only turned around and left the room.

"FUCK," Todd said. "Oh, Gabe."

"The cheating never stops," Gabe said quietly. "It rules the world, doesn't it? My first boyfriend cheated on me. Then Daniel and Brett. Joan cheated on you. It's the way of the world. Is that all people do?" Gabe cried. "David from the Bible cheated! Catherine the Great. Mark Anthony. Benjamin-fucking-Franklin. Henry VIII. Einstein! Mother skeeter! Can you believe that? He must have been a lot better looking when he was young."

Todd bit his lower lip. "I…. Yeah…."

Is he laughing at me? Gabe wondered. "Lyndon B. Johnson and Dwight Eisenhower," he continued. "How do you like that shit? Ashton Kutcher cheated on Demi. Brad Pitt cheated on Jennifer. Jennifer Aniston! What straight guy would cheat on the cutest, sweetest girl ever? LeAnn Rimes cheated! That talent-free little bitch from *Twilight* cheated on that vampire guy!"

Todd's eyes went wide and he sucked his lips in. *He's trying not to laugh*, thought Gabe. And before he knew it, he was the one that was laughing. Todd let out a blast and joined him.

"Bitch from *Twilight*?" Todd managed to get out through his laughter.

The laughter didn't last long. The conversation had been pretty serious after all. Nothing to be dispelled with anything less than hysteria, and hysterical they weren't.

But it lightened the mood a bit.

"Well, at least now you know you didn't ruin the evening," Gabe said. "I helped."

Todd's eyes went big again. "And I he-ulped," he said, mocking the ancient Shake 'n Bake commercial, and they laughed once more.

"How do you even know that commercial?" Gabe asked. "That was before your time. Hell, it was before mine."

"YouTube," Todd said. "Where do you think?"

CHAPTER **SEVENTEEN**

"WHAT happened to them?" Todd asked as Gabe parked the car in the Oscar Wilde's lot.

Gabe turned to him. "Thought we were done with that."

"We aren't," Todd said. "And I want to know before we go upstairs."

"Why?" Gabe asked him.

Because I want to change the mood, Todd thought. "So we don't take it home."

Gabe gave him a little smile. "Home?"

Todd smiled back. "You did ask me to move in. I got that, right? At least temporarily?"

"Yes, Todd," Gabe said. "And you can stay as long as you want. We'll set up your bedroom and you can live there forever if you want."

"Then finish. I did. I saw Austin fucking Joan and I moved to KC. You found Daniel in bed with Brett. What happened?"

"It's only going to make things worse," Gabe said.

"No, it's not." *Tell me. Tell me, Gabe. Get it out.*

Gabe gripped the steering wheel and looked out into the night. The sky had gone clear at some point—there was no snow—and a quarter moon hung over them, silver and flawless. "They moved out," he said finally. "They left that night. Brett didn't even say anything to me. Daniel said something… not sure exactly. 'Sorry' or some lame ass thing, and they were gone. Daniel came back a few days later and I gave him a couple things—most of his stuff was in the storage locker. I guess the two of them had been fucking for a while." He shook his head. "And Brett a minor!

"Then two weeks after that, Daniel wanted to move back in. He said he caught Brett in bed with someone else." Gabe snorted. "Can you believe that shit? I can."

"Did you let him come back?" Todd asked.

Gabe turned to him, aghast. "Are you crazy? No way." He looked back out the window. "It was over. It had been over. I can't even blame Daniel. He wasn't getting the loving he deserved. But Brett! He said *I* was Daddy One."

I'll call you Daddy if you want me to, Todd thought and then blushed.

"And the worst part of it all?" Gabe said.

Todd waited. It got worse?

"He's a hustler now. He works the park near you."

Todd jerked in his seat. Hustler. In the park?

"I was going for a run when I saw him. Stopped me dead in my tracks." Gabe shuddered and he gripped the wheel even tighter.

Shit. This is *bad*, Todd thought.

"He offered me a deal. Said he was really experienced now, and he'd make my eyes roll he was so good." A tear welled up in Gabe's right eye and slowly rolled down his cheek. "He was snapping his fingers and acting really gay. I mean he was always a little effeminate, but now he was acting like the complete stereotype of a gay man. It was disgusting. I wanted to puke. Not just from the way he was acting, but all of it. I started to leave, and he brought the price down. So I asked him. I asked him if he had ever loved me. I told him that I had fallen completely for him. And you know what he told me?"

Todd found he was afraid to ask.

"He said sure, he loved me. But not like I loved him. And that the whole Daddy One and Daddy Two thing had creeped him out. *Creeped him out!*" More tears began to run down Gabe's face. "He said I should have known better. That his daddy molested him, so why would he want me to call him that?" Gabe dropped his forehead to rest on the steering wheel. "God, it was like he was *stabbing* me, Todd. It hurts now. I thought I was past it, but damn it hurts."

"Gabe," Todd said, laying a hand on his shoulder. "Gabe. It's okay. Come here." He tried to give the man a tug, but of course, he was like stone and there was no moving him.

"Todd, I *never* did anything to hurt him. He was the one that started calling us Daddy. *He* was the one!"

"Gabe! Come here." Todd pulled at the wrist resting on the wheel. "Come here."

"I told him that. I said, 'You're the one who called us Daddy' and he said it was so he could get out of the cold. Oh Todd!"

Somehow Todd pulled Gabe's hand away from the wheel, and Gabe looked at him then, face wet with tears. He tugged again and held out his arms. "Come here, Gabe."

"He said horrible things to me. Said I was always walking around with a boner looking at him, and that I was no better than his own father. Todd, I *promise* you I never took advantage of him."

Todd leaned into Gabe and took him into his arms. It wasn't easy in the confined space in Gabe's little car. "I believe you, Gabe."

"But I've been doing it to you! Walking around with a hard-on. Like I have no fucking control of myself."

"Shhhh," Todd said. "You've got control of yourself. You haven't done anything. You wouldn't do anything when I started it."

"Of course not," Gabe said, pulling back slightly. "It was thank-you sex. I couldn't do that. I might as well have paid you, and you had to know I helped because I *wanted* to."

"I know that," Todd said, and pulled Gabe close again.

"I thought you were a hustler."

Todd nodded. A new understanding was hitting him. How weird and confusing all this must have been for Gabe. Crazy, even.

"I thought you were a hustler and I turned Brett into one."

"You did not." Todd began to stroke the back of Gabe's head.

"That's what Brett said. And he told me he had HIV. That it was his only way to make a living. He's HIV positive, Todd."

Todd froze. Something clicked. "His name is Brett, you said?" *He said he was mixed....*

Gabe nodded. "Brett Charles."

Fuck, Todd said to himself. *Charles.*

Chaz. The kid in the park who had tried to talk Todd into being a hustler. Gabe's ex.

"Todd, I'm a terrible person."

"Don't be ridiculous," Todd said. "You are wonderful." He kissed Gabe's cheek. "You are amazing." He kissed it again. "And I love you."

Gabe stiffened in his arms. Slowly pulled back. "What?"

Todd looked into those beautiful eyes and then repeated himself. "I love you," he said. And kissed Gabe on the mouth.

At first Gabe tried to pull away, but Todd wouldn't let him. Gabe was stronger than him, but he used all his own strength to keep the man in his arms. To keep Gabe's mouth against his own. Then with a cry, Gabe kissed him back.

All it took was that kiss for Todd to know. The other kisses were just a hint. But as Gabe opened his mouth to Todd's, as their tongues tentatively touched and then began to tangle and twist, as Todd grew lightheaded and felt his heart began to pound and his cock grow hard and felt the world melt away, he knew.

He was gay.

"God," Gabe moaned. "Todd, I'm trying not to take advantage of you, but there's only so far you can push me."

"Dammit, Gabe. I want this. Can't you tell?"

"You do?"

Oh, God, Gabe! He took Gabe's hand and pressed it against his crotch, letting Gabe feel his hardness.

"Oh God," Gabe groaned.

Todd dropped his hand into Gabe's lap and yes-yes-yes! He was hard. This was real. No fumbling. No doubts. Gabe's mouth fell open and his breath was coming in quick, deep pants. And his mouth was so sexy. So real. And none of that damn, slimy lipstick.

Todd began to stroke the hard tube of flesh in Gabe's pants and the man moaned again...

"Oh Todd."

... and had anything ever felt so sexy? It was like with Austin but so, so much better, even though he couldn't really get to the man's cock. Gabe gripped back and Todd thought he would cum in his pants he was so excited. Nothing had ever felt this amazing, and they didn't even have their clothes off.

"Gabe," he said, voice horse. "I think we need to go upstairs now. I don't want my first time to be in your car."

THEY made it upstairs. Barely.

They flung off their coats and Todd practically climbed up Gabe's body. *God, he's so big*, Todd thought. Huge. Everywhere.

Gabe spun around and all but slammed Todd against the door. Kissed him hard, mouths wide, tongues fighting, teeth clashing.

And I thought sex was boring? Todd would have laughed, but he couldn't with Gabe's tongue so far into his mouth. Gabe tasted like spices and wine and sweet coffee, and wasn't it wild that even that was sexy?

Todd didn't say anything. He didn't know what to say. He only knew he was going to do this—*Am I really going to do this?*—and he was harder than he'd ever been in his life.

Gabe began to suck at Todd's neck and his head fell to the side, giving the man access. He moaned in pleasure, only to realize Gabe was moaning too. Gabe was pulling at his shirt, yanking it out from where it had been tucked, and then his hands were sliding up inside, up his torso and chest. Gabe's hands felt amazing against his skin, and he thrust his crotch forward to meet Gabe's. Hard. He was pressing his hardness along Gabe's. The man was turned on. The man wanted him.

How many times had he wondered if Joan only had sex with him because that was what they were supposed to do. She never seemed that enthused—*Any less than me?*—but Gabe! Gabe wanted him. The hard-on left no doubt. And who knew just pressing your cock up against another man's cock could be so frigging hot?

Gabe pulled back suddenly, his eyes wild, but lids heavy. "Last chance," Gabe gasped.

"For what?" Todd managed, breathing labored.

"To get out of this," Gabe said, locking eyes with him.

"Are you crazy?" Todd asked, and once more tried to crawl up the man. Gabe put his arms around him, lifted him, and Todd wrapped his legs around Gabe's waist, felt the man's hardness against his ass. Gabe let out a long groan and then hefted Todd higher so that his spread cheeks were bumping Gabe's tummy, and the man began to carry him down the hall, kissing him the whole way.

Let's see Joan do this!

They reached the door, lurched through it, and then Gabe was practically throwing Todd onto the bed—that vast bed Todd had thought about so much in the last few days. Gabe stood, yanked his shirt off over his head, at least two buttons flying into the air. He wasn't wearing anything under it and there was that massive chest—as big as Todd's favorite weightlifters from his magazines—*and look at that eight pack. That tight tiny navel.* Todd gasped at the sight. So hot. So beautiful. Gabe's nipples were small and hard and only slightly darker than his skin, and Todd found his mouth watering, wanting to taste them.

Gabe fell on him, kissing him again, and Todd felt his own cock growing harder and harder. It almost hurt. Like the skin could split he was so hard and he suddenly, desperately wanted to get his pants off. He reached down, trying to get his hands between him and Gabe so he could open them. Before he could, Gabe grabbed his wrists and pinned them high and to the side. He kissed down Todd's neck, down his chest, sucked and nipped at one of Todd's nipples. Todd surged up against that mouth, tried to get away, pressed back again. He could feel his skin crawling with pleasure.

I fought this? I fought this! Was I insane?

("You a faggot or something?")

Yeah, you asshole. I think I just might be one after all.

Somehow the thought only made Todd harder. Made him smile. Made him happy that what was happening would sicken his stepfather. He almost wished the man could see.

Gabe began to lick and kiss up Todd's left arm and then buried his face in Todd's pit. Todd squealed in delight, laughed—*it tickles so!*—because it felt oh so good.

Gabe ran his kisses and tongue down Todd's arm, across his chest (making sure to suck on the other nipple) and then up his other arm, sucking and licking his other armpit.

Then Gabe was kissing him, releasing Todd's arms. Todd wrapped them around Gabe, ran his hands down Gabe's unbelievably muscular back. So smooth. So hard. So alive. He could feel the muscles moving, flexing. So real.

"Oh, Todd. I want you so bad."

"Me too," Todd said, and marveled that he was saying it aloud. Admitting it to the both of them.

Gabe stood and shuffled a moment. Todd heard clunking, knew the man was kicking off his shoes. Then Gabe unbuckled his belt, unzipped his slacks, and they fell to the floor, leaving him standing in a pair of his sexy underwear. Todd recognized them—figured he probably had some pictures of them on his laptop—but who cared? It was the huge tubular bulge that was what was so damned hot.

Why hadn't he been able to tell Austin how hot his cock was?

Won't make that mistake again.

"You are so fucking hot," Todd grunted.

"Not me. *You*," Gabe said, and scooped him up again and literally tossed him right into the center of the bed.

Gabe started to crawl back on top of him, but Todd shook his head. "No. I want to touch *you*."

He pushed against the mountain of one of Gabe's pecs, an immovable object for sure, but the man relented and rolled onto his back. Todd leaned up on one arm and looked over the length of the man next to him. He had never seen anything so sexy in his life. Anything so gorgeous. That handsome face, beautiful eyes, sweet mouth. Todd's eyes traveled down Gabe's body, the plains of muscles, oceans of flawless skin, and then the huge erection filling the man's tiny underwear. It was throbbing, actually lifting the band of the underwear with each pulse. Todd lay his other hand in the center of Gabe's smooth chest, marveled at the feel of the warm flesh—God, it was so smooth. So hard. How could human flesh be so hard? It wasn't at all soft like Joan's breasts—ran his fingers everywhere, touching, skimming, pinching at the nipples—all of it making Gabe jump—and then down, down—*Oh God, this is it!*—to finally grasp Gabe's cock.

"Oh, God," moaned the big man, and Todd felt a thrill of excitement. Gabe was really turned on. He wasn't faking it. Todd kissed him, kissed him hard, pushing his tongue into Gabe's mouth and tangling it with his. Gabe had the tiniest bit of stubble on his lip, and it felt so different from any kiss Todd had ever experienced. But it felt really good.

Gabe moaned again, and then abruptly, he was pushing Todd back onto the bed and pulling himself on top of him, covering Todd with his massive, comforting, safe masculinity. He could feel Gabe's cock, grinding into his thigh. Something wild ripped through Todd's chest as he looked up into Gabe's face. It was scary and exciting.

I'm gay, thought Todd. *No doubt about it. Not straight. And no, little girl, I'm not bi.*

I'm gay.

A thrill raced down Todd's spine at the inner words.

Gay. I'm gay!

Not even homosexual.

Gabe leaned down to kiss him, but Todd stopped him. "Wait!"

Gabe sat up, freeing Todd. He looked desperately disappointed.

Todd smiled. He began to unbuckle his own belt, and Gabe smiled back and helped him slide his pants down and off his legs. Todd blushed, shy suddenly, seeing that Gabe was looking down at his erection, which tented out his underwear. But the lust in Gabe's eyes dispelled any shyness. He felt a rush of affection and gratitude and a deep need to give back just a little of what Gabe had given him. He lifted his ass off the mattress and squirmed out of his underwear. His hard-on sprang out. He dropped his hands and spread them to his sides, offering Gabe whatever he wished.

"Oh, Todd."

"It's not as big as yours," Todd whispered.

"Todd, it's huge." Gabe leaned down and kissed his face, his chest, and then his belly and then…. Gabe reached his cock, grasped it in his fist, kissed the head of it, and as he took it into his mouth, they both let out long moans. "Hot cock," he murmured, releasing Todd's erection for a moment. "Fantastic, beautiful cock."

Beautiful? He said my dick is beautiful? A penis can be beautiful?

Of course it can, he realized. How could he deny it? He'd known the truth forever but had avoided it somehow.

Pleasure raced through Todd in a huge wave. Gabe's mouth was so smooth and warm and wet. He couldn't believe how good it felt. Gabe's tongue flexed and rolled over and down Todd's shaft, sending sparks of pleasure all through him. He looked down and watched his cock disappear and then reappear from Gabe's face. Strangely, it didn't decrease his masculinity at all. If anything, it made him look even more masculine. That manly face bobbing up and down on his hard cock was one of the most exciting things Todd had ever seen. No, it *was* the most exciting. And what was crazy great was that he could see Gabe was getting as much pleasure from sucking him as he was getting from being sucked. He was enjoying it. He was getting off. Gabe was loving sucking his erection and loving Todd's reactions. This was what oral sex was supposed to be. Not something you were supposed to do, but something you wanted to do. Not furtive and rushed, but deliberate and pleasurable for both lovers.

What would it be like to do the same to Gabe's? What would it feel like? Taste like? Would it be pleasurable? The idea didn't repulse Todd; it made him so hot he felt like he might cum.

"Gabe," he panted.

Gabe stopped sucking and looked up.

"Kiss me."

Gabe leaned up and pressed his mouth against Todd's. They kissed for the longest time. And then Todd pulled back. He smiled up at Gabe, and then, as Gabe had done, began to kiss first his mouth and face, and then move slowly downward, scooching down the mattress as he did. He'd explored the man with his eyes, touched him, and now he was doing so with his mouth. The skin was so smooth and silky, yet it covered a body that was so hard. He reached a nipple, kissed it, then began to suck it, gently at first and then harder. Gabe cried out, and Todd felt goose bumps rocket over his arms and shoulders.

He released the nipple and moved under and over to suck in the other one. As Gabe moaned, gooseflesh again shot out over Todd, this time well down onto his back. *Yes!* he thought. *This is the way it's supposed to feel.* Making love to another human being is supposed to feel as good as having them make love to you.

Todd pushed up and guided Gabe so that the man fell on his back once more. Todd began to kiss and lick Gabe's entire pectoral, marveling at its size. It was so sexy. Gabe's chest was so strong. Pleasure washed over Todd and several times he thought he was about to cum, even though the only friction his leaping cock received was as it pressed against Gabe's body. He'd never felt like this before.

Todd kept moving down, feeling Gabe's hard cock rubbing his body and then finally, there it was, in Todd's face, straining those underwear, trying to get out. He pulled on the top of them, and down, and Gabe's erection burst out to meet him. The skin of his hard-on was stretched so tight it was shiny. The meaty head—circumcised, just like in Todd's dream—flared out much more than Todd's. It was very wet, and there was an enormous droplet of clear liquid balling up at its tip. After a second or so, it began to slowly slide down the thick shaft. The balls were large and hung low in a nearly hairless sack—*mine are so hairy compared to his.* Todd took them in his hand, holding the elastic band of the underwear back by catching it under them. He weighed and fondled them. Gabe moaned again. Shivers of pleasure continued to roll over Todd, and his toes curled tightly in response. So fucking hot. And then there was the scent of Gabe. It was so strong and rich. It was the smell of sweat and soap and precum. It was the smell of man.

Todd's mouth began to flood with saliva, and he knew the moment had come. He wouldn't chicken out this time. Wouldn't run. He had nothing to be afraid of. No reason to run. This was where he wanted to be and what he wanted to do.

He kissed the cock, wetting his lips in the precum. Gabe cried out in pleasure.

"Todd, are you sure?"

Todd laughed. "I'm sure," he said, and kissed it again. *It's so hot. Like it's on fire.* "Your cock is so warm," Todd said. And it was so hard. He kissed it again, and then stuck out his tongue and slowly licked the shaft. It was nothing like he'd expected. It tasted vaguely sweet and salty at the same time. He shut his eyes. *Do it,* he told himself. *You want to.*

Taste Gabe. Taste him like you've been taught.

Then Todd licked the shaft again, but this time he lapped up the new dollop of precum from the slash across the cock's tip. It was so thick and warm. Todd ran his tongue all over the large head, cleaning it thoroughly and covering it with spit. It was incredibly smooth. As smooth as glass. The flavor of Gabe's cock and natural lubrication saturated Todd's tongue and he groaned in pleasure. For one blazing moment, he once more thought he was going to cum, but somehow didn't. Then he opened wide and took the head in. Deep moans passed from both of them as for the first time in Todd's life, he took a penis into his mouth. Then, completely out of control, his head began to bob up and down on Gabe's cock and his hips began to thrust against

Gabe's leg. He couldn't stop. He rose higher and higher on the waves of sensation, and suddenly—

"Todd! Stop! I'm going to…!"

—both cocks exploded in orgasm, Gabe's cum jetting and filling Todd's mouth to overflowing and Todd's covering Gabe's muscular calf.

Todd thought he was passing out from the pleasure. The pleasure of cumming and the erotic sensation of Gabe's cock throbbing in his mouth—he could actually feel the semen jetting up its length—and then across his tongue, into his mouth, and before Todd even knew he was doing it, he was swallowing it down. He didn't even have time to register what had happened, no time to be afraid—only to absorb what he'd done afterward.

Never had anything felt so good, so sexy, so powerful, so… right.

Todd was feeling everything he'd ever wanted to feel.

As he collapsed, the heavy taste of Gabe blazing across his tongue—so thick and musky—the pounding of his heart, and his swimming in a sea of sensation, he knew that being with Gabe was what sex was supposed to feel like. Fantastic. It was everything his classmates had talked about. The earthquakes and fireworks were all there. He felt like he was floating on clouds.

This is why Joan had seemed so wrong to him. There wasn't anything wrong with her. Girls just weren't right for him. Straight men loved everything he had hated about her. The guys back home hadn't lied. They did like sex with women, and it wasn't boring to them, as hard as that was to believe. But the problem was that he had been with the wrong sex. Trying so hard not to be what his stepfather despised, he'd cut himself off from what he'd always needed. Sex was great.

He just needed to be with a man.

This was no choice. He hadn't chosen this.

This….

Todd grinned.

This had chosen him!

Somehow he found the strength to roll over onto his side and up into Gabe's muscular arms to snuggle onto his fabulous body. He felt so content. Suddenly the snow and the fact that he didn't have an apartment didn't seem important anymore. He didn't know what tomorrow would bring, but one thing he did know.

His life was finally beginning.

TODD woke up to Gabe's mouth. It surrounded his cock, and it was totally amazing. He moaned in pleasure and looked down on the incredible hotness of Gabe sucking him. Did anything in the universe look as sexy as that?

Then Gabe looked up at him, eyes filled with lust.

Now what? Todd wondered. And on the tail of that: *Bring it on.*

Gabe got the message and straddled him. He spit heavily into his hand and then reached behind him. *What's he doing?* Todd wondered, watching Gabe's chest and shoulder flex. Gabe's eyes were flickering, little gasps escaping his lips.

Todd's eyes widened when he got it. Just in time to feel Gabe sliding something down his cock. *Condom. He's putting a condom on me.* He'd no sooner acknowledged that when he felt his cock nudge and then force its way into Gabe. Gabe shut his eyes tight, stopped, gasped, gave a grunt, and then Todd's cock was surrounded, gripped by an incredible warmth.

So tight. My God—so tight.

They both cried out together and then Todd felt even more of himself slide into his lover.

My lover. Gabe is my lover!

Then Gabe's ass settled firmly against the base of Todd's cock. Gabe shifted and then laid his hands on Todd's chest, let his thumbs run through the patch of hair that grew there. "God I love your chest. The hair," Gabe said softly.

Todd laughed. "I love yours," he said. "I love how smooth it is."
Like the men in Todd's magazines. He laughed again. *How the fuck did
I deny this? How did I pretend I wasn't gay?*

("*It don't make no sense a boy your age having so many of these.
You a faggot or something?*")

He'd told his stepfather he just used the magazines for exercise
tips. Todd laughed again. *How did I not know?*

"What's so funny?" Gabe asked, looking down at him with those
country-sky-blue eyes.

"Nothing," Todd said. "I'm just happy."

Gabe grinned. "Then let's see what this does." And he began to
rise and fall, letting his ass grip and squeeze Todd's cock.

Todd thought he would die from the pleasure. He'd just cum—
well, who knew how long ago. A minute? Ten? An hour? He'd be
out—and yet he knew it wouldn't take long to cum a second time.

Gabe moaned, and God, he wasn't just doing this for Todd. Gabe
was enjoying it. It was making him feel good to fuck himself on Todd's
cock. Something about prostates? He'd read that, right? The one or two
times he'd dared skim a gay-sex story online.

Gabe was muttering to himself, moaning, bobbing ever faster,
those miles and miles of muscles shifting and flexing. Todd reached up,
grabbed those pecs, squeezed them, felt them move under his hands. *So
hot. So fucking hot.*

Gabe rode him longer and harder and faster, all of it somehow
lasting and lasting, and then finally Todd knew it was almost over. He
was going to orgasm again. "Gabe!" he cried and Gabe's eyes flew
open, looked down into Todd's, and he quickly grabbed his own cock.
Then Todd was cumming, and Gabe must have already been close
because with only a few strokes, long ropes of semen were jetting out
of him, rising and landing in long splashes on Todd's chest. It only
made Todd cum harder at the feeling and the sight.

His vision went black for a moment, and then, slowly, as the
orgasm quieted, Todd opened his eyes again to see wavering spots and

the face of his love. The man was looking at him with tired eyes and smiling and saying something... what was it?

"I love you, Todd."

The words were total joy.

"I love you too," Todd said.

Then they curled up together, and Todd drifted off with the tickle of Gabe's breath against his neck.

CHAPTER EIGHTEEN

THEY were at the five-story building that housed the storage lockers, and Todd was in heaven. It was a pleasure to watch. It was all Gabe could do not to laugh in joy.

Todd pointed at the rickety bed. "Will we need this?" he said, eyes sparkling.

Gabe knew he should say yes. According to that book Peter had given him about limerence, taking Todd to his bed could be a bad thing. Especially so fast. It was such a stereotypically lesbianish thing to do. One night of sex—some of the best sex he'd ever had but one of night of sex to be sure—was pretty fast to tell Todd to leave his own bed in storage.

But when he looked into Todd's beautiful face, those huge doelike eyes, Gabe knew he couldn't refuse him. And after all, they weren't getting rid of the bed. If worse came to worse, they could retrieve it.

But Gabe was going to go on instinct this time—going with what Peter had taught him. This wasn't just limerence. What he was feeling wasn't just some kind of uncontrolled state of mind. It was more than hormones. It was more than romantic attraction. This time he didn't need another person to return his feelings. He was just happy that it was true.

This was love. He had to believe that.

"Let's store the bed for now. Then think about making a guest room later."

"Just as long as you don't fall for any other strays," Todd said with a shy grin.

"I think I've fallen enough," Gabe answered. "Besides, it's time to have a spare room. I don't need all that space. And you need a place."

"No I don't," said Todd. "All I need is you."

Gabe walked up to him and gave him a kiss, not caring what the men unloading the big truck thought. "Yes, you do. Even if it is only to write up your recipes or something. A place to decorate just how you want. It was ridiculous for me to need a home office and workout space. They can all fit nicely."

Todd looked doubtful, but apparently wasn't going to argue.

"Besides," Gabe added, "this way if family comes to visit, they'll have a place to stay."

Todd's smile wavered. "I don't know about that."

Gabe held up a hand. "A drunken friend, then."

Todd smiled again and nodded. "Whatever you want."

Gabe pulled him tight and gave him an especially good kiss. "We. What we want."

Todd sighed happily and then ran back over to the truck to direct the movers. He was laughing over a very large toy spaceship—Gabe wasn't sure which one it was, only that it was from *Star Wars*—when Gabe got the call. When he pulled out the cell phone, he saw it was Peter. Now what could he want?

"Hey, Peter," he said after excusing himself and stepping away from Todd, who had just ordered his ugly coffee table to be taken into the storage building.

"Good day, Gabriel. And how art thou?"

Gabe smiled. He looked over at Todd, who was digging quickly through some boxes and then pointing to the building or to the side of the truck. Gabe had already let the men know they had two stops and not just one. They weren't happy until he handed them a hundred-dollar bill. That made them smile. Just how little had "William" Racine paid them?

Todd looked so happy. All for a bunch of used-up furniture.

But for want of a nail a war was lost? For want of his own personal, meaningful possessions, who knew what could have been lost?

"Actually, I am doing better than I have in a long time, Peter," he said.

"So you two decided to consummate things, did you?"

Gabe almost gasped, but somehow stopped it. How did Peter do it? Read his mind even over the phone.

"Say no more," Peter replied. "I am happy for you. I am sure this bodes well. There is nothing better or more precious than new love."

Gabe glanced over at Todd again, who was shaking his head at a small TV. Gabe stepped around the moving truck and whispered. "This feels so real, Peter. Can it be finally? Can this be it?"

"And whatever that love is, perhaps an illusion of a new love, I want it, I can't resist it, my whole being melts in one kiss, my knowledge melts, my fears melt, my blood dances, my legs open."

"Shitfire, Peter. Who is that?"

"Anaïs Nin. Who else? And yes, I think this could be the real thing. I think you know it too."

"I was wrong with Daniel. I was wrong with Brett."

"You loved them both, you did the right thing, you let go, you waited, you behaved just as you should have. But this is different. Toddy is different—"

"You know he doesn't like to be called that," Gabe said.

"—I feel good about him. Don't you?"

"I do, Peter."

He stepped back from around the truck. Todd had a funny look on his face. Was everything okay?

"We must celebrate."

"That would be nice, Peter." And it would. Peter would come up with something amazing and Todd needed some amazement in his life. Lots of it. Tons and tons.

"What are you two doing tonight?"

"Well, Todd has something in mind. Some special dinner he's cooking."

"Excellent! Perfect, in fact. You must invite me!"

Todd was looking through some drawers. He didn't look good.

"Peter. I might have to go…."

"What time do you wish me to arrive?"

"Peter, I think Todd had something romantic in mind." Todd was starting to throw things on the ground. Socks. Underwear.

"Gabriel. Trust me. You want me to show up. Do not doubt. My presence is called for."

"Seven, then. I have to go." And he hung up and dashed over to Todd. "Baby! Are you okay?"

"No! I'm not okay," Todd cried. He was shaking.

"What is it? Tell me."

"Money," Todd said. "My money."

Money? "I thought you said you were broke."

Todd began to go through the drawers again. "This was special. My most magic money. The stuff I was saving for my most important dreams. It wasn't a lot. Three hundred dollars. Not enough for a month's rent. But it was all I had. It was wrapped up in some black socks and in the back of this drawer." He yanked it out. Waved the clunky thing in the air.

"Are you sure?" Gabe asked. *Oh, Todd. Not another piece of bad luck.*

"I'm sure," he shouted.

Gabe spun on the movers, who were standing back, mouths open, hands raised before them. "We didn't take nuttin'," the biggest of them said. "Honest Injun."

"Oh, Gabe! I wanted to do something for you with that money," Todd sobbed.

Gabe took a step to him, laid a hand on his arm. "Todd, it will be okay."

"No. No it won't."

"Todd," he barked, sorry that he was so harsh. But he had to get through.

Todd stopped, looked up at him.

"It will be fine. We are fine. Money means nothing. We have each other now. Do you hear me? I would rather be homeless and be with you than rich and be without you."

Todd froze. His eyes grew soft. "Really?"

Gabe pulled him into his arms. "Really."

Todd laid his head on Gabe's shoulder. He trembled once but didn't cry. Good. There was no more room for tears.

Then he got an idea. He looked over Todd's shoulder at the moving men. "Question," he said.

"Shoot, boss."

"When you moved the dresser down all those stairs, did you take the drawers out?"

The men looked at each other, a skinny one nodded, and then the big one answered. "Yeah. It was heavy."

So they could have dropped a rolled up sock.

Or....

He grinned.

"Do you know if you put them back in the same slot?"

The big guy shrugged. "We put 'em where they fit."

Todd raised his head. Looked up at Gabe with hope on his face, then back at the dresser. He walked up to the drawer he'd been looking through. "This isn't the right one," he said. He walked over to the left and pulled out the second one down. "Oh... oh, oh...." He rummaged through it and then let out a shout. In his hand was a rolled up pair of black socks. He quickly unrolled it, not caring how he did it, and then froze, a look of happiness on his face.

Todd turned to Gabe, smiling. In his hand was a small roll of money.

GABE was trying to help Todd in the kitchen when the phone rang. He was surprised to see who it was. "Hey, Tracy," Gabe said after excusing himself and stepping away from Todd, who had just pulled a roast out of the refrigerator. It was in a big deep casserole dish and seemed to be marinating in something.

"Hi, Gabriel. Um...."

Um? Tracy said "Um?" She might as well have said "shit" or "damn" it was so uncharacteristic. She was constantly on any team member who used the word. She said it sounded like weakness. If there was one thing Tracy wasn't, it was weak.

Gabe was getting a bad feeling already.

"What is it, Tracy? I'm kind of busy." He looked over at Todd, who was looking in one of the cabinets and pulling out some spice bags, as well as what looked like peanuts. No. Was that shelled pistachios?

"It.... Well...." Again, Tracy was being totally uncharacteristic. Hesitating wasn't within her killer style. Funny that she could move in for the kill but wouldn't swear. "You don't have to be trailer trash to be successful," she would tell him. "And swearing is tacky."

"Spit it out, Tracy."

There was a pause. "Only if you promise not to hate me," she said.

Gabe counted to ten. "You know I don't like to promise," he said through gritted teeth. This was getting worse. And something told him it was about Todd.

"You make promises all the time," she said. "Most of which you can't possibly keep."

"Wrong, Tracy. Most of them are promises people think I can't keep. But I always do."

"Then promise."

Gabe sighed. "Okay. I promise."

Another pause. "It's about your friend. Todd."

Gabe shut his eyes. Rubbed them. Of course. He'd known it. Hadn't he known it? "What about him?" he said, trying not to growl.

"Todd Burton, that's his name, right? From a town called Buckman? Graduated two years ago?"

Gabe froze. "Yes," he said stiffly.

"Gabriel, you promised."

"I also said I don't like to make them." He glanced over at Todd again, who was now placing the roast in a big roasting pan.

"You have the best-stocked kitchen! I just love it," Todd cried.

Gabe stepped out of the kitchen and moved down the hall and dropped his voice to a harsh whisper. "What is it, Tracy?"

"Well...." She cleared her throat. "This would be so much easier if we were face to face. Where are you?"

"It wouldn't be easier," Gabe said. "Tell me."

"Mother skeeter!" One last pause and then she plunged on. "I did a little background check on him—"

"You what?" Gabe asked, barely keeping from shouting. Tracy did a background check on Todd?

"Yes. And I found some interesting stuff."

I don't want to know. Damn you, Tracy. He began to pace.

"And Gabriel. There's nothing bad, okay? I'm not calling to tell you 'I told you so.'"

Gabe stopped in place. Held his breath.

"I mean, from the little I've found so far, he seems like a great kid. He's never been in trouble. Not even a parking ticket, let alone for speeding. He did really well in school. In fact his principal said he volunteered every year for all the school events. Food drives. All kinds of things. This guy is squeaky clean. The only bad thing about this boy is his credit. It *was* good, but in the last few months it's gone to heck and back."

Gabe let out a sigh of relief. For one horrible second there, he had actually feared Tracy might say something that would change everything. He so believed in Todd. He had no reason to. Not really. He didn't *really* know him. Couldn't figure him out. Couldn't de-code Todd like he did with people when he was going into a business situation. But that instinct had told him Todd was a good man.

"But there's more, Gabriel. I think if I hadn't found out this shit I might not have called."

Gabe froze. Shit? Had Tracy said "shit"? Now she had his attention.

"Seems like there just might be something weird going on with the parents. Didn't you say this kid didn't have any money? That he was flat-out broke?"

Gabe nodded. Then: "Yes."

Tracy cleared her throat. "Well, he shouldn't be. And it's more than that. Wait until you hear this...."

Gabe listened and couldn't believe what he was hearing. It was good news. Very good news. Unbelievably good news.

"Thank you, Tracy," he said when they were finished. "And you'll check up on those other things?"

"Already in the process," she said.

Of course, he thought. She was Tracy, wasn't she? Tracy-Mega-Efficient-Creighton? "Thanks again."

"Not mad, then?"

Gabe shook his head. "You're lucky it all came to this. I would have been pissed as hell if it had been anything else. I should still be pissed. But this might be the answer to all of Todd's prayers. I can't be mad at you."

"Thanks, Gabriel. I only did it because I love you."

"I love you too," he said, and hung up.

"You love *who* too?" Todd said, an eyebrow raised.

"Tracy. It's just Tracy," Gabe said, chuckling. He liked Todd's possessiveness. Daniel never had a shred of it. It was nice to be wanted.

"And this is a female Tracy, right?" Todd asked.

"Yes, baby. No worries."

"Yeah, well, that's good," Todd said.

SHIT, Todd thought to himself. *What am I gonna do with all this?* He turned and looked up into his lover's eyes. "Look at this, Gabe. This roast I bought the other day. It's enough to feed an army. I'd planned on getting lamp chops but got this joint of lamb instead. We'll have leftovers for days."

Gabe's eyes went wide, and he bit his lower lip. *Something's wrong*, Todd thought. *Is he mad I bought too much lamb? The price was so good.*

"Shit," Gabe said.

"Did I do something wrong?" Todd asked.

Gabe shook his head. "Baby...."

Baby. He liked the sound of that.

Gabe pulled out a kitchen chair and sat down. He patted his big thigh. "Sit down."

"I'm too heavy."

"Ridiculous. Sit down in my lap."

Oh, just look at those eyes, Todd thought and felt his dick stir. *Oh, the things you do to me.* He got an idea. Gave his man a wicked grin and then crawled up into his lap, straddling him.

"Uh oh," Gabe said.

"No uh oh," Todd said and kissed him.

Gabe laughed. Kissed him back. "And that is what I was about to say to you. I don't want you to ask me if you did anything wrong, okay? You couldn't do anything wrong. We might make mistakes, but we're building a foundation right now, and the key is just to talk things through."

"Okay." Todd's cock finished its climb to erection. He pushed it against Gabe's belly.

"Uh oh," Gabe said again.

Todd dropped his head back and chuckled.

"Todd, I already forgot to tell you something, and now you are going to make me forget again." He grabbed Todd's ass and squeezed it.

Todd felt shivers. Sooner or later he was going to have to find out about his prostate and see if it felt as good to be fucked as Gabe made it look. Of course, Gabe's cock was a whole lot bigger than his. Could a human being even take such a big thing? Todd began to rub his cock against Gabe's flat, strong belly.

"Todd! I have to tell you something," Gabe said.

Todd pouted. "What?"

"You have to promise not to be too disappointed."

Todd narrowed his eyes. *Disappointed?* "What?" he asked.

"Peter invited himself over for dinner tonight."

Todd slumped in Gabe's arms. "Gabe," he whimpered. "I wanted this to be about us."

"I know. But he seemed to think it was important. And I've learned not to argue with Peter when he's insistent. Forgive me? I'll make it up to you, I promise."

Todd looked into those sweet eyes and knew he couldn't deny Gabe anything. "It's okay. We have a lifetime of special nights, right?" he asked. *Right? Tell me I'm right.*

"A whole lifetime," Gabe said. "We can have a special afternoon if you want." Gabe grinned at him lasciviously.

Todd felt his cock pulse. "You let me put that roast in the oven and you got it. After all, I want it to be perfect. Peter Wagner is coming to dinner!"

THE loving was amazing. Gabe did things to him that he'd never imagined people did. Hot things. Naughty things. Sucked his toes. Licked his hole. Gabe had actually licked his asshole. Who'd a thought people did that? Thank God he'd showered.

And oh, it had felt good. So good.

Then Gabe did magic things with his fingers. Very magic things.

At first it had been a little uncomfortable. It had made Todd feel like he had to go to the bathroom. But Gabe assured him that: a) that was normal, and b) his fingers were up inside Todd and he could tell Todd did not, in fact, have to go to the bathroom.

"Just relax," he told Todd. "Relax."

Two fingers had turned into three and then God, four after that. He felt huge back there and wild. Crazy wild. *Oh, my God, wild!* Something amazing was sending little shocks all through him, up his spine and down his arms and through his fingertips. It made his scalp tingle and his toes curl and *God, oh God, it felt good!*

Then Gabe pulled him into arms, curled him up like a baby and kissed him, and Gabe did more things with his fingers, playing deep into his ass. "Oh God," Todd panted. "What are you doing?"

"Making you feel good," Gabe panted into his ear. "Making you feel really good."

Todd felt like he was crawling out of his skin, but it was good. So good. His heart was leaping and his cock was like steel and he felt like he would cum if Gabe did it any more. "So close," he said. "I am so close."

"Are you ready? Do you want to?" Gabe asked him.

"Is-is th-this wha-what it f-feels like to be fucked?" Todd stuttered.

Gabe chuckled. "My cock can't tickle you like this—" and Gabe wiggled his fingers.

"Oh God," Todd cried.

"—but it can feel good. And I can't get any closer to you than having my cock inside you. But you have to be sure, Todd."

They looked into each other's eyes.

"There's no going back, Todd."

Todd thought he would get lost in those eyes. He wanted to. "I don't want to go back," he said.

Gabe kissed him again, deep and slow, their tongues slowly caressing, breathing into each other's mouths.

Gabe slowly pushed Todd onto his tummy, gently urged his legs apart, and ran his fingers up and down Todd's crack, teasing his balls, teasing his hole, slipping one inside and gently massaging his prostate. Todd thought he would die.

Then Gabe was reaching for a drawer in his bedside table, pulling out a foil-wrapped package. "Do you have to use that?" Todd asked.

"Yes," Gabe answered.

"I want all of you in me. No plastic. You. And I want you to cum inside me."

"I do too," Gabe replied gently. "But not this time. I am pretty sure I'm negative, but I want to test clear a little longer."

"I trust you," Todd said. *With my life.*

"But I don't know if I trust my body," Gabe said. "Brett had sex without condoms. Daniel had sex with him. I know they used condoms the time I caught them, but I don't know if that was their first time. I can't trust a thing Daniel said. If he cheated with Brett, who else did he cheat with?"

"Oh...," Todd moaned sadly.

"And Joan cheated on you. Who knows if it was just once? We need to be sure."

Todd sighed.

"Don't be sad, my love."

His love. I'm his love.

"We can make love without condoms one day. When we know we won't hurt each other. When we know we want only each other."

Todd rolled on his side. "Do you think I could possibly want anyone but you?"

Once again they locked eyes. "I can't imagine wanting anyone but you," Gabe said. "I know I'm not in love with being in love this time. I am in love with you. But we'll wait. *Because* I love you."

"Then do you mind waiting?" Todd asked with a tear in his eye. "Can we wait to do that again until we don't have to use them?"

"If that's what you want," Gabe said. "If that's what you want."

So they kissed, and Gabe placed his fingers deep in Todd again and coaxed the most powerful orgasm out of Todd that he'd ever known. Todd was gripping Gabe's cock by then, and he came seconds after Todd, spilling himself in Todd's hands and on his belly.

I'm in love, was the last thing Todd thought as he drifted off to sleep, tangled with his lover.

CHAPTER **NINETEEN**

THERE was a ring of the intercom, and when Gabe went to answer it, it was Peter. He buzzed the man in, and Todd flew about the kitchen making his last minute preparations. The wine was out and ready to open, room temperature, not chilled like the Schwartzbeeren. Gabe had run to the store to find something right—two bottles. It was a red wine called malbec—Todd had never heard of it. But if the liquor store clerk was right, from his description, it would go perfect with dinner. Maybe some afterward.

Gabe answered the door right at the knock, and when he opened it, Todd noticed him freeze. *Now what's that about?* Todd wondered.

"Peter?" Gabe asked, surprise in his voice. Maybe something else as well?

"Yes, my boy. And I brought a guest."

A guest? Oh for God's sake, Todd thought. *Does Peter do this kind of thing all the time? Thank goodness the roast is so big. But there isn't enough dessert. I could cut one in half. It would be small portions....*

"I hope you don't mind," Peter was saying. "I ventured a guess that if Todd could make his chicken dinner stretch for three, he could make a dinner for three work out for four."

Todd stepped out of the kitchen, towel in hand, and then his mouth fell open in near horror. Standing just to Peter's left and one step back was Izar Goya.

No. Oh, no. How could he? Not her. Peter!

She was carrying a small box, and when she turned to Todd, she gave a nod and said, "I don't know what you've prepared, but I hope this will make a good dessert. Or you can save it for later. It's from the Jatetxea. I made it this morning."

Dessert made by Izar Goya herself? Todd couldn't believe it. Somehow, it shocked him enough to make him step forward and take it. "Thank you."

"I believe you two have met already," Peter said with an amused raise of his brow. "Not on good terms I understand, but I trust this evening will be better. Let's pretend this is the first time you have ever met, shall we?"

Izar nodded. She wasn't classically beautiful; she could disappear in a crowd of nondescript people if she wanted to—at least before she started to become a local celebrity. She had long thick hair, a brown so dark it might as well be black, and large dark-brown eyes. Her chin was perhaps a bit too narrow and her teeth might not be perfectly straight. But standing there, she felt like a force of nature to Todd. He had to admit she scared him. She pursed her full lips and responded to Peter's challenge. "Thank you for having me in your home," she replied, her voice deep and musical.

"Izar Goya?" Peter replied. "This is Todd Burton, the young man who so impressed me. And this is Gabriel Richards, the master of this domicile. Toddy? Gabriel? Izar Goya."

It was all Todd could do not to bow.

"We're pleased to have you here," Gabe said and flashed Todd a sympathetic look. *I'm sorry*, those eyes said.

Todd only shook his head. *Not your fault.*

They took their guests' coats and Gabe led them to the couch. "May I get you a cocktail?" Gabe asked as Todd put the coats away and dashed back into the kitchen. "If you like them, a Manhattan would go perfectly with what Todd has prepared."

A Manhattan goes with lamb? Todd knew he would have never known that. Since he couldn't really drink, except for what he and his Buckman friends had kyped from their parents' liquor cabinets, how would he have known something like that? Thank God Gabe knew. Izar Goya was here. Everything had to be right.

Izar Goya is here. For dinner. My dinner? Ohmygawd. He peered in the oven at the roast, knowing it would be ready any minute. But did he dare slice it to see before bringing it to the table? Of course not. Meat needs to rest after it comes out of the heat to redistribute the juices He couldn't. Plus, presentation was everything. But what if it was dry? What if it was overcooked?

Well, it's too late to worry about that, he answered himself.

Leap. Trust your instincts. Isn't that what Gabe always does?

He made the last preparations for the appetizer by spreading the cranberry pesto over fresh organic goat cheese atop some fancy crackers and further decorating the plate with a few dried berries. The frozen ones just weren't pretty enough, and he'd decided they might be too mushy. Fresh berries were just not available this time of year, even though their season had barely passed. And it was a pretty plate if he did say so himself.

("Can't you just make a goddamn burger or a friggin' meatloaf? What is this supposed to be?")

It's something classy, you ass, he thought. *Something you wouldn't know anything about.*

There wasn't a lot (he'd originally only planned for two) but when he brought the plate out and laid it on the coffee table there were enough "oohs" and "aahs" that the hated voice of his stepfather vanished in an instant, like ashes being blown away in a breeze. Then, to Todd's delight, they each took some and the pleasant noises continued. Did this mean he did well? He had made a few changes in the recipe he'd found months ago, especially by using dried fruit.

Todd went back to the kitchen to get the lamb out of the oven. It looked beautiful, and he hoped the crushed pistachio crust would taste as he imagined. His mouth began to water as the aroma hit him full in the face. He covered it with the glass lid and called everyone in for dinner, the small appetizers already gone.

Soup was their first course, a chunky tomato that not only complemented the appetizer in appearance, but started taking the taste buds to a different place as well. Again, the portions were small, but he wanted there to be room for the lamb. It wasn't quite what he'd hoped for, but again, it was the wrong time of year for really good tomatoes. Luckily the grocery store that Cody had taken him to had some grown in a hothouse. Maybe he was just being picky?

Peter cried out in poetry over it, and Todd couldn't help but be pleased. "Ah, Gabriel, thou art a lucky man having this prince to feed you every day." The lanky man stopped, tilted his head toward his friend and employee, and said: "I trust the couch has gone back to its traditional usage and Todd will be cooking for you for some time to come? I do sense that in the air? Love? *L' amour? Liebe? Alofa?*"

Of course, Todd blushed, but when he turned to glance at his lover, he saw Gabe beaming at him, l'amour pouring from his eyes. That made Todd's eyes grow wet, and he knew there was no hiding what was happening between them. A quick look at Izar showed she was busy with her course, and politely doing nothing to embarrass her hosts.

When they were finished, Todd brought out the roast, placed on a fancy platter he'd discovered on top of the kitchen cabinets. He drizzled the natural juices over top and was thrilled to see the meat was practically falling apart, and proud that he'd managed to transfer it without a mishap. Then he served the couscous, which he'd finished with some lightly pan-toasted pine nuts while Gabe cleared the table of the first course. The grain cooked almost instantly, so it had to be prepared at the last minute, and he hoped the nuts gave it a little crunch, again complementing the crust on the lamb. At least he hoped it did.

As with the rest of the meal, Peter used poetry and uncredited quotes to describe his feelings (and compliments)—"If more of us valued food and cheer above hoarded gold, it would be a much merrier world!"—and Gabe simply glowed. Todd was starting to think he could have done no wrong with his new love, though. The feeling was incredible. Like coming home.

Goya, on the other hand, said little to nothing. It was driving Todd insane. It was like he was being interviewed for God's sake.

But at least Todd liked the meal. No. Despite his nervousness, he loved every bite (including the soup), and it was all he could do not to scrape the roasting pan for more of the lamb-sautéed pistachios.

The wine was a perfect fit, just as the liquor store clerk had claimed. It was plummy and reminded Todd of some dark berry pie with clove and maybe some vanilla. Not overly sweet like the Schwartzbeeren, but far more subtle, going well with the crust of the lamb and the couscous.

Todd watched nervously through the whole meal. Goya did seem to be enjoying herself, but was she? Was she just being polite? After all, she was in their home.

Their? Todd smiled despite his nervousness. He was saying "their home," if only to himself. He was absorbing all of this: what had happened in less than a week, falling in love, the miracle of love returned—love from another man—and now simple things, like them working together to make a good meal.

And their guests treated them like a couple. A real couple. They were two men, and by the grace of God—or something out there—they were a couple. More than once, Gabe had reached over and placed his hand over Todd's. No eye blinked, at least not in derision or shock. The sparkle in Peter's eyes could not be missed. More often than not, Todd's heart was pounding. Would it always feel like this? Would it last?

Goya did share a tale of her childhood. Apparently, cooking and the kitchen were not the traditional domain for Basque women. Men did the cooking. They cooked for their family and wives, for friends, or happily, themselves. But on certain days, a woman was allowed, and once, when she was just a girl, her father had let her cook with him.

"I was so happy," she recalled, real emotion filling her face. "Just to be with him in the kitchen, let alone helping him cook. I had always wanted to cook, but that wasn't a girl thing."

Todd sighed. "And here, my stepfather claimed that cooking isn't a boy thing. He made such fun of me. Wanted to know why I couldn't just make a meatloaf, if I had to be a fag."

Gabe flinched at the word, and Todd turned to give him a silent apology.

"Your father is a foolish man," Izar said, and Todd stifled a gasp. Was that a compliment?

"*Step*father," he corrected.

"Anyway," she replied. "Something magical happened that day. Everything came natural to me, and my *aita*, my father, noticed. Soon we were wordlessly dancing around each other, fingers touching spices and cutting vegetables, and feeding each other as we did so. I remember it like it was yesterday, although I am sure that the years have colored that day with more romance than might have actually been there. On the other hand, from that day forward I was always welcome in my father's kitchen. My life had been changed forever."

Todd smiled happily. He knew just what she meant, and when they locked eyes, he saw that she was acknowledging a shared experience. Magic.

They decided to go with Goya's dessert. It was simply polite, and Todd had only prepared enough for two anyway. The other choice was three pieces of cheesecake from The Cheesecake Factory that Gabe had gotten when he went out for wine.

The dessert was miraculous, of course. It resembled a buttery rich shortbread, and once tasted, revealed a subtle almond-flavored filling. Izar called it *gâteau* Basque, a traditional Basque dessert. It was simply irresistible.

It makes my food taste like cardboard, Todd thought.

But when they were done and had decided they were going to have coffee instead of more wine, Goya dabbed at her mouth with a napkin, leaned back in her chair, crossed her legs, and said...

"What a wonderful repast."

Todd almost missed her words. He'd been busy noticing that Gabe was using the coffee beans from The Shepherd's Bean. Todd saw on the brown paper bag that it was the Kenyan variety he'd tried the other day. *It'll be the perfect ending for the meal*, he was thinking, when Goya's words sank in.

Todd's mouth fell open.

"It's too bad you didn't stand up to me," she said, eyebrows disappearing into her dark bangs.

"Stand up to you?" Todd asked.

She gave a very short nod. "Yes. You gave up too easily. When you were so audacious to ask me to teach you to cook. You fled like a frightened child when I refused you. It's too bad for both of us. Who knows where you and I could have progressed by now?"

Todd's mouth fell open again. *What? What was she saying?*

"You need teaching—yes. But after this evening, had I not known already, I would never have guessed you have no teaching. The lamb was juicy and so tender I barely had to use my knife. The pistachios were a wonderful idea and suited the entrée perfectly. The tomato soup was good. Just a dash too much salt perhaps, and maybe just a bit more coriander? But perhaps not. Close. Very close. I liked the pine nuts with the couscous and the sultanas were an excellent touch. The average customer would have called it perfect. But what could we do if we experimented together? Would you like to learn with me, Mr. Burton?"

Todd clenched his jaw to keep his mouth from falling open again. "Y-you're serious?"

"Quite," she said. "If you say yes, I think we could have quite an adventure ahead of us."

"Yes," Todd all but shouted. "Y-yes! Of course!"

She smiled. "Most excellent. But you would have to promise me something."

"Anything," Todd squealed.

"You must stand up to me," she replied, eyes turning to steel. "Argue your point if you believe in what you are doing. And there is nothing more important than believing."

Argue with Izar Goya? How? But that look on her face. She meant it.

"Yes," he said. "I will."

"Then a new chapter of our lives is about to begin, *nire lagun berria*, my new friend."

THEY retired to the living room, where Gabe already had a fire blazing. Outside it was snowing again, huge flakes, like puffs of cottonwood. No moon, but Todd knew how it would look. He'd seen it just the night before while kissing his lover in that tiny silver car.

Peter told more tales and soon had Goya talking of home, growing up in Basque country. And of marrying and coming to the United States. Of her husband's early death, and how she'd taken the insurance money and opened her jatetxea.

Todd told them about making pancakes for his mom on Mother's Day, but not about throwing them away. Goya loved the story and said it was proof he was thinking of the palate when he was but a child. That he had a gift for it.

"This is a marvelous young man," Peter said. "He's changed so just in a few days. He's had a terrible time and somehow endured. You remind me of something," said Peter.

"Oh?" Todd asked. More poetry? Who knew with Peter? But he couldn't help but hold his breath in anticipation.

"Yes," Peter replied. "There is a moth. It lives in the coldest of places. *Gynaephora groenlandica*, I believe."

He believed? Todd almost laughed. Peter didn't "believe." He knew exactly the right word and name.

"They live under the harshest conditions, sometimes in areas that drop to as low as minus sixty degrees Celsius. Can you imagine? And we thought it got cold here in Kansas City. It is one of the longest lived of the lepidoptera on this planet. Its caterpillar is known as the Artic Woolly Bear—I dearly love that name!—and takes somewhere between seven and fourteen years to reach its full adulthood. Amazing!

Imagine. A fourteen year old caterpillar. It gets frozen solid for as long as ten or eleven months at a time. Frozen. Solid!" Peter laughed. "There are only a couple of months in the height of summer that Mother Nature allows them to defrost so they can grow. Finally, after all that time, they spin a cocoon of silk, and a few days later—only a few days!—they emerge as moths."

Peter took a drink of his coffee before continuing.

"Think of that, Toddy. Think of your hard years, think of them as hibernation. Think of them as your frozen years, where there were only short times when you could be free and grow. Then you spun your cocoon. You came here. And finally, you emerged as the man you are today. Transformed by so many things—chance, belief, love—into something new and glorious. Of course, you are much lovelier than the Arctic moth. It is rather plain. But not you. And somehow, I think you are ready to make a much bigger impression on this world. We will have to see if the world is ready for you, Todd Burton. I dare hope it is."

The words stunned Todd into speechlessness. He thought he would cry. Struggled not to. Not with Goya here.

Then Peter changed the subject, as he was wont to do. He "shuffled through his memories" and told stories that had them laughing. Tales of frolicking youth, and tales of watching the next generations frolic as well.

It was a lovely evening. What company they shared. Who ate dinner with Izar Goya, after all? She was only one of Kansas City's most famous chefs. And after all, who sat around spending an evening with Peter Wagner—who Todd was just discovering was not only wealthy, not only extremely wealthy, but actually one of the richest men in the country. Gabe thought he was in the top one hundred. What was really cool was that Peter had done it himself. He'd been born into privilege, yes, but it was his ideas, his business sense and investments, that had catapulted his family's money to its present wealth. What blew Todd away was that most of Peter's investments were in people. Musicians, artists, writers, people with ideas and no real venture capital to get them off the ground. Peter provided that capital. Then when those people became successful, Peter was invested in them. In dreams.

And those people became connections that helped Peter help other people. Peter had once helped Izar start her restaurant. And here she was now helping Todd.

A circle. Putting money and time and resources into circulation.

It was simply amazing. Just *like* magic.

So, no. It hadn't been the quiet evening for two Todd had imagined. But there would be a lifetime of romantic evenings. Somehow he knew it. A lifetime.

CHAPTER *TWENTY*

GABE woke to find himself curled around Todd, the young man's back to him. He had his arm around Todd and with a happy smile, pulled him closer. He loved Todd's size. Not a small man, but just small enough that Gabe could cradle him in his arms. He certainly wasn't small anywhere else.

Happy. I'm so happy. He never thought he could be so happy. And all for helping a kid get out of the snow.

What if I hadn't?

What if I hadn't gone down for the mail and seen he was still in the lobby?

What if Todd hadn't pretended to be my boyfriend and the building super hadn't brought him here to see if it were true?

All for want of a place to get out of the cold. All for the fact that he'd let Todd in, not only in out of the cold, but deep into his heart.

Just a week ago I was alone. A week. The world can change so much in one single week!

Todd stirred, wiggled closer, his sweet, round, furry butt back against Gabe's crotch. *Oh be careful, baby. You'll make me want you.*

As if he didn't already want Todd every minute of the day.

Sure enough, Gabe's cock began to rise and Gabe had to shift his ass back, pull his crotch away from the sweetness of that bottom, to help calm the beast.

Why did I promise to wait until we can fuck without condoms?

Todd stirred again, slipped his hand in Gabe's, and he took it, smoothly and easily. *Don't wake him up. Let him sleep.*

Gabe loved the sound of Todd's breathing. *So alive, this man in my arms.*

Love you, Todd.

Such a miracle. So many miracles. That they'd found each other in this cold, cold world. Two people alone and hurting.

Please let this be real. It's gotta be real.

But he knew it was, at least for himself. Now he just had to wait and find out if it was real for Todd. First times could be powerful, heady stuff. It could feel like love when it was often just that wonderfully drunken feeling that came from mutual chemistry and such great sex. Gabe felt his cock stir again at just the thought. *Dammit. Think of something else.*

So he turned his thoughts to work, and immediately he remembered Tracy's call from the night before.

He could have told Todd about it, but there was so much more going on. He didn't want to tell Todd in the midst of his panic about dinner. Then there was the wondrous revelation of Izar announcing she was willing to teach Todd. How excited Todd had been, and justifiably so. Gabe was proud of him, excited for him. No. He couldn't. The night had been too good. Why destroy it with uncertainty? The information Tracy had stumbled on could be a big deal, but first there was all kinds of information that needed to be gathered. So much unresolved. So many things to check up on. He didn't want to start something before he knew all the facts. There was no telling how Todd would react. Wait to say anything. That's what his business sense told him.

But Todd wasn't "business." Todd was a person, a man he loved. A human being with feelings.

But in this case, it was best to consider this business. Gabe would know more soon. Tracy was on it and she moved fast. Left little or nothing to chance. She didn't believe in chance, only facts. That, among other things, is what made her such an asset.

I'll wait.

I should get up. Go into the office. Do what I'm paid for. Get the details of what's going on with Todd if nothing else. And dammit. See what's going on with the AbledRides account.

But do I tell Todd what Tracy found out?

No. You've already made up your mind on this. Best wait.

Yes. Wait until you have all the info. That's the ticket.

TODD woke up with Gabe curled up behind him. He felt like a peanut in a shell and couldn't remember when anything had made him feel so safe.

He slipped his hand in under Gabe's—it was so much bigger than his own—and in his sleep, Gabe grasped his fingers.

Let him sleep. This is nice.

Protected. Yes. That is what it was. Todd felt protected. Nothing could hurt him now. Not really. Not when he had this man in his life.

Does this make me "the girl"?

Then he remembered Gabe—mountain of masculinity that he was—sitting down on his cock.

Gabe liked having my cock inside him. He liked it a lot. So did I!

No. I am not the girl. And Gabe wouldn't want me if I was. Gabe wants me. Todd felt his cock stir at the thought. *We are two men who want each other. We want men. Wow. Gorgeous. Intelligent. Successful*—normal. *He's not sick, not disturbed, not a freak. He isn't interested in children. He wants a man. He wants me.*

"Baby?" *Gabe. He's awake.*

Todd turned in his lover's arms, over onto his back, and looked up at Gabe.

"I need to go to work. I missed all day yesterday."

"I don't want you to go." Todd pretended to pout. It was hard not to giggle, though, despite the fact that he *really* did mean what he was saying. "I want you to stay here with me. Want to make love." And he did. His cock began lengthening as if in witness to the thought. Or proof of it.

"Oh, my," said Gabe, noticing. "Damn. I guess we have time for a quickie."

Todd stuck out his lip playfully again. "No. I want a long time or I'll wait until later."

But then Gabe was sucking his cock and his intentions were tossed to the wind.

TODD showered and padded naked to the kitchen for coffee. Amusing. The only place he'd ever really been comfortable naked before was his secret place in the woods. A week ago he would have never been able to walk through the apartment naked. Why, he wasn't sure. It wasn't like anyone would see him.

But a lot had changed, hadn't it? He had done some transforming.

What had Peter said? That he was like a moth? There was no way Todd could remember the scientific name, but it had been an Arctic moth. One that survived for months frozen in ice and took years to reach maturity. That was him, wasn't it? It was like he'd been frozen, unable for one reason or another to change.

But change he had.

Wasn't it crazy he was denying he was a "faggot" a week ago, and now he was practically begging Gabe to have sex with him? More, to make love with him?

Crazy world. And oh how one could change and how fast they could change, even if they didn't want to.

He hadn't wanted to. He'd fought it. As a matter of fact, he'd slapped on some blinders besides. Super Glued them on. He could only marvel at how blind he'd been.

How did I not know?

All those muscle magazines. His downloading of underwear ads. How he'd told himself it was just shopping, that he was just planning on the day he could afford them. It was just underwear, he'd told himself. Just underwear. But if that were true, then why hadn't he been satisfied with tighty-whiteys from Walmart? Why save pictures of beautiful men with big bulges in expensive underwear? Especially the mesh one where you could see their penises? He was never going to buy, let alone wear, anything like them.

What about his aversion to Joan's body? All women's naked bodies? Why hadn't that been a clue?

And most men liked women. Liked them a lot. He supposed that was a good thing, otherwise what would happen to the human species? But it was also good to finally know what was wrong all these years. There wasn't a damn thing wrong with women. They were just wrong for him.

How had he not known he was gay? It was insane!

Why hadn't his experience with Austin told him? It had been—up until then, that is—the most exciting sexual experience in his life. Why oh why hadn't he put two and two together?

You did. But you were still afraid of what your stepfather would think.

And now it's the last thing I care about—he's *the last thing I care about.*

I am gay.

I have a man *who loves me.*

I am working for Izar Goya.

I've got it all!

And he owed it all to Gabe. A sweet, gentle giant who had let him in out of the cold.

If there was only something he could do to thank him. But what?

Just like that, the name "Chaz" popped into his head.

And just like that, he had the answer.

TRACY wasn't at the office when Gabe got to work. Strange, she always beat him there. Sometimes he teased her and said she had an army cot in her office and never went home. She'd shuddered at the idea.

"Me on an army cot! Can you imagine?"

The truth was, no, he couldn't.

So when he didn't see her an hour later, he called her on her cell phone.

She answered right away. "Yo!" she said.

"Where are you?" he asked, first thing.

"Well good morning to you too," she said cheerfully.

"Good morning," he replied, exasperation shading his words. There was a lot on his mind, most of it this business with Todd. And despite the lovemaking of the night before, he'd still had dreams ghosted with everything she had told him so far and all she had yet to find. "Where are you?"

"Buckman," she replied matter-of-factly, as if she went there every day.

"Buckman?" he asked. Todd's hometown.

"Yup. I brought Wilfred Cooper with me—"

Wilfred Cooper? Gabe wondered. From Peter's lawyer firm—Baily, Cranston and Watch? Well of course, he realized. That made perfect sense now that he thought about it.

"—and we've already discovered whole bunches of interesting stuff."

TODD found the young man in the park—he hardly had to look at all.

His sidekick Doug was nowhere to be seen. Turning a trick perhaps? At least it was a beautiful day, in the upper forties. Just like Kansas City: it could snow heavily one day and be halfway to melted the next. Chaz couldn't be too cold.

"Well, look at Miss Thang!" Chaz crooned when he spotted Todd. He walked up to Todd and reached out and felt the fabric of his coat between thumb and forefinger. "Nice."

"Thanks," Todd replied.

"That had to set you back. Did you finally get you-self a job? Is that why I ain't seen ya?"

Todd opened his mouth to explain, and then it hit him. "Well, actually," he said and couldn't help but grin. "I do have a job. I'm going to be a cook."

Chaz shrugged.

Todd almost explained just what a big deal it was and then stopped. Chaz probably wouldn't know Izar Goya from the man in the moon and how would he explain? Tell this young man who was selling himself on the street he would be learning under such a famous chef? Rub it in? Why? It would be cruel.

"Well, goody gumdrops," Chaz said and smiled dazzlingly. The smile changed his whole face. Maybe that is what Gabe had seen?

"I'm pretty happy."

"It must be a pretty high-paying job for you to get you-self a coat like that." Then one of his pierced eyebrows shot up. "No. Waits. You didn't buy that did you? Somebody got it for ya, didn't they?"

Todd was surprised at the perception. How had Chaz known? Todd blushed.

Chaz nodded. "Yuppers. That it, baby. Youz got you a sugar… what? Daddy? Mommy?"

And how did he answer? Was Gabe his sugar daddy? He balked at the idea. But was it true? He didn't really think so. Soon he'd be making some good money on his own. And he planned on paying back Gabe every single cent. But did he explain all that?

"Sorta."

"Sorta?" Chaz returned. "Eithers you do or you don'ts."

Todd shrugged.

"At least you all is admittin' you is gay."

Todd smiled, blushed, then threw his head back. "Yes," he said. "Wow. At least I am finally admitting I'm gay."

"So what you doin' here then? He already bored you and you lookin' to come to me for some fun?"

Todd laughed. "No. That's not it, Chaz." He paused. "I mean Brett."

Chaz's mouth fell open. "What you call me?" His brows came together in one angry line.

"Are you denying it?" Todd returned.

Chaz opened his mouth, hand raised high, fingers ready to snap—and he slumped. It was just like a puppet with its strings cut. How many times in his life had Todd heard that phrase, and it wasn't until that moment he'd actually witnessed it. Even the stern look on Chaz's face fell. Like tiny little knots breaking and letting go at once. The high-raised brow, the half smirk, the thrust-out chin. Gone.

"How did you know my name?" he asked, voice quiet and lacking his usual attitude.

"We have a mutual friend," Todd said.

"Oh?" A brow tried to raise and fell in defeat.

"Gabe Roberts."

"Gabriel?" Chaz snapped, his inner bitch showing again.

Todd nodded. "I thought so. It's you. What a damned small world."

Chaz turned his back. Took a deep breath, raised his shoulders movie-star-queen high, and turned back, chin thrust out once again. "Ya, baby. It a small world after all. That your sugar daddy? Did Gabriel find you on some street corner? Did he pitys you? Did he take you in?"

It was hard not to get mad. It was exactly what Gabe had done, but Chaz—Brett—acted like it were an offense. Todd took a deep breath and regained his composure before he'd quite lost it.

"He did" was his answer.

"Gabriel Roberts. The knight in shining armor. The hero," Brett/Chaz said, the expression there, the tone not. "What he hold back? What he *not* give you?"

Todd raised his shoulders, thrust out his chest. "Nothing," he said. "He didn't hold anything back."

"Well good for you, bitch" came the response.

"He also told me about his broken heart," Todd said. "A heart *you* broke."

Brett (Chaz?) trembled again, gulped. "Me?"

"He told me he fell in love with you, but he wouldn't make a move on you because you were underage. He told me how he waited until your eighteenth birthday and came home and found you in bed with his lover."

Chaz's eyes narrowed, he trembled, then closed them.

"He said he told you he loved you, and you told him you didn't love him."

There was a long pause. "That ain't what I said." Another pause. "I said I didn't love him like he loved me. That is what I said."

"Okay," Todd acknowledged.

"I knew what I wanted. I wanted him. And he made me wait. And when I couldn't stand it any longer, I went for Danny-boy." He closed his eyes again. "Stupidest mistake I ever made."

"Then why did you do it?"

Chaz's eyes flew open. "I was a kid when we met. I acted like one!"

Todd furrowed his brow. "You saying this is his fault?"

"I'm saying he could have tried just a little harder!" Chaz turned away.

An eternity passed.

"How is he?" Chaz asked.

How do I answer? Todd wondered. *Why with the truth, of course.*

"He's good," Todd replied.

Then: "Good." Another pause. "I fucked up good there. Hell. I never even got a chance to try him out."

"But you had Daniel," Todd said quietly, without any accusation.

Chaz shrugged. "Boy was that trading in a dollar for a penny. Dumb, dumb, dumb."

Interesting that nearly all of Chaz's style had vanished. Todd had suspected it was just a persona.

"I guess I'll never have him now."

"Probably not," Todd said. *Not if I have anything to say about it.* "So is it true?"

"Is what true?" Chaz asked quietly, lazily. No accent. No finger snaps.

"Are you HIV positive?"

Chaz jumped. He spun, obviously ready to back into character. Todd just stared at him with a no-nonsense level glare. Chaz slipped away and Brett returned. "I don't know. Probably. I let a trick fuck me bareback a few times. They pay a lot for that. But Doug got on me about it. Don' do that no more."

Anger flared, but he reeled it in. "Then why did you tell Gabe you were when you don't really know?"

Chaz shrugged.

"Why don't you get tested?"

Chaz shook his head decisively. "No way."

"Why not?"

"Scared" came the quick response.

"Then take someone with you."

Chaz laughed. "Who? Doug?" He laughed again. "Yeah. Right."

"I'll go with you," Todd said, surprising himself. *Now where did that come from?* "I'll get tested too."

Chaz's mouth fell open. "You would do that?"

"Sure," Todd answered, and meant it.

"You would really do that?"

"I would. Want to go now? Isn't the free clinic close by?"

Chaz nodded.

A moment later they were on their way.

WHEN Gabe walked into the apartment, the last thing he was expecting was to see his new lover sitting on the couch with his ex-almost-lover. He stopped dead in his tracks, door still open.

"Brett?" He barely got the word out. He could not have been more shocked.

"Hey," Brett said just as quietly.

"Todd!" Gabe said, tearing his eyes away and looking to his lover. "What is he doing here?"

"I brought him," Todd said.

Gabe felt his heart breaking—just a little bit. "Why?" he managed.

"He has something to tell you," Todd replied.

Gabe looked back at the young man who *had* broken his heart two years before. "Brett?"

Brett opened his mouth, shut it, opened it again, shut it once more.

"Brett?" Todd said.

Brett stiffened, sat up straight, then cleared his throat. Finally: "I don't have AIDS," Brett said in a rush.

Gabe staggered. "What?"

Brett's eyes grew glassy. "I-I only said I had it."

Gabe finally closed the door and leaned against it for support. He felt like falling down. He didn't think he'd make it to the chair. He glanced back at Todd. *You brought him here? To my home?*

A tear rolled down Brett's face. "Todd found me in the park. He went with me to the Free Health Clinic. Talked me into getting tested."

"We got tested together," Todd replied.

"Together? You got tested too?"

"It was so fast," Brett said. "They just pricked my finger. They let us sit in the same room. We had to tell them we were boyfriends."

Gabe looked over at Todd again, who mouthed the word "Sorry."

"And God, Gabriel. I'm negative."

This time Gabe really thought he would fall. He made himself walk into the living room and let himself fall into the chair next to the two young men. "Negative?" The relief Gabe felt was enormous. *Not positive. He doesn't have AIDS.*

"Of course, they told me I'll have to come back at least once more before they can be sure." Another tear rolled down his cheek. "If Todd hadn't talked me into it, I wouldn't have known." Brett turned and grabbed Todd's hand. "I owe him. I owe him big. I told him that too. Told him I would do anything."

Brett looked back at Gabe. "So he told me to come tell you the truth."

"The truth?" Gabe repeated.

"I only told you I had HIV. I was so mad at you." More tears began to flow.

"But why?" Gabe asked. "I didn't do anything."

"I know!" Brett cried out. "But I couldn't be mad at myself!"

Brett reached out a hand, it wavered in the air, then fell back into his own lap. "I fucked up big time. What I did was the biggest mistake of my life. I know you can't forgive me, but Todd was right. I had to come tell you. I am so sorry, Gabriel. I messed up so bad. I screwed everything up."

Gabe could hardly believe what he was hearing. Surprisingly, he couldn't find it in him to be mad. Only relieved. Only happy. "You didn't do it alone. I messed up too. And Daniel messed up big time."

Chaz reappeared long enough to snap his fingers. "Tellz me about it!"

In another time or place, Gabe might have laughed. But all he could do was smile. That's all he had. He looked over at Todd. There was a part of him that was mad. Springing all this on him. Couldn't Todd have at least waited in the hall and warned him? Or had Brett wait in a back room?

But no. That would have been stupid. And whatever else Brett was, he was a human being.

"Can you ever forgive me?" Brett asked. "One day."

Then a thousand thousand of Peter's stories and pieces of advice filled his head. But it was the quote by Martin Luther King that floated up above them all. "Forgiveness is not an occasional act, it is a constant attitude."

What would Peter say? That what we give is what we get in return.

How could he not forgive? What about all the things he himself needed to be forgiven for? Like putting the boy in situations he was not quite ready to deal with. He could argue he had gotten him off the streets. But hadn't he and Daniel played with Brett's emotions? Decided they knew better than he which direction the boy's life should go? By what right? Maybe his way hadn't been Brett's?

"Of course I can forgive you. Just please forgive me."

"You?" Brett sobbed.

And then Gabe stood, walked to Brett and pulled him into his arms. They hugged fiercely, cried on each other's shoulders.

After, with Todd now laying back in Gabe's arms and Brett on the opposite end of the couch, they talked of the future.

"I'm going home," Brett said. He laughed. "Golly. This morning I was thinking about turning a trick, and now I not only know I'm not HIV positive, but I've decided just like that to go home!"

"But what about your father?"

"I can take care of *him*," Brett said.

"Do you need bus fare?" Gabe asked.

Brett shook his head. "A friend loaned me the money," he replied and looked into Todd's face. "My new friend Todd."

Gabe gripped Todd in surprise. His special money? He had given Brett his special money?

"Who would have known so much could happen so fast?" Brett asked.

Gabe looked at Todd. "We know," Gabe said. "Don't we, Todd?"

"We sure do," Todd said.

Brett didn't stay much longer.

"I can't, Gabriel," he said. "It's too...."

Gabe nodded. "Todd, can I have a couple minutes with Brett?"

"Sure," Todd replied and damn, if Gabe couldn't read his lover's face. *Please have him not be upset.*

"What a great guy," Brett said after Todd walked away.

"Yeah."

"I'm happy for you, my angel." Brett reached out and touched Gabe's cheek. "He's a great guy. Amazing. But I can't watch."

"Watch?"

"Not yet. I have other things to face first."

"You're really going home?" Gabe asked Brett.

Brett nodded. "For now. I may be back. But I have to face my past so I can face my future. My father is just part of it."

Gabe shook his head. "You're unbelievable."

"No. Your boyfriend is. I can't believe he did what he did for me. It seems impossible. When he walked up to me in the park and started talking about you, I thought he was going to punch me there for a second. Instead he helped me out."

Gabe smiled. "He is pretty incredible. But Brett, so are you."

Brett grinned and snapped his fingers in a Z formation. "You bet I is!"

Gabe couldn't help but laugh.

Brett leaned in quickly and gave Gabe a quick kiss on the cheek. "Bye-bye, my almost love."

"Bye-bye, Brett."

Then fast as could be, Brett opened the door and was gone.

Gabe stood and stared at the door for a moment before calling Todd back. Then all Gabe could do was hold onto him. "Thank you, Todd."

"I love you," Todd replied.

"You really do, don't you?" Gabe said.

"I do. I think I fell almost the minute we met. That crazy kiss you gave me when Mr. Martinez brought me up—"

"Which I shouldn't have done," Gabe said. "I feel guilty about that. I took advantage of you."

"Nonsense," Todd said. "I deserved it. No. I was lucky. When you had me sleep on the couch instead of making me sleep with you. *That* would have been taking advantage. And wow... when you stood up tall to get me those towels and flashed your incredible ass at me—"

Gabe blushed. "I hope you know that was an accident."

"The lust I had for you in that moment... I know now it was already more than that. I don't know how it happened, Gabe. But I fell in love with you this week. I love you."

"I love you too," Gabe said and felt his heart simply zing. They hugged tightly. "But next time you bring someone like Brett back into my life, give me a warning? That was a hell of a shock."

"Sorry," Todd said. "It just sorta happened."

"Promise me anyway?"

"Of course," Todd assured his lover.

Gabe pulled Todd closer, kissed him hard, and just as he was about to suggest they take things to the bedroom, they were both startled when the apartment buzzer sounded once more.

"Now who could that be?" Gabe said, disentangling himself from Todd and walking to the intercom. "Hello," he said, pressing the call button.

"Excuse me" came a strange man's voice. "Is there a Todd Burton here?"

"Why?" Gabe asked.

"Because this is his parents. We're looking for him."

Gabe turned toward Todd, who stood there, eyes wide, hand to his mouth.

CHAPTER **TWENTY-ONE**

"DON'T let them in!" Todd wanted to shout, but of course he didn't.

Because.... Because it was his *mother*. Todd didn't give a shit about *him*—his stepfather—who could rot and die for all he cared.

But his mother....

In one split second, he found himself once more hoping for her approval. He wanted a smile from her. An "I'm proud of you, Son." Something he couldn't remember ever getting from her.

"Todd?" Gabe asked when Todd looked at him; he suspected Gabe had said something he'd missed.

"What?" Todd answered.

"You really don't want me to let them in?"

Son of a bitch, he thought. *I* did *say that out loud.* "I... I...."

"Todd. I think we need to let them come up."

"Why?" Todd cried.

"Trust me," Gabe said in way of an answer.

It made Todd wonder. He looked up at this lover and knew, or thought he did, that something was up. But what? "Don't want to see them," he said, his mind caught up in confusion. What were they doing here? "Haven't seen them," he said out loud. "They don't want me. *Why* should I see them?"

"Todd... I suspect this is important."

Why would you suspect anything like that?

"Because they're here, Todd. Today. I don't think it's out of the blue."

I did it again. Said something out loud I thought I said to myself.

"Hello?" came the voice of his stepfather. "Hello?" The second time more insistent.

"Don't want them here," Todd said. "Let's go down there."

"Todd, if there is one thing I know, it's that it's always best to have them come to you. That's why I always see business associates in *my* office. It's the home field advantage. If we go down to them and there's a scene...."

"Trust me," Todd replied. "There'll be a scene."

"If they come up here, it's your territory. And you can always kick them out."

"But it's not my territory," Todd said. "It's yours."

"It's *ours*," Gabe said firmly and pulled him close.

"Ours?" Todd asked.

"Of course it is," Gabe said, and touched Todd's forehead with his own.

Todd felt tears threaten. *God. Ours? Really?*

"Dammit! Is this thing working?" came that horrid voice again, making Todd flinch even floors above and hearing the voice only over an intercom.

Can't hurt me. I'm in my territory. Our *territory.*

"I'm here for you, Todd. I won't let anything happen."

Here for me. He pressed himself against Gabe's mass of muscles and then knew he would be okay. No matter how bad it might get, it would be okay. Todd nodded. "All right," he whispered.

Gabe pulled away, but only slightly, and buzzed them in. "Come on up, Mr. Burton," Gabe said. "Apartment...."

"We know which one," snapped Todd's stepfather. "And it's Sandburg, not Burton."

A moment later they were there. Gabe had opened the door and then filled it with his giant self, waiting, like a guard at the gate of a castle.

Protecting me. No one's ever protected me.

Todd almost gasped at the sight of his mother. She was wearing what for her was her Sunday-go-to-Jesus clothes, as if she were going to the church she never did. The dress, gray from both age and a million washings, hung on her like a sack. She wore a heavy coat (warmer than anything they'd bought him recently) and her hair, turning white, was pulled back in a fierce bun, in an old-lady way. And it was that which had so surprised Todd. *She looks old. Ten years older than the last time I saw her. It's only been six months.*

His stepfather, on the other hand, looked the same. Tall, wide, with a receding hairline that looked neither more nor less withdrawn from his bushy brows. His eyes, steel blue and not the country sky blue of Gabe's, were flat and cold. He'd shaved, miracle! And he wore a suit of all things. A suit. When had Todd last seen his stepfather in a suit? Five years? Ten? The way it hung on him made Todd realized he had changed some after all. *He's thinner.*

"Welcome to our home," Gabe said while Todd tried to think of what to say.

His stepfather's eyes narrowed and he stared up into Gabe's face. Gabe was taller than him, Todd saw. He'd never thought of anyone as being taller than his stepfather. But now, suddenly, Todd could see that he himself was no more than an inch, maybe not even that, shorter than his stepfather. When did that happen?

A long time ago, some part of him answered.

His stepfather all but pushed his way in, and his mother followed. They stopped just inside the door and stared at the big room around them. *Just like I did the first time*, Todd thought. *God. Was it less than a week ago?*

"Sit down," Gabe offered. "I'll make some coffee. It's cold out."

"That'd be right nice," Todd's mother said, and hesitating only a second, sat on the couch—not hugging Todd first. Todd's stepfather had barely glanced at him before joining her.

And now there they were, sitting on one end of the couch while Gabe sat on the other end. Todd sat on one of the recliners. Away from them. They were drinking the coffee Gabe had made and were making small talk. All Todd could do was wonder: *What are you doing here?*

"This is a very nice place," Todd's mother said. "You live here, Todd?"

Todd nodded stiffly. "Yes," he said, just the one word.

"You come a long way, Son," she continued. "I'm proud a you."

Todd felt something hitch in his chest. *Oh, my God. She said it. She actually said it. Proud of me.*

"That you could amount to something like this...."

Todd nearly gasped at the cruelty of the words, intentional or not.

"Shit. I'da never dreamed it," she continued.

"That's because you *never* believed in me," Todd said. The words were out of his mouth before he could stop them. *Where had that come from?* He'd surprised himself.

"Don't talk to your mother that way," said his stepfather

"It isn't any of your concern how I talk to her," Todd snapped. *You. You! How can you even be here?*

The man sat up straighter, his hand gripping his thigh. "It ain't respectful," his stepfather said.

Todd shrugged. "It's the way it is," Todd replied.

"Todd," Gabe whispered. "Take a breath."

Todd glanced at his lover, heart pounding but in all the wrong ways. He saw all Gabe was doing was trying to calm him down, and as long as he was looking into Gabe's eyes, it might work. Unfortunately, that wasn't possible.

"This is such a surprise," Gabe said, saving Todd from having to come up with something. "How did you two find Todd here?"

"We come to visit him at his apartment," his mother said. "Only he weren't there. The super said he moved out and gave us your address. Said you might know where he was."

"That was taking quite a chance," Gabe said. "You must have really wanted to see Todd."

"Well of course," she said stiffly. She clenched her purse. "He's my son. Why wouldn't I wanna see him?"

Gabe gave a hard nod, and Todd couldn't help but think his lover wanted to say something else, but didn't. *What's going on?*

"Mom," Todd said. "I have to tell you, you've surprised the hell out of me—"

"I hope it's a good surprise," she said, smiling awkwardly. "I missed you, Son."

Todd just sat there, more confused than ever. *Missed me?* It was not something he expected to hear. He'd figured she was in heaven with him gone.

"Those sure are some shoes you got there," his stepfather said. Todd looked down and saw they were the ones with the brightly colored friendship bracelets pattern. "Kinda faggy, aren't they?"

"Urston...!" Todd's mother hissed.

"Can I use your john?" his stepfather asked abruptly, no preamble as per his way.

"Sure," Gabe replied. "It's just down the hall."

The man nodded, rose, and walked past them.

"Mrs. Burton...," Gabe began.

"Mrs. Sandburg," she corrected.

(And oh, Todd hated that. Mrs. *Sandburg*. His stepfather's name. She'd taken that name nearly fifteen years ago, and Todd had hated it then and he still hated it now)

"Mrs. Sandburg," Gabe replied. "May I ask why you're here?"

(But Todd hated it even more when someone—naturally, of course—assumed Sandburg was Todd's last name.)

"Todd says he hasn't heard from you in months—"

(But didn't it give him a secret pleasure when every year a new teacher used "Mr. Burton" when meeting his stepfather? Not that the man deserved to get to use the name—but he knew the man hated it just as much as Todd hated being referred to as Sandburg.)

"—that you didn't even call on Christmas."

"That's cuz it ain't cheap to call Kansas City," she replied. "We ain't got a lot of money."

"But surely, not even on Christmas?" Gabe asked. "What is it? Five cents a minute?"

Todd goggled at Gabe. Was he criticizing his mother?

Todd saw Gabe had slipped into business mode somewhere along the way. He was acting official and not at all as if he had guests. Is this the way he was in his boardroom?

"If the big shot can afford to live here," his stepfather said, returning to the room, "then he could afford to call us."

"Urston!" said Todd's mother.

"What, Betty?" his stepfather said.

"Let's be nice. We have things to talk about with Todd."

The man grunted and sat beside his wife.

Now let's see what they say, Todd wondered.

His mother cleared her throat, glanced at her husband, then back at Todd. "It's about your father," she said quietly.

"Urston isn't my father!" Todd snarled.

She shook her head. "No. I mean your father. Him that helped make you."

Todd slumped back in his chair. "My real dad?" he asked.

She nodded. "Yes," she said. "He done somethin' for you 'fore he died. When you was just a baby."

"He... he did?"

"He... he set you up a trust fund. And we been watching it. Waitin' for it to... to...." She looked at the man beside her. "What's it called? Mature? I think that is what it's called. It comes to you on your twenty-first birthday, and that ain't far away."

"A trust fund," Todd said, stunned. "He left me a trust fund?" Todd could not have been more surprised if she'd told him his father were still alive and was president of the United States.

His mother looked at her husband, eyes flickering. Then back at Todd.

"A trust fund," Todd repeated. "But why didn't you ever tell me?"

"We didn't want to worry you none," she replied. "What was you gonna do about it before now?"

"Well, there is the matter of the allowance," Gabe said, and she turned to him, mouth falling open.

Todd turned to Gabe. "Allowance?"

Gabe nodded. "The two hundred dollars a month Todd was supposed to receive all this time."

"That money," said Todd's stepfather, "has been used to take care of Todd. We got a lawyer, and he said we could spend it to take care of Todd until he's twenty-one. You think kids are free? You think his clothes and food and stuff were free?"

"Clothes?" Todd exclaimed.

"You mean like that cheap fall coat you bought for him three years ago?" Gabe asked. "And how you claimed you couldn't afford to get him a warmer one?"

Todd's mother's face had gone completely white, and her husband's turned a bright red.

"There is electricity and gas and all kinds of stuff!" the man barked.

"But surely with the cost of living in Buckman and all the years you've worked selling combines and tractors and such for Newsome Farming Equipment. I understand you do well."

Todd raised a fist in front of his mouth, trying to hide his expression. His stepfather's eyes had grown wide and seemed ready to pop from his red face. "How did you know where I worked?" he barked. His mother tried to calm her husband with an open palm patting his knee. How many times had Todd seen that? It had surely spared

Todd a black eye a time or two, an injury he would have explained as a fall against a doorknob or some such lie. Had anyone ever believed his stories? In retrospect he figured that in a town like Buckman, you just didn't ask.

"And these last six months?" Gabe asked. "I suppose you've set that twelve hundred aside? Since Todd wasn't living with you?"

"Todd moved out!" his stepfather barked, jumping to his feet, hands clenched.

"And therefore the money should have been saved for him. Was it, Mrs. Burton? *Sandburg*, I mean." Gabe looked at Todd's mother instead of his stepfather. Todd was frozen. He was in too much shock to speak.

"I… we used it to get a new roof for our house," his mother said.

"You mean *Todd's* house, correct?"

The woman's face paled even more and his stepfather's turned an even brighter shade of red. "Todd's house?" he shouted.

Gabe leaned back—relaxed. "Well, it will be in a few months, according to the will. I believe it says something about if his mother remarries by the time Todd is twenty-one, then he shall inherit the house since you, Mrs. Sandburg, have someone to support you. A man who makes a very decent living, as a matter of fact."

Todd's stepfather took two steps forward, one hand raised in a fist.

Gabe raised an amused eyebrow, sat up straight, massive chest flexing.

"My house?" Todd cried. *My house?*

Gabe turned to him. "Yes, Todd. Your house."

Todd thought for a moment he might faint. It was all too much. All of this was too much. First his mother and hated stepfather showing up out of the blue. Then all this stuff about a trust fund and allowance, and now the house belonged to him?

"He ain't got no right to the house," his stepfather said. "We took care of him all these years. We took care of the house, kept it up."

"With Todd's allowance," Gabe replied.

Todd jumped to his feet and walked up to his stepfather, chest thrust out as if it were as large as Gabe's, hands gripped tightly at his sides. He furrowed his brow. "You son of a bitch!"

The man gave Todd a shove and Todd shoved back. Hard. So hard the man staggered and nearly fell. The look on his face was pure shock.

"Todd," his mother blubbered.

"All this time," Todd said. "All this time you should have been taking better care of me, and you've been using me, my money, instead." Trust fund! His father, his real father, had set up a trust fund for him? He wanted to cry. The man had loved him! Had taken care of him. He'd set up a trust fund. But how much? And then out loud: "How much? How much is the trust fund?" he demanded.

The man opened his mouth, shut it with a snap. Looked down at his mother.

"Well?"

"Tell him, Mr. Sandburg," Gabe said.

Todd's stepfather shook, anger and outrage written all over his face. But there was something else too. Todd could see it. Was it fear?

"Todd, it's for twenty thousand dollars," Gabe said quietly.

This time Todd did sway, almost fell down. *Twenty thousand dollars? It couldn't be!*

Todd's stepfather sat down. His mother cleared her throat. "Yes, Todd. And that is why we're here."

"Betty!" said her husband.

She gave him a surprising glare. "You didn't think he'd find out you... you...."

"Watch your tongue, woman!"

"You watch yours!" Todd roared, and the man flinched. Yes. Fear.

"Todd, we're here today for two reasons. One, to give you your paperwork." She patted her large purse. "It explains it all." She gulped, eyes growing large and wet. "And second... Todd. To ask for the house." Her head bobbed. She looked around the room. Waved at it.

"You don't need it. You have all this. I've only ever lived in one place. That house. Except when I were a little girl."

Todd trembled. *She wants the house. She wants the house I grew up in. My house.* He laughed. *My house!* He laughed again.

"What's so friggin' funny?" his stepfather asked.

Like he wanted the place. Like he ever, ever wanted to see that house again. His or not, he'd rather it burn down first. He looked at the man who he had hated so long and opened his mouth to tell the man what he thought: about the house, about what a horrible man he was. He wanted to tell the man he could live on the streets for all he cared. Tell him just how much he hated him. Revenge. Oh, for the first time he finally had the chance to get back at the son of a bitch.

And then something happened.

He thought about Gabe. The beautiful man who had done so much for him. He thought of Peter Wagner, about all the man had done to change the world. About how Peter said that Todd had been transformed.

Then he saw his hated stepfather.

Really saw him.

A scrawny, ugly punk. A nothing. A man who had spent his life making Todd miserable, and for what? A tiny, grisly two-bedroom house, no bigger than Gabe's (*our!*) whole apartment. A house in a tiny town on the edge of the universe. A house that *if* there were a bright center to the universe, it, and the town of Buckman, was farthest from.

It was all nothing.

His stepfather and all the rest: Nothing.

He turned to his mother. "The paperwork," he said stiffly. "Give it to me."

She flinched, ducked her head, and opened her purse. Dug through it. Brought out an old manila envelope. She raised her eyes, almost flinching again, and held it out, hand shaking. "Todd," she whispered.

Todd almost snatched it away, but took a deep breath, took control of himself instead. He reached out, gently pulled it away from her, and without looking, handed it back to Gabe. "You look it over," he said. "You seem to know so much about it." Suddenly he couldn't look at this man who had become his lover. Who had been holding something back. Todd was trying too hard to get a hold of his emotions, and he didn't need to be getting mad at the man he'd fallen in love with.

Fallen in love....

He felt the envelope taken from his fingers. He swallowed. Took another deep breath. "Mom," he said.

She straightened in her chair. "Toddy?"

"Do not call me that," he said quietly, but with steel in his voice.

She drew back, bobbed her head. "You never liked being called that."

"No," he said. He closed his eyes, opened them. Willed himself to relax. "I've never liked it. Told you that a million times! But you do it anyway." Todd shuddered. Used his anger to block back the tears of hurt and shock. "You've spent years lying to me, stealing from me, and letting him pound on me and tear my dreams apart. For what?"

"Todd, no...."

"Yes! Tell me why I should I give you what you want. You wouldn't have told me about the trust if Gabe hadn't leaned on you!"

Todd's mother began to cry.

Weak. She was weaker even than the man she had married. He shook his head, felt tears threaten again, and forced them down and down and down. Enough. He had had enough. "Keep the house," he said. "Do you think I want it? You think I want to live in that horrible town? That I ever want to see it again?"

She gasped. "Todd?"

"I don't want it. You take it. Live in it forever for all I care."

He turned to his hated—no, not hated—stepfather. "And you! You ignorant piece of...." *Shit. Look at him! A weak old man. And I was afraid of him. Him!*

No. He wouldn't waste one more bit of emotion on the man. What good did it do? It was poisoning him, hating this empty man.

This man he'd been so afraid of. Who had kept him cringing and in fear and from being his real self. Of cooking and singing—who cared if he could sing or not?—and being a "faggot."

Of being gay.

"Cocksucker," the man muttered.

"What did you say?" Todd asked, stepping forward. "I can't hear you."

"Cocksucker!" he spat. "I knew it. Always knew it! Saw the bedroom. Only one! You been sleeping with this faggot here, haven't you!" He pointed at Gabe. "You his little wifey? Letting him stick his cock up your ass?"

"As a matter of fact," Gabe said quietly, finally speaking again. "Todd is the one who fucked me."

Todd's mother gasped and his stepfather's mouth just dropped open again, snapped shut.

Todd smiled. "He's got a *great* ass," Todd said.

His stepfather's mouth fell open once again. He looked like a fish.

"I want you to go," Todd told the man. "I want you to leave right now. I don't want to see you again."

He turned to his mother who now had her hands covering her mouth, her eyes wide. "You should leave with him. You've got what you want. You've got the house, and you've gotten rid of me."

"Todd!" she sobbed. "I never wanted rid of you."

Todd shook his head, refusing to rise to the lie. "You never wanted me."

"That's not true!" she said, tears beginning.

Her husband rose to his feet. "Come on, Betty. Let's get out of here before we catch AIDS or something!"

Todd felt Gabe rise up behind him, like some powerful force. "Yes, Mr. Sandburg. I think you should."

Todd's mother was trembling, started to rise, fell back. "Todd...."

He husband pulled her to her feet and began to drag her to the door. Suddenly, she yanked herself away from him and went to Todd. "I never wanted rid of you."

Her move couldn't have surprised Todd any more.

"I love you, Todd."

He shook his head, looked over at his stepfather. "Why, Mom? Why him? Why did you marry him? Why did you let him...."

"I had to!" Tears began to roll down her face. "I couldn't do it. Be alone. I couldn't."

Todd just stared at her. Clenched his teeth. Then made himself relax once more. "Why did you let him...."

"He was the man!" she said. "A woman doesn't argue with her man."

"What would your son know about how men and women are supposed to be?" her husband asked.

She turned to him. "Enough, Urston." Then back to Todd. "I am so sorry," she said. "For all I done. For all I didn't do." She shook her head sadly. "Don't hate me."

Something released inside of Todd in that second. Not with a snap, but with a simple unknotting. Quiet and easy.

"I don't hate you," he said then. "I don't respect you. But I don't hate you."

He saw her step forward, raise her arms—*to hold me?* he wondered—and he stepped back, stopping her.

"You need to go now, Mother."

She gave him a long final look, then walked away, her husband already going out the door. It was there she stopped, turned back once more. "I love you, Son," she said quietly.

He froze. Said nothing. Finally nodded. "Good-bye, Mom."

"Good-bye, Toddy... Todd."

And then she was gone.

CHAPTER **TWENTY-TWO**

GABE swept Todd into his arms an instant after the door closed.

Todd trembled, almost pulled away. "You knew they were coming," he whispered.

"No, Todd. I didn't. But I wasn't surprised."

Not surprised. Why weren't you surprised? "How did you know all that stuff about me? The will. The money?" *The money. Twenty thousand dollars!* Maybe that wasn't a lot to someone like Gabe, or Peter for sure. But twenty thousand dollars was a hell of a lot to him.

"I found out a little last night, just before Peter and Izar got here. I didn't think it was the time."

"And after they left?"

Gabe pulled him closer. "I'm sorry. It just didn't seem the time either."

Todd looked up into his lover's eyes. "Maybe. But you should have."

Gabe bit his lower lip. "Maybe."

"No maybe," Todd replied. "You said it before. The time you bring someone like my mother and stepfather back into my life, I need to know. I need a warning."

"It was a hell of a shock?" Gabe asked.

Todd nodded, pressed his face into the cleft between Gabe's pectorals.

"Sorry," Gabe said. "It just happened. But I promise."

"Good," said Todd.

"I mean it," Gabe said. He lifted Todd's chin, looked down at him with those gorgeous country-sky-blue eyes. "We have to trust each other. Build a foundation. One built on rocks and not sand. One that will allow us to withstand anything."

Todd sighed. His heart raced—

"I love you, Todd."

—then skipped a beat. "I love you too."

They kissed.

But for only an instant, when there was a knock at the door.

No! It's them!

"Gabe! Todd?" came a voice from the other side of the door. "It's me. Tracy."

"Tracy?" Gabe said, and pulling out of Todd's arms, opened the door.

Todd saw a tall woman there, thick but stunning, wearing a red dress and long dark coat. "I missed it all, huh?" she asked. "Those two nearly mowed me down outside. I did get in, though." She leaned against the threshold. "Wow, what a day!"

"Tell me about it," Todd said.

She looked at him with large dark eyes. "So you're Todd?" She looked at Gabe. "He's cute, all right," she said.

"Todd, this is Tracy. She's the one who set all this in motion."

"All this?" Todd asked.

She rolled her eyes dramatically. "Yeah. That's me all over." She slumped. "Was it crazy?"

"Pretty crazy," Gabe said.

"Frigging insane," Todd added.

"Look, sorry kid. I didn't mean all this to happen."

"All of what?" he asked her. "What did you do?"

The was a cry in the hallway.

"I'll explain it all," she said. "But first, I got something for you." She went into the hallway and came back in with a small animal carrier. "Is this yours?"

Todd looked down, surprised. *What the hell?* He squatted, looked into the plastic box and then his eyes went wide in shock. "Leia!" he cried.

He quickly opened the container, and a squalling ball of white-and-black fur launched up into his arms, crying piteously. "Leia!" he sobbed and buried his face against her shoulder. "Oh, Leia!" He rocked her in his arms, then looked up at Tracy. Damn, she was tall. "How?"

"Well, when I was in Buckman—"

"You were in Buckman?" Todd asked, astonished.

"—and I was talking to your neighbors, I saw this cat. Made me remember Gabe talking about how much you loved yours. And any man who loves a cat is okay by me!"

"But how did you know she was mine?" Todd said laying his beloved Leia over his shoulder. Gabe had stepped up and was holding out his fingers, which she sniffed curiously.

"The one I saw wasn't her. But I asked the neighbors—an older couple who say you used to mow their lawn all the time—they told me what she looked like. Said she came to their back door for food."

So the son of a bitch did kick her out, Todd thought and snuggled his cat closer. She was purring up a storm now and nudging her face against Gabe's hand.

"So I went to the Wally Mart and picked up this carrier and came back and waited. Sure enough, she came along—finally—but she sure as heck didn't want to go in it." She held up a hand showing several scratches.

Todd laughed. "Well, she's out of it now." He turned to Gabe. "Can I keep her?"

"Of course you can," Gabe said, and kissed Todd's forehead. "Thank you, Tracy."

"Oh, yes, Tracy, thank you!" Todd said, and hugged her, Leia pressed between them.

"It was the least I could do, huh, Gabe," she said.

"You done good, Tracy. You done good."

Todd went to the couch and sat down, and his cat instantly flipped over belly-up, demanding a good petting. Todd didn't know whether to laugh or cry as he scratched her tummy. He looked up at his lover, and even Tracy. Sighed.

Wow. It was true. What Gabe had said.

The only way had been up.

And how could it ever get better than this?

EPILOGUE

TO THE casual observer, the kitchen of Izar's Jatetxea might have looked like chaos, but that wasn't the truth of the situation. Todd Burton was directing the apparent bedlam like a conductor over his orchestra. Everything was going just as it should. Pots simmered or boiled, per his carefully organized plans. Cooks and helpers were all doing just exactly as they should, as if choreographed. Todd had learned quickly and well, responding to Izar's teachings like a prodigy. In fact, she had recently given him control over the lunch crowd: Izar would let no one else have her kitchen for dinner; it was a part of her pride. It suited Todd perfectly because he had every evening with Gabe. And it suited the restaurant even more: a recent reviewer had praised the lunch venue, and Izar was considering letting Todd make more serious changes.

"Change can be good, right, *maitia*?" Izar had told him.

The comment could have no less surprised him than if she had announced she was going to get rid of the restaurant and sell used cars. Izar was pretty set in her ways!

Todd smiled at the endearment. *Maitia.* Sweet. Honey. Could he have imagined the woman who threw him out of her kitchen a year and a half ago would use such a word about him?

"Todd!" He turned as Janice, a young woman he had convinced Izar to hire a few months before, ran up to him as per her habit. She held a big spoon with one hand cupped beneath it.

"What do you think?" she asked, holding it up for him to taste.

"What do *you* think?" he asked, as he sampled the spoon's contents.

"Well…." She hesitated. "I think it needs just a touch of fennel. I think the saffron is perfect."

"I think the same thing," he replied and winked. "Trust your instincts."

"I'm learning, but you're still the general," she said with a grin.

"The general?" came Izar's familiar voice, "Not the colonel?"

Izar? What was she doing here? he wondered.

"Then am I no longer first in command?" She was coming up the main isle, her thick dark hair pulled back, and she was shoving it into a net as if she was ready to cook.

"Miss Goya!" Janice cried. "I didn't mean any disrespect."

Izar smiled and waved her hand. "Go on, Janice," she said, chuckling, "I only tease."

Janice giggled and ran back to her station.

"You were right about her," Izar told Todd. "What would I do without you?"

"You did just fine before."

"But I do better now!" She grinned. "Thanks to you."

"I think I'm the one who owes you the thanks."

"Enough with the thanks! We are beyond that now. Okay?"

Todd nodded.

"Are you nervous, *maitia*?"

"Nervous?" he asked. *What for? Everything was going just fine.*

"About the papers. Everyone's here, you know. In the dining room."

Papers? Todd's eyes flew wide. *The papers!* That's why Izar was here.

He dashed out of the kitchen and into the main dining room, and there was Gabe, looking stunning in his business suit, and Kent—their Realtor—sitting at a table with a stack of papers in front of him. Kent rose when he saw him. "Todd. You ready to become a homeowner?"

He nodded to the other man who was sitting there, someone Todd could only think of as The Man from the Bank.

Gabe stepped up to Todd and kissed him, "Hey, Babe."

"Was this today?" Todd asked, surprised.

Gabe chuckled. "I'd thought you remembered after the way we… ah… celebrated last night."

Todd blushed furiously, Kent looked away—obviously a little embarrassed himself—and when Todd glanced Izar's way, he saw her leaning back on the bar, arms crossed across her chest, an amused look on her beautiful face. The Man from the Bank had no expression at all.

He's like a robot, thought Todd nervously.

"Let's do it," Gabe said and pulled out a chair.

Papers. I'm going to own a home. That reminded him of the night long ago when Gabe had told him why he didn't own a house…

"I don't want to find a house until I find him," he'd said that day.

And then…

"When I find him, I want us to find a house together. So it's more than a building made of wood or stone or brick. So it's a home. Our home."

Now they were going to own that home together.

So they signed what felt like a thousand different pages, and when they were finally done and The Man from the Bank checked once more to make sure there wasn't an unsigned or uninitialed page, he finally smiled and handed them a set of keys. "Congratulations. You are now both homeowners." He rose and held out his hand.

Todd discreetly wiped his on his pants leg as he brought it up from his side, a trick Peter had taught him. *Never ever let anyone shake a sweaty palm.*

Then the man was packing up his briefcase, like an extra in an off-Broadway play, and disappearing into—as it were—the wings.

Izar came forward, and behind her Janice wheeled a cart with a bucket of ice and a bottle of Champagne. "Congratulations," she said, beaming. "I'm so proud."

She popped the cork and the rest of the crew ran out for a glass, even if it was fast and they only had an inch. A watched pot never boils, but an unwatched pot can boil over and make a complete mess.

"To Todd and Gabriel and their new *exte*, casa, home. May it hold more than a pillow to rest their head, be more than a fortress to protect them, but a place where their love can thrive and grow even more beautiful than it already is. Congratulations, my friends!"

The group broke into applause and then toasted the couple. Todd and Gabe interlinked their arms and drank from each other's glasses. When they had drunk, they kissed to a second round of applause.

"I love you, Todd."

"And I love you, Gabe."

"Shall we go check out our new home?"

"Well...."

"Go! Go!" said Izar. "You have the day off my *mutil maitagarri*."

And so, hand in hand, Todd and Gabe left the restaurant. But they had one more errand to do before they went to their new home.

WHEN they pulled into the driveway, matching folded pieces of paper in their pockets, whom should they see but Peter, sitting on their front stoop, those great gangly legs crossed, hands folded at the wrist over his knees, and holding his always-present cane.

"Ah, my boys! I didn't miss you! Alas, I cannot stay, but I have something for you!"

The "something" turned out to be a second bucket of ice complete with Champagne. It was something called "Taittinger Comtes de

Champagne Rosé" and somehow Todd guessed it had to have cost at least a couple of hundred dollars—that's just the way Peter played.

"Did you want to come in?" Gabe said, and knowing him the way he did, Todd knew his lover was just being polite. Gabe didn't really want Peter to come in. And in this instance, Todd knew why, and he felt just the same.

"There's the pity, but no—I cannot tarry. But I wanted to provide a means for you to christen your nest. But please drink it and don't break it on yon doorframe."

"Don't worry, we won't," Todd said, picking up the bucket and cradling it carefully. "You sure you don't want to come in and see the place?"

"See it later I shall." But then Peter wavered. Neither standing still nor going to his car. Obviously, there was still something.... Then it hit Todd.

"You told him?" Todd asked Gabe.

Gabe sighed. "Yeah, baby. Sorry."

Todd grinned. "It's fine," he said, pulling his folded piece of paper from his pocket and opening it. "Well, get yours out too," he said. Gabe nodded and followed suit.

And what they showed Peter made the man grin even wider than usual.

"Excellent!" Peter cried, and standing up, hugged them both.

It was their HIV results. Negative on both counts.

"This certainly means I must part company with you boys. I believe this means you two have an entirely different christening ceremony in mind!"

As per usual, Todd turned pink.

"How charming," Peter said. "That after more than a year spending time in my presence, you can still blush. I knew you were a prize, my boy!"

Peter spun around and, swinging his cane like a baton, went to his little Porsche 959 (stunning and sexy and oddly appropriate for the elegant man), but then with his usual style, stopped and leaned against the car. "Remember this, my sweet friends, that where we love is home, home that our feet may leave, but not our hearts."

"And who was that?" Todd asked.

"That was Oliver Wendell Holmes," he said and with a final "Adieu," folded himself into his car and pulled down the driveway and out of sight.

"I just love him," Todd said. Then he turned and saw the way Gabe was looking at him. Wow. His heart started pounding.

"I love you," Gabe said.

Todd's heart leapt in his throat. "I love you too," he replied.

Gabe pulled him into a sweet kiss—just enough to make things start happening to Todd, but not enough to scandalize the neighbors.

"Ready to 'christen' our new home?" Gabe asked, a sensual grin on his face.

"I sure am," Todd said.

And that's exactly what they did.

AUTHOR'S NOTE

SPECIAL thanks to the amazing poet Michael Lee for allowing me to use some of his words at the beginning of this book. We wanted to make sure you had a chance to read his entire poem, and you will find it below.

Please check him out on the Internet. You will be happy that you did. This young man is simply inspiring. Especially check out his poem "Pass On" at YouTube. You are not going to believe it. http://www.youtube.com/watch?v=PZ7-rgfu-2s

Thanks!
B.G. Thomas

Bloom Backwards   —Michael Lee[1]

When we were young we were whispers:
soft, but resonating like giants clapping across the ocean floor.
We were mystics with a faith softer than dusk
believing a cape, juice boxes, and our limited vocabulary could bring
     world peace,
"let's all just be friends".
We were small like songbirds, a little less quiet, but just as much
     orchestra.
We were instruments knowing so little that there was mystery to
     everything,

but these days we are yells.
We know so much and it is so heavy.
We are moving faster than whispers,
though we forget where we are going;
it doesn't matter. There are no mysteries in a place this loud.

---

[1] Bloom Backwards © 2010 by Michael Lee. Used with permission of the author. All rights reserved.

Growing up is a whisper bursting into a yell.
Regaining your childhood is blooming backwards.
So bloom backwards.

Open your mouth, swallow a swarm of fireflies,
hold your breath until they freeze into street lamps.
It is dark, but we are not lost yet.
Yell back down your own throat,
there are still echoes that sound like footprints,
a rifle pulse in every toe until it is only a tremor beneath your feet.
You haven't stopped running since you forgot where you were going.

Reshape your liver, broken from the nights spent drinking
trying to lose yourself never knowing you'd actually do it.
Replace your chest with a cello bending
in the dusk, calling music to your stomach,
smelling like rain that won't come until tomorrow.

Now, close your eyes. Go on
and close them. Imagine waking up
at midnight on a bicycle. You are seated backwards
yet somehow pedaling forwards, your arms are stretched out
and cradling the handle bars behind you. Pedal faster.

Watch as your neighborhood disappears into itself.
Watch as the grinning slick of a spring road becomes one blur
like every moment of a lost freedom finally returning to your feet.
Watch as every responsibility is sucked back into a sandbox,
look over your shoulder. Watch as life approaches your back.
Do not let your future live behind you.
Bloom backwards, and open your eyes.

We have grown into umbrellas, upside down,
catching rain like we forgot our purpose:
grab thunder and swallow it.
Plant flowers bottom up, their roots digging outwards
like there is a storm in your palms and God wants his lightning back.

Douse yourself in gasoline. Wear steel-toed boots,
dance on flint and count the colors. You are a burning building,
shower yourself in sand until you are a castle made of glass.

A whisper is a river drinking the world,
it is the string can telephone connecting you to your neighbors bedroom,
the line vibrating so hard with laughter the night snaps back into
    morning.
We blink over 22,000 times a day, and I bet you thought you only woke
    up once.

A yell is an ending. A block of ice that remembers
it was happier when flowing. It is a voice box
break dancing in front of anyone who will watch fearing its words
are not good enough of their own so it must flicker like an earthquake.
Remember when you were young, when you still believed
you had something to say worth listening to.

Find someone who you can grow young with.
Kiss him, kiss her, on every finger fluttering
like a songbird accordion
not knowing which way is up, slide your lips
across their body, make harmonicas of their skin
piano keys of their teeth, play your tongue
across every note and remind the both of you
together you are symphonies.

You are the youngest sound since the moon
swallowed the sun and held its breath till spring.
You are a yell sucked back into a whisper.
Love.

B.G. THOMAS lives in Kansas City with his husband of more than a decade and their fabulous little dog. He is lucky enough to have a lovely daughter as well as many extraordinary friends. He has a great passion for life.

B.G. loves romance, comedies, fantasy, science fiction, and even horror—as far as he is concerned, as long as the stories are character driven and entertaining, it doesn't matter the genre. He has gone to literature conventions his entire adult life where he's been lucky enough to meet many of his favorite writers. He has made up stories since he was child; it is where he finds his joy.

In the nineties, he wrote for gay magazines but stopped because the editors wanted all sex without plot. "The sex is never as important as the characters," he says. "Who cares what they are doing if we don't care about them?" Excited about the growing male/male romance market, he began writing again. Gay men are what he knows best, after all—since he grew out of being a "practicing" homosexual long ago. He submitted a story and was thrilled when it was accepted in four days.

"Leap, and the net will appear" is his personal philosophy and his message to all. "It is never too late," he states. "Pursue your dreams. They will come true!"

Visit his website at http://bgthomas.t83.net
or his blog at http://bg-thomas.livejournal.com
or contact him directly at bgthomaswriter@aol.com.

Also from B.G. THOMAS

All Snug

B.G. Thomas

http://www.dreamspinnerpress.com

Also from B.G. THOMAS

How Could Love
Be Wrong?

B.G. Thomas

http://www.dreamspinnerpress.com

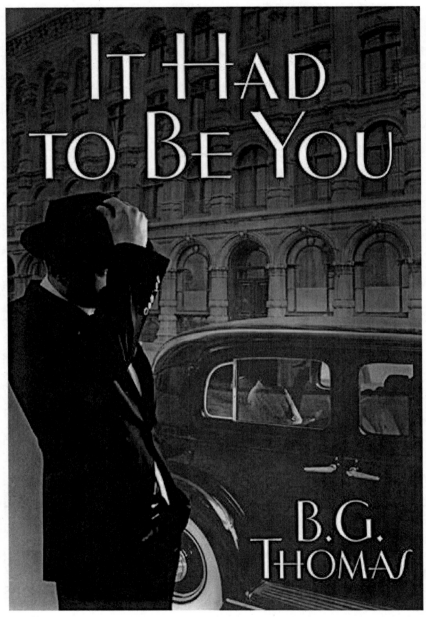

Also from B.G. Thomas

Baiu en Sāhuf or

SOUL OF THE MUMMY

B.G. Thomas

http://www.dreamspinnerpress.com

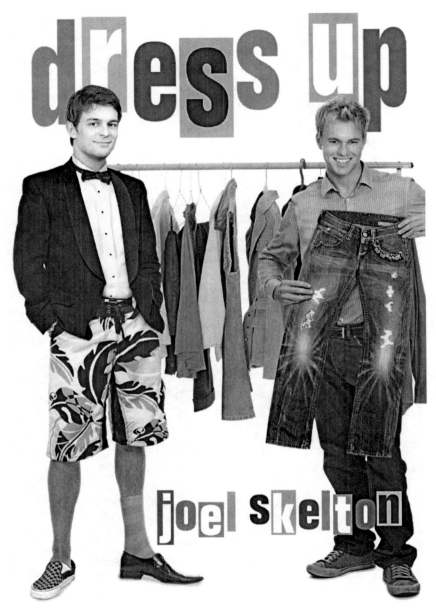